The Maid

and the

Minister II

Putting Ghosts to Rest

Angela Halliday

Fiction Romantic Comedy.
British Cataloguing in Publication Data

13-978-1-8380030-1-2
10--1-8380030-1-2

Cover by the author

Cover Picture: Some of the cast. By Angela Halliday

First published 2020

Forever Books
21 Heol Felyn Fach
Tondu
Bridgend
CF32 9DE

Published by Forever Books

The Maid and the Minister II

An Introduction.

My life had changed so dramatically since moving from London. Now happily married to a vicar, a lovely caring man who desperately tried to look after his flock, often under difficult and stressful conditions due to what could only be described as idiotic activity by a small group of residents. However, on the whole life was good and usually relatively peaceful in this sleepy village on the edge of Westmoor County, the nearest bustling city being Exeter. But often situations can develop that are out of the ordinary, even becoming extraordinary, especially when dealing with Mister Richard Drummond and his pals. The 'excitement' referred to suddenly erupted during a fete and developed steadily from there into another of those Miss Marple situations. The slight altercations this year began turning into a double event, emanating from accusations of theft, the disappearance of a young lad and just to make things more chaotic, coupled with the usual catastrophes caused by Dick and his cronies that wreck both the vicar's and my own social lives as well as upsetting the whole village. As you read, remember this is in a period before mobile phones and much is spoken with West Country and Irish accents. During the book, regression is used to solve a problem, so the viewpoint changes slightly as the explanation of past events are retold. Whatever madcap events occur, just enjoy and allow them to wash over you.

Contents

Contents

And by the Grace of God!

A new Start

Life as a married woman suited me, it had to be admitted. Dominic was a perfect husband, exactly as my feminine intuition had sensed he would be the moment we first met. That seemed ages now, although having moved here just about eighteen months, much had happened in that time, events that had made it an adventurous, trying but also happy period.

Dominic suggested we lived at the vicarage, letting my cottage out to rent rather than sell it, so keeping it as a small investment in the background should we ever need it. We also renamed it Briar Cottage rather than Periwinkle, as there wasn't a Periwinkle in sight while briars abounded in the field beyond. Thus far, it had remained empty and I was beginning to wonder about the wisdom of our decision.

Dick and Margaret were about to move back into their cottage now it had been rebuilt as well as extended, allowing Annabel to move in with them. I was sure they would all settle remarkably well together, which, when I mentioned it to Dominic, was a tremendous relief for him, making his life a lot easier, although how long that state of affairs may last, was open to question knowing Dick's propensity for, shall we say, 'accidents'.

Dominic broke into my thoughts. "Haven't Margaret and Annabel made a wonderful job of the garden, planting shrubs and flowers, even a small tree? It looks positively civilised now. If Miss Sharpe was still next door, she would have no reason to keep complaining to me. Annabel has helped a lot and the sisters get along fine. Although, I wish Annabel would get out a little more to enjoy life instead of gluing herself to the kitchen sink or ironing board, she is still a relatively young woman, but dresses so drably."

"She got hurt very badly, remember? Margaret told us when she was making her wedding dates the first time, so I'm not surprised she acts that way. Nobody wants to suffer emotional trauma any more than they need, hopefully if one doesn't have to. Once in a lifetime is quite enough. But you're right, I'll have a quiet word one day soon."

He nodded absently. "Dick has been quiet too, now you mention the word. I hope he's not ill. Haven't seen him or Jack about the village at all for a month or two, now that really is out of character."

"The pair were walking towards the Manor green the other day, he seemed okay then, surprisingly sober, too."

"Good heavens, he *must* be ill, in that case," Dominic quipped with a laugh. "I wonder why they were going there. That reminds me, I need to talk to CHS about the fete, still lots to organise on that score. Fancy a wander?"

"Why not, it's a lovely day."

Lady Celia Hornby-Smythe, known to most by her initials, owned the Manor together with the riding school. The establishment was most impressive, kept on top form by her gardeners and indoor staff.

Dominic rang the bell.

Olga opened the door. "Good morninks, vicar, a lovely day it beinks, no?"

Celia had told me one day at a Women's Institute meeting, that Olga came from eastern Europe somewhere, coming here without a job so had accepted Celia's generous offer, settling here as her maid.

"Oh, um, yes, of course it is," Dominic stuttered.

A smile was hidden. Olga had that effect on most men. To say she was very attractive to them was an immense understatement. Their knees went to jelly the moment she flicked her long eyelashes. Jack Sweeny, Dick's friend and almost constant companion, had been mesmerised the moment he saw her. However, although my husband didn't fit into that category, he seemed to feel uneasy when in close proximity.

"May we have a word with her Ladyship, please?"

The maid ushered us into the hall. "Be vaitinks moments, please."

We vaitinked moments.

"Good morning, vicar," Celia boomed as she entered the vestibule. "What can I do for you? Need a horsie again?"

"Um… no, no, nothing like that, thank you for the kind thought, Lady Celia," he replied a bit too quickly for decency, obviously not fancying another set-to as had occurred during the incident at one of Dick's wedding attempts, when Dominic involuntarily took to point-to-pointing on a horse called Mercury. "We've came about details for the fete to be held in your grounds."

Celia beamed at us. "Well done, vicar. It can go on the main lawn. Appleyard, my head gardener will ensure it is mown and suitably prepared."

"Will Master William be home?" I ventured.

"Yes, Jane, boarding school breaks up then. You must meet him, a charming little boy."

That wasn't an opinion shared by most people. Whenever home, everybody became fair game for some mischievous prank or other. He and Dick were a well-matched pair. With that in mind, I looked forward to this meeting with a certain amount of trepidation in my heart.

"How wonderful for you, Lady Celia," I tactfully replied.

"Oh Jane, call me Celia. After all, we both work hard for this community." She beamed again.

"Thank you, you're most kind." In fact, it was a high honour. Not many enjoyed such a privilege. However, when Celia said work what in reality she implied, was organising everybody else from the stage at the village hall, much as Maude Masterson and Penelope Bragshawe, the Major's wife, did. It should also be pointed out, anyone less like a Penelope was unimaginable, as the woman was more akin to an Amazon Warrior than a dainty female. It was Margaret, Annabel, Cynthia Wrackham and Miss Maybrook, plus one or two other minions including me, who did the donkey work. Still, we made a good team, getting on well.

Dominic seemed relieved. Now, having been given carte blanche use of the lawn, which rather surprised me, as it was maintained in pristine condition. Allowing a hoard of people and animals right of way over it was seriously pushing her luck. We left Celia to her horses.

"I'll see you shortly, my love, I'm going to the shop."

Dominic nodded, leaving me at the vicarage gate.

As the store loomed into view, surprise took me when bumping into Dick Drummond by the Memorial Green. It was barely nine o'clock.

"Morning Miss Jane," he chirruped, again unusual that he should be so cheerful at this hour.

"For goodness sake, Dick, call my Jane. I'm not a Miss anymore, haven't been since last year when our weddings, which I am sure you must remember, it being something of a special day. The vicar and I, do not live in sin."

"Oh ah, that be right, um… Jane. It's just that oi got in the habit, you sees."

I did 'sees. When Dick got something stuck in his head it was virtually impossible to get it out, even if one of those things for getting stones out of horse's hooves was available. "Where are you off to this time of day?"

"It be a big day for us, a-moving back into moi cottage."

"Us?"

"Moi Missus along with Annabel, Miss Jane. Oi had an extension made where the old shed used to be out the back, you remember the old shed? Then they decided they wanted to stay together, so Maggy said her sister could live in there.

It's got all modern things, so she'll be okay, live in with us most of the time, the sisters are close, you sees."

The memory of that broken down, ramshackle mass of oddments he called a shed full of useless junk had been etched in my mind. "I'm sure she will, Dick. Good to see the village settle down again, too. What will Annabel do with her house?"

"She only rented that, so it will save her money for a rainy day, won't it?"

After the dreadful fire, Dick and Margaret had been given shelter by Annabel until his place was rebuilt, so this was probably a show of gratitude on Margaret's part. As Dick had pointed out, the sisters had always been close. How the village had changed since that terrible day. Miss Sharpe burned to death, me moving to the vicarage and Dick's house torn down. But now they would be together again, which meant one house full once more. It left mine, Annabel's and Miss Agatha Sharpe's vacant.

"Are you okay, Miss?" Dick's voice jerked my mind back.

"Oh, yes, thank you, Dick. Just thinking of things that have happened here. Are you looking forward to returning?"

"Oh ah, Miss, we all are. Be good to get back to normal, won't it?"

"Yes, it will. I hope everything works out for you, too."

We parted, as I watched Dick disappear down the lane while making my way to the store, the milk was collected.

Mister Leggett smiled. "That scallywag is moving today, then?"

"Apparently, Mister Leggett."

"What about the other empty places? It's nice to have a vibrant village, not a half dead one, Jane."

He was fishing. "I haven't decided about my place yet. Miss Sharpe's will go on the market most likely though, Annabel's up for rent again."

"The Colonel said he knew of someone wanting to move into Sharpe's place. I wonder who that might be."

14

A shrug of my shoulders was all the information given in reply. "He hasn't said anything to us, so I'm as wise as you are, Mister Leggett."

"I can't believe those two layabouts are looking for work," the shopkeeper continued. "Doesn't seem natural to me somehow."

"Just goes to show they aren't layabouts, doesn't it? Is there any work here?"

"Not much, most of the jobs are farming so all taken. Maybe that's why they are just looking," he ended with a laugh.

The Colonel was leaving as I returned to the vicarage, politely holding the gate open for me. He could be a stuffy old stick most of the time, an ex-cavalry officer who liked, no, that's not right, demanded things done with his military precision. Unfortunately, if the two lads were involved in any way shape or form, that frequently failed to materialise, the job ending in chaos, much to the Colonel's chagrin. At least he was polite, nobody could fault him on that score.

"Good morning, m'dear."

"Good morning, Colonel, are you well?"

"Fit as a fiddle, Jane. Had my constitutional earlier."

"Well done, Colonel." I wondered why people applied that expression, 'as fit as a fiddle'. Are fiddles known for being fit and taking daily exercises?

Dominic's worried brow attracted my attention on entering his study.

"The Colonel's been," he said in a distracted manner.

"Yes, met him at the gate, he seemed in a good mood. Is there a problem, my dear, you look concerned?"

He sighed. "Yes and no. Its Miss Sharpe's place, the Colonel has let or sold it, not sure which yet. All he said was someone was moving in and would most likely want to join the church community."

"Oh, surely that's good news? Be some help perhaps at the WI."

"It's the person who's going to move in, that might cause something of a problem, my love."

"Really, who might that be?" My curiosity was piqued.

"A Miss Sharpe."

It was such a shock, I stood staring at him. "Ber…but she's dead!"

"Not that Miss Sharpe, my dear, a Miss Clara Sharpe, a sister of Agatha's."

"Good God! Does Dick know there are two of them?"

"It has nothing to do with Dick, has it? It's a vacant property that has been let or bought, but the Colonel never explained that. He came because she's a churchgoer so will want to join our congregation."

"Let's hope she has a better disposition towards her neighbour than the last one had, that's all, otherwise sparks are likely to fly, then you'll be sitting on top of a powder keg again. Remember, sparks and powder don't mix." However, I mused to myself, surely two sisters couldn't be exactly the same? Hopefully this one isn't as vindictive as the last. "At least his place is tidy, so nobody could complain about that and the accusations aimed at me had been resolved, so I had little to worry about, either. It might actually work out well. What do you think Dick might say?"

Miss Clara Sharpe

"What!" Dick screeched as Dominic broke the news. "Crikey, revrund, oi never thought there were two of those old crows. Where did this one spring from, out of hell?"

"That's unfair, Dick. We don't know what she's like, she might be a very pleasant person for all anybody knows. We thought you might like to be prepared, that's all."

"Come on, Dick, she might be okay," I encouraged. "Her move can't be stopped in any case, she's already on her way."

"Oi needs a drink, Miss Jane," he uttered, collapsing onto a seat with his head slumped forward.

I felt for him, considering recent events. He wasn't that bad, well, only sometimes, yet made up for it at others with his irrepressible character, humour and joyful outlook on life. He was always willing to help out, unfortunately with oft dire consequences, but that wasn't his fault. People never gave him a chance, were far too quick to point an accusing finger if anything went awry, especially Constable Bracknell and often said very publicly, loudly, nor without justification. Many could take a leaf out of his book and be the better for it. Yes, it had to be admitted there was a place in my heart for the scallywag.

"Come on girls, we'll go to the inn," he said, a brighter glint in his eyes at the thought.

"Oi'll stay to do this ironing, else it'll build up." Annabel stated. "Don't like the inn much in any case, it be all smoky. You three go, oi'll catch you later."

By three, she meant the two lads and Margaret, which meant her tied to the house again. Annabel was a concern to me. She had lived an almost monastic life at the other house, now it looked as though she intended continuing doing it here. She needed to be brought out of her shell. The poor love had suffered at the hands of a two-timing lover several years ago, which plainly must have hurt a lot, to the extent she kept away from people as much as possible. She's a sweet young woman so should have a little social life, after all, not all men are mean sods causing that amount of emotional pain, are they?

"You sure, Annie?"

"Yes, our Dick, oi'll be fine."

"See you later then," Margaret called.

"Annabel?"

"Yes, Jane?" She seemed somewhat surprised at my interest in her, having rarely spoken much before.

"How about if we went into the big town one day, just us two, a girly day. Have a lunch there, after that a look around the shops?"

"Oh, oi'd like that, thanks, Jane. You don't mind if oi calls you Jane, do you?" she asked nervously.

"It's my name," I replied with a smile. "Better than Miss Jane, considering I'm a vicar's wife."

She sniggered. "Yes, he do call you that, don't him? Oi've told him several times, but it's got stuck in his head and won't budge."

"Yes, I know, thank you for trying. Dick won't change, will he, perhaps that's just as well. It isn't a problem, we all know who I am, don't we?"

"That be true. When shall we go?"

"Perhaps after the fete, because Dominic and I have a lot of organising to do, so we'll be busy. But as soon as possible. I'll look forward to it. We can use the vicar's car; we'll have a fantastic day."

"Oi do too, make a nice change to get out of the village.

Thank you, Jane." She gave me a hug.

That was good, she seemed excited about venturing out. Fears had lurked she would have baulked at it. But no, she welcomed the chance. Perhaps there had been nobody to go with, so Annabel might have felt lonely. Now I had plans to make a few changes in her appearance, too. It was just she didn't know it yet.

As we left their home, a large lorry drew up. "Marigold Cottage?" A man asked from its cab.

"You're right next to it, just there," I answered, indicating the place.

He touched his forehead as a thanks, drew the truck on a bit farther, stopping. Out jumped the crew to begin opening the doors.

We left them to it.

"I wonder where the new occupant is." Dominic mused.

The Colonel's car chugged into view, stopped by the gate in front of the truck and out stepped the promised Miss Sharpe.

I froze. She was the exact likeness of Agatha, right down to her spectacles along with that hooky nose. Maybe that was a characteristic that ran in the family, more like an affliction, I thought.

"Good morning, Colonel," Dominic greeted.

"Ah, vicar," said the Colonel. "Allow me to introduce Miss Clara Sharpe, the sister of our dearly departed."

The woman glared at Dominic. "You're the reverend of this village?" Her high-pitched voice demanded almost imperiously.

It was a stupid question, as he had just been introduced as such. "Um, yes. I look after St Mary's church just along the way. Will you be attending my congregation?"

"Yes, but only if you're not one of these new, progressive clergymen, who think that anything goes?"

"I'm sure Dominic isn't like that," I replied, springing to his defence.

"Who are you? Can't the vicar answer for himself that he needs a lacky?" She looked me over disdainfully, as if inspecting some ragamuffin begging on a street corner or ridden with an incurable vile, contagious disease.

"This is the vicar's wife," the Colonel put in. "Jane Chantril."

"Oh, I see, one of those parishes, is it?"

Goodness knows what she inferred by that statement, not only that, it grated with my sense of fairness and loyalty.

"Excuse me, I've things to do," Dominic uttered abruptly, a hint of annoyance in his voice.

Clara Sharpe caught sight of Margaret, Dick and Jack, entering the inn. "Who are they?" came another demand.

"Your next-door neighbours," Colonel Masterson replied.

"How awful, I'm being forced to live next door to a band of drunkards."

"They are hardly that," just villagers, the Colonel said, uncharacteristically sticking up for Dick. "Young Drummond does a lot of work in the village."

Clara Sharpe snorted, leaving us to go shout directions at the removal men as they carried a sideboard in.

It was not a good start. What did she mean by 'new and progressive', that could imply anything? Dominic was silent all the way back, excused himself at the vicarage gate making his way into the church, probably to offer a prayer as he often did when going quiet.

Dick's attitude worried me, he hadn't even met the woman yet, what then? Perhaps he should know, so took a wander to the memorial Green. They were sitting at a table outside. The general air boded ill.

"Oi saw the bitch just now," Dick stated. "Came out with the Colonel a-goin' to his. It looks like the old routine again, Miss Jane."

"I sincerely hope not. She can't complain about your garden or anything else, it's all been done, hasn't it, Dick?"

"She looks just like the other old scarecrow, mean and nasty, to oi. We were a-hopin' for a nice new neighbour; someone we could be friends with."

It was pretty plain to me, that wasn't going to be the case with this odd woman, having already had a dig at both Dominic and me. "She's not very nice, I'm afraid, was rude to the poor vicar, even though he had hardly spoken a word. Try not to worry, we will stand by you if anything happens."

"She gave oi a look that could have buried an herd of cows, so oi guess oi'm not very popular. S'pose her sister told her all kinds of horrible things about oi. Now we're out of cash, so will have to go home," he muttered, glumly.

"I'll ask Charlie to bring a couple of drinks out, on me. Try to cheer up, please."

"Oh ah, you're a true lady, Miss Jane," he beamed.

A smile went back. It was nice to see the Drummond grin again.

Dominic was in his study when I looked in. "Everything okay?"

He smiled and nodded. "The Colonel popped in while you were out, said he had organised a parachute drop for the fete along with some military hardware of some sort. Every bit helps."

"Did he say anything about Miss Sharpe?"

"No, and I decided not to push it."

"You were very wise, my love."

"We had better draw a ground plan out. Has that section of the Manor got easy access for military vehicles? What if it's a great big tank thing? That would chew the ground up, wouldn't it?" Dominic found a clipboard and paper.

"We had better look in that case, my love. There's a lane running alongside her land, but it's very narrow, I wonder if that's wide enough for that sort of thing?"

"Come on then, no time like the present, Jane."

A Count

*I*t was indeed narrow, more like a track.

Dominic took measurements, grunting a lot through the exercise. "It's barely a wide footpath even. Wonder where it goes to?"

A walk brought us out to a grassed field farther on from Celia's land.

"Who owns this?" I queried. "I don't think its Celia's, not looking by the state of it."

"It belongs to farmer Rogan, he used to keep pigs here. Celia complained about the smell, so he moved them to the other end of the village beyond the inn."

A light laugh left me. "I bet she did."

"We need to know what vehicle is coming. Let's pay a call on the Colonel."

"A tank!" he exclaimed at Dominic's question, displaying great surprise. "No, no, vicar, an armoured car or something small, with a gun on it. I was in the cavalry, not the tank corps. Stop worrying, it's organised."

A sigh left Dominic. We both knew how wrong the Colonel's organising could go from the debacle with the choir, he was totally unreliable.

Back at the vicarage we discovered a message on the answerphone. Please call the estate agent as there was news of a letting for Briar Cottage?

"A foreign gentleman," the voice said down the phone line. "Sounded keen, never argued about the rental price.

Would like to move in immediately if possible?"

"Yes, that would be fine, it's fully furnished. We have agreed how the payments will be made, through my bank. Once that is signed, no problem." Hanging up, my attention turned to Dominic. "Seems like I've rented the cottage," my call to him went. "Foreign people, they said."

"Which country? I hope they look after it, darling."

"The agent didn't say. Paul would have vetted them, made sure they weren't bloodthirsty criminals," I joked.

"Let's hope he has, but it might be difficult if they come from abroad."

"Don't say things like that. It's only along the lane, we can keep an eye on it."

"Now then, the fete, my love. I phoned Miss Wrackham, found she has several stalls organised, the usual fete stuff, shies, tombola dips and raffles, yet one is a Madam Zala, she does fortune telling. Goodness where Cynthia knows her from, she can be a dark horse sometimes. Perhaps she should tell Dick's, although on thinking about it, his future is pretty predictable. CHS assured she will set up a mini farmyard with some animals loaned from various friends, a donkey ride as well as an arena for horse jumping, too. Oh, and a dog competition of some sort. Fred knows a local band that have volunteered to play. Not sure what they are like though. Charlie is providing a drinks tent that he says is big enough for the WI to serve tea and cakes in as well. His wife, Sheila, is getting a dance team together, but again, don't know much about that. The Major thinks he can get Newtown Army Cadets to run a rifle range with air guns, need to confirm that, he also says he knows a regiment that will run a paraglide drop, whatever that is, too. Seems to be coming along well."

"Dick isn't involved, is he?" My question was asked tentatively.

Dominic laughed. "No, only guzzling Charlie's beer, I expect. Margaret said she'll help out on a stall, she's persuaded Annabel to come along to help. Be good for her to get out of the house."

"What about first aid?"

"Doctor Monday will get a small team together for that, so it's covered. That's a weight off my mind."

"Wow, you've done well," I said, giving a cuddle. "What about somebody to open it?"

"Haven't a clue. Maybe CHS would, she is a Lady, after all?"

The phone rang. Dominic quickly took it away from his ear, so guess it must be Celia bellowing down it.

"Well, what was that about, not a problem, is there?"

"No, the opposite if anything. A French Count has asked her to put him up for a while, comes from the wine region of Macon. However, she has suggested he rents Annabel's old house, it has been refurbished with an extension since she moved out to be with Dick and Margaret, so more than suitable for a Count. Perhaps he would open the day?"

My eyes took on a dreamy look. "Mmm, Macon, I spent time there, a lovely region. France is a beautiful country."

"Really! You amaze me at times, Jane. What were you doing? Not espionage?" he asked with a wide grin.

"It was an international crime case, I worked as a liaison officer with the French police."

"The police! Don't let Dick know, he'll have a heart attack," Dominic said through a loud guffaw. "CHS said he had a vineyard out there. As you were in the vicinity, you may know the label?"

"How lovely. What is it?"

He shook his head. "She didn't say. To be honest, she seemed a bit overwhelmed about having a French Count here."

"She is a Lady, after all, I suppose a Count is on her level of society. By the way, I've not seen Dick or Jack for a few days. Not ill, are they?"

"Apparently, they have got work on CHS's property for a couple of months while Jim Appleyard has a bit of time off.

He's probably ducking out of being around when the fete is on, you know how particular he is about the state of the grounds."

That revelation stunned me! "Is he! I mean, he is? Are you sure? You said Celia couldn't stand Dick."

"Her hand has been forced by Jim Appleyard's absence. She did try official channels, but nobody was interested. So, with great misgivings, she sent an underling to ask the pair. They should be okay, it's just garden work together with a bit of window cleaning before the fete."

"Didn't Dick have a dubious past with window cleaning? Does Celia know that?"

Dominic shrugged his shoulders. She must, its common knowledge in the village, although the tales have become exaggerated over time, people like to embroider his lifestyle a lot."

Casting him a glance, I asked, "Does it need embroidery?"

He roared of laughter. "Probably not, my love. Come on, we had better get there."

"Where?"

"The Manor. CHS asked me to keep an eye on the pair. She still has deep misgivings about them."

The morning dampness still permeated the air from the early dew and a light shower, causing me to shiver.

We found the pair at the front of the house. There lay a long ladder on the ground.

Dominic looked at it, then at the pair. "What's that for?"

"She wants this big plant cut back a bit, reverend," Jack replied. "Says it's cutting light out from her bedroom."

"Please take extra care, Jack. Who is going to do the trimming?" I asked nervously.

"Oi will, Miss Jane. Jack's a bit nervous up ladders, so we agreed it be oi."

"Oh. In that case take even more care. Don't want any accidents, like at the church tower, do we?"

"A-corse not Miss. Jack'll hold the ladders steady while oi snip some of the growth away."

"Shall we stay a while," I whispered to Dominic.

The pair lifted the ladders, propping the top against the wall, then lifted it back to slide the extension up beside the offending Wisteria, leaning the tip on bricks beside the window.

Dick tested them. "Seem firm to oi, our Jack. You hold them tight though, the paving stones are wet and slippery, don't want the bottom moving away, do us?"

Jamming a foot against the bottom, Jack gripped the wood. "Go on, get up. Shouldn't take long. Got the secateurs?"

"Rightyo, oi'm on moi way."

He went up full of confidence, arriving at the top to begin work, happily snipping bits off.

We watched, but Dick seemed to be doing well as lengths of the plant fell to the ground.

"Are you done yet?" Jack called.

"One more long thick bit. Oi needs to lean over to get it, so hang on properly a-corse my weight will be sideways." He stretched, unerringly gripping the branch.

At that moment, an incident occurred that set off a train of events. The heady scent of Olga's perfume came to our nostrils.

It had a magnetic effect on Jack, who appeared to go into a trance.

Olga stopped beside him looking at the ladders, trying to decide whether or not to walk under or around. She blazed a smile at Jack as she turned to walk behind him.

Jack had his mouth open and stupidly let go of the ladders to follow Olga's shapely form as she walked on.

Without any form of restraint, the ladder's base slid away across the damp paving slabs, departing the wall at the same instant.

I admired Dick's quick reactions as he did about the only

thing he could, grabbed the plant's branch he had been about to cut, hanging on for dear life. Suddenly, he found himself in mid-air and reminiscent of Tarzan in a faraway jungle, swung on the Wisteria, feet first, straight through Celia's bedroom window accompanied by a shattering of glass and splintering wood frames, disappearing from view with a loud shriek.

"Get that ladder up there, quickly," Dominic shouted. "He may be injured."

A head appeared. "What the bleedin' hell did you let go for, you great hairy corncob?"

"Well, I was… I mean… Olga went off with a wiggle…" Jack spluttered.

"Can you climb out? The vicar will give Jack a hand putting the ladders back for you," I called up.

"Oi think so, Miss Jane. There be a lot of broken glass in here. CHS b'ain't going to be very happy about it."

No, she'll be absolutely bloody furious! Poor Dick will get the blame as usual, only for a change, it wasn't his fault.

He climbed down looking very crestfallen.

"We'll tell Celia it was a set of circumstances, you never had anything to do with it," I said, trying to give him support.

"Neither it t'were, Miss. Jack let go of the blinkin' ladders. Oi only had that last bit to cut off, too."

"Have you been cut or injured anywhere?" Dominic enquired.

"No, oi be okay, revrund. What am oi to do now?"

That question was rapidly solved when Celia came tearing around the corner of the building like a charging rhino in full-blown anger, plainly after somebody's blood. The culprit was soon identified.

"Drummond! I might have known it. Why I ever let those people talk me into engaging you, I don't know. Obviously, it was a bad mistake. Look at my bedroom window, smashed to pieces with a fete in a few days. Get off of my property immediately."

"It wasn't his fault. Somebody let go of the ladders

causing them to slide, Celia," I added, glaring at Jack.

"I don't care, the man is a disaster, always has been and always will. I'm sorry Jane, they are both dismissed." She stormed off.

"Really Jack," Dominic chided. "What on earth got into you?"

"It was Olga, giving me the come-on, like that," he moaned.

"She smiled at you, that's hardly a come-on, is it? You could have just said hello or something and concentrated on what you were doing."

It was common knowledge Jack had the hots for Olga, so a blazing smile was a major alluring temptation as far as he was concerned. In any case, she only had to flutter her eyelashes to have that effect on most men.

But the damage was done, all in a moment of fascination with the rear end of a woman. As I pondered that fact, a movement caught my attention the far side of the Manor. "Who was that flitting about in those bushes?" I asked Dominic.

He shook his head. "I didn't see anyone. Are you sure?"

"Yes, a scruffy looking individual. Came from the kitchen door area."

"Are they still there?"

"No, gone now. Maybe a tramp looking for a meal?"

The important thing was Dick had somehow miraculously survived without getting hurt, yet again. It had to be admitted, he did lead a charmed life.

Dreadful Fete

The next day as we walked to the store, a black car drew level with us, grinding to a halt. The driver's window lowered to show a swarthy face, dark hair, a trilby hat set at an angle.

"Briar Cottáge?" the person asked in a gruff, deep foreign voice.

"Just along the lane a little, on your right. It has a gate, a path leading to a porch, you can't miss it," I confirmed.

The window slid up again as the vehicle moved off without a word.

"Good Lord, are they the people that have rented your cottage?" Dominic gasped. "They don't seem to have many manners. I noticed a strong French accent."

"I'll have a word with Paul, he made the arrangements so assumed it was fine."

"Morning reverend, Jane" Mister Leggett greeted. "How are you two today?"

"Fine, thank you. A pint of milk, please," I replied.

"Celia engaged a local firm to repair the damaged window, so that's secure again," Dominic said, as we stood chatting in the store.

"The mysterious Master William hasn't put in an appearance," I viewed as we left. "He was supposed to be a menace so people claimed, used a catapult to great effect on unsuspecting victims, put worms down girl's blouses or any other prank he could get up to, so Mister Leggett said." I laughed. "He and Dick are a well-matched pair. From the picture Celia showed me, the lad looked angelic, as often scallywags do, take Dick for example. But mainly, as Master William is Celia's only offspring, I expect he usually gets away with blue murder."

At last, after all the work and effort, last minute hiccups or other niggles that had to be solved, the day of the fete dawned bright and sunny. That was a relief, meaning people would flock from miles around to see some of our unusual exhibits and events.

We had gone early to oversee the general chaos as order gradually began to surface. The only reservation Dominic had, was about farmer Rogan's prize billy goat. "It's on the rowdy side to say the least, so had to be tethered outside the farmyard pen that was put aside for other, gentler animals. The wretched animal nibbled or butted everything in sight, so is being given a wide berth."

"What time is the fete due to open?" I asked.

"I expect early, although the official opening won't happen until about twelve o'clock, that's to give people time to get here."

"Did Celia get anybody?"

"I believe the Count is going to do the honours," Dominic answered. "Apparently he has never seen a traditional English fete before."

"Mmm," I mused, "he'll likely get a rude awakening in that case."

"He only has to say a few words, it's not a difficult task. I hope he speaks English…" Dominic added thoughtfully.

"Most upper-class French does. Stop worrying. Oh look, the hot air balloon is being inflated. It looks dangerous with all those flames spurting into it."

"The chap will get enough hot air into it, just to have it light on the ground but secured by a rope to a peg driven into the lawn. He'll leave a pilot light on in case the balloon needs topping up during the day, a tug on a cord sets it off, he said. Don't want any accidents with that wafting away, do we?" Dominic ended with a laugh.

Celia appeared. She didn't seem her normal boisterous self somehow, although I couldn't put a finger on the reason. Perhaps still smarting over the broken window. Notably Master William was nowhere in sight, which surprised me. However, true to her upbringing, she soldiered on, introducing the Count.

There was a click as the microphone became live.

"Ladies and gentlemen, welcome to this year's wonderful fete here at the Manor. We are very honoured to have the Comte du Fontaigne, all the way from Macon in France, who has agreed to open the proceedings. Please show a grateful welcome to our shores with a show of hands. The Comte du Fontaigne."

"Merci, Ladee Celia, for such a warm welcome. Please let it be known, I have donateed a case of my best vin to 'elp raise le funds. I now declareds theese fete, Ouverte."

He dressed well, looking every inch a count and equally as full of his own importance, I suspected.

"Now's your chance to see the label," Dominic grinned. "Shall we sample a glass?"

It looked good, tasting as a wine should from the region, but I didn't recognise the label at all. "A little dry for a Chardonnay," I commented.

"Maybe a bad year," Dominic viewed. "Perhaps that's why he's giving it away?"

"I have suspicions, don't know why, something wrangles with me. I'll drop Phillipe a line, see what he thinks."

"Who is Phillipe?"

"The officer I dealt with during the liaison. He'll check for me."

By eleven, the place was filling nicely, looking as if everything would go to plan, culminating in a successful day for Celia.

"The para drop should be coming in soon, Chantril," The Colonel said, as he came to us. "Planned to land just beyond the stalls, over there," he motioned with an arm as he scanned the sky.

"Isn't that rather close?" Dominic questioned. "A breeze or hiccup, then they'll land in the middle of the people."

"Humph", went the Colonel. "These men are experts, been training for years. Stop being so pessimistic, vicar."

The drone of an aircraft came to our ears. Arms pointed as it circled high in the sky, finally picking a course in a straight line. Soon, a few tiny black shapes appeared, falling, falling, down and down.

"Aren't they supposed to have parachutes?" I wondered aloud.

Suddenly they opened, odd square shaped things, nothing like I expected them to be.

"There Chantril, I told you so," the Colonel uttered pompously. "They guide them in to the landing point, just as they would in a war situation."

True to the Colonel's predictions, the men landed exactly where the cross on the ground had been marked. A sigh of relief left me. Perhaps things would go off without a hitch after all.

The Count was beside Celia with Olga close by.

In an attempt to distract Jack's attention from that group, I moved to his side. "No Dick?" I asked, casting around.

"He's helping Josh Rogan move some pig manure into the far field with a horse and cart. Soon be done, it's only just up there," he said, indicating the fields the far side of Celia's garden.

"Don't you think someone should warn Miss Sharpe about standing that close to the farmer's Billy goat? I am told it is a little on the aggressive side."

Jack snorted. "It's up to the miserable old moo, ain't it? She had a go at Dick about his drinking earlier, he had only had a swift pint. Puritanical old cow, if you ask me."

"Oh look, here comes that paraglider man, the Major organized."

"Looks a bit off course, if you ask me," Jack replied. "I

thought they could control where they landed. He's going too far left, it's the lane he's heading for."

True to Jacks forecast, the man and chute disappeared behind the line of trees that separated the lane from our field.

A loud shriek followed… a pause… then, as they say, everything popped at once.

In an eruption of twigs, leaves or other detritus, a horse closely followed by its cart burst through the hedge completely out of control completely driverless, to hurtle through the throngs of folk who went diving in all directions to avoid injury. The filthy old cart collided with the blacksmith's lovely carriage that he had allowed to be displayed, clipping it with a resounding thud taking off some woodwork that went curving through the air gracefully. The dreadful contraption continued straight for the animal pen, tearing the frail fence down.

Miss Sharpe screamed her head off, swinging a handbag at the rampaging nag, stupidly missed hitting the Billy goat a hefty clip around an ear.

The animal wasn't very pleased about being attacked for no apparent reason, so promptly charged, head down, straight for her.

I had to admit she surprised me, as the woman valiantly tried to defend herself, failed, then took to her heels with a greater alacrity one would ever have expected of her.

She had almost made the tethered balloon when the goat caught her from behind with a perfectly timed butt that sent her flying to land head first, half in, half out of the balloon's basket, legs dangling helplessly, frantically yelling for help.

In the meantime, some very brave soul had managed to stop the horse and cart, out of which emerged two human beings. At least, I assumed they were, but judging from the state they were in, the pair could have been a couple of Martians straight out of some tar pits.

"I must assist Miss Sharpe," Dominic said, dashing to her rescue in a lively run. He struggled, but she refused to budge.

"I'm caught on something in this basket," she wailed.

"I'll try to free you," he replied, clambering in.

At that very moment, the goat felt it should run amok again and in its attempt at making an exit, got its horns trapped in the balloon's tether. Annoyed at restriction, the beast flicked its head, removing the retaining peg from the ground as easily as a champagne cork from a bottle, and in so doing freeing the whole issue from any form of restraint.

The basket jolted, ruining whatever grip Dominic had managed to gain, so desperately attempting to stay upright, he took hold of the first thing coming to hand, which happened to be the cord controlling the amount of heat that went into the balloon. Before anyone could utter a word of warning, the whole issue took off for destination unknown.

At the sound of igniting gas, the owner shot out of the beer tent to see his pride and joy disappearing into the great blue yonder.

While this was going on, the mangled mess beside us had sorted itself out into Dick and the paraglider man.

Each stank to high heaven having been sloshing around in the cart amidst the mostly liquid pig manure.

"Should the revrund be a-flyin' that? Be he havin' a licence?" Dick stated.

An enormous, very irate blacksmith appeared, gripped Dick's clothes to lift him off his feet with one hand.

It in itself was a courageous act, considering the state Dick was in, covered in slimy dung from head to toe as he was.

"You broke my carriage!" the giant of a man exclaimed in a voice so loud, it probably startled the pigs in the next field.

He was about to hit Dick, when for some reason, he slipped from his grasp, bolting for cover.

"Help!" Yelled Dominic, his cry refocusing our attentions back to the errant balloon.

"Let go of that rope," the owner shouted back.

He did, as if it had become red hot, which it may well

have done, considering the volume of flame in such close proximity.

Shouted suggestions were bandied about and eventually, to all our reliefs, the balloon began descending. It landed amid the pigs, tipping its occupants out head over heels.

The errant pair returned to the fete, going into the drinks tent for a sit down and cups of tea, as well as a quick medical from Doctor Monday's team.

"I've always hated flying," Dominic uttered between sips.

The Colonel entered, asking if Miss Sharpe was injured.

"No, I'm not," she snorted. "Furthermore, Masterson, I shall be going back to London as soon as possible, forever! It was your dreadful idea I should come to this God forsaken hole in the middle of nowhere, look how I've been treated. That man Drummond is exactly the menace my poor departed sister, said he was."

But it was an accident, Clara," the Colonel blustered, possibly trying to rectify the situation."

"I am not interested, Edmund. Order that removals lorry back immediately>"

That was unfair. Poor Dick had been knocked off his perch driving the cart by the man from above, misjudging his landing so badly, in which case it had not been his fault at all. However, as Dominic often said, God moves in mysterious ways… Dick would be free of Clara's presence next door.

"That bloody Count is making eyes at my Olga," Jack muttered in the angriest way I had ever heard a mutter, muttered.

As far as I could see, the boot was on the other foot. Perhaps Olga saw an opportunity to better herself. As far as I was aware, she had come from one of the eastern bloc countries so was probably poor. She had plenty of feminine attributes to make up for that, as Jack had already noticed, although I believe he considered her out of his league. Goodness knows why, he was a handsome man with a nice disposition, honest, reliable and would make a good husband for the right woman. However, he had no permanent job here, due in the main, to the health reasons he had been advised to move from the smoky city that plagued him, so a shortage of cash was most likely the governing factor.

"I wonder where Dick went to?" I said, hoping to distract him.

"Who? Oh, Dick. Hiding probably, in case he gets a right-hander from the blacksmith. Now look at him, he has his arm around her waist."

My ploy plainly wasn't working. I also sensed Jack's temperature was rising rapidly.

The Count and Olga began circulating. I expect she was explaining, in French, I knew she could speak the language, what each stall or sideshow did and how it worked, although, there appeared to be a familiarity between them that annoyed Jack, no end.

The pair arrived at this tent.

"*Allow me to procure you a drink, mademoiselle,*" Count Thingamajig said, smarmily.

Olga's long eyelashes fluttered like a flag in a strong breeze. "*I am thanking you, sir.*" She obviously loved the attention.

As the Count returned, Jack moved sideways to collide with him violently. Drinks went all ways.

"*Messieur, you spilléd my glassés. You will apologise,*" the Count demanded.

"Stop bloody moaning, it was an accident," Jack returned.

"*It was intentional, messieur.*"

"Are you accusing me of lying?" Jack snapped, turning menacingly upon his up-coming adversary.

"*You knocked der arm on a purpose, beink,*" Olga retaliated.

The pair stood looking at each other like two bull elephants.

It was obvious to even the dimmest person around, Jack was after a fight.

Grabbing his arm, I somehow dragged the hulk of a man

away. "Stop it, Jack. It would ruin the fete. Then you'll be blamed, driving the young lady farther from you than ever."

"He's being a pain, Jane."

"You are just jealous. You have no claim on Olga at all, as well you know. If you're that keen, you should plight your troth, or whatever Dominic would say. In the least, chat her up."

Lady Celia had seen the incident. "Find that other dreadful man and then leave my grounds, Mister Sweeny," she demanded. "How dare you insult the Count, a guest on my property? Go, now, otherwise I shall call the police to have you forcefully ejected. That man Drummond stole my jewellery, I saw the muddy footprints all through the kitchen, up the stairs right into my bedroom. I shall have to get carpet cleaners in to get that mess off," Celia ranted.

That was that. Celia had put the lid on Dick's future here today, possibly at any other time, intimating he was a thief. Why he should have had muddy feet was beyond me. When Dominic and I were there his shoes were clean, so he could not have possibly made muddy footprints anywhere. In any case, Dick hadn't come down the stairs, he had used the ladders and only been inside for the blink of an eye.

"Go and find Dick, please. He needs a bath anyway, so can't stay here stinking the place out. His unusual aroma should give you a good idea where he has holed up."

He was in some bushes behind the drinks tent.

"T'weren't moi fault, Miss Jane," he muttered. "Oi'll get it in the neck off moi Missus too, yet oi never did anything."

That was perfectly true, but his phrase, *T'weren't moi fault'*, was one heard far too frequently when a calamity occurred. Usually, it wasn't, as Dick rightly claimed, although he appeared to have a propensity for getting into scrapes that caused chaos, placing him in the spotlight. In that bright beam of attention, too often for his own good, he got elected the guilty one.

Dominic had recovered, so accompanied us all to the

vicarage.

"Do try to curb your ambitions towards Lady Celia's maid," he chided Jack. "As Jane has pointed out, you have hardly spoken to her, so don't expect the woman to fall over herself for you. Now it seems, you are hardly ever likely to get near her again, having been banned from the Manor's grounds. I can't understand you, normally such a mild-mannered man, yet you get this bee in your bonnet about a woman, then go off the rails."

"Sorry, reverend. I'll try not to do it again."

"Trying isn't good enough, Jack, a promise never to indulge in such activity would be better."

Jack stood like a scolded schoolboy, head hung, face a picture of misery.

"Cheer up," I put in. "Plenty more fish, it's just finding one."

"She's beautiful, Jane…" his words trailed off.

"Better you take Dick home, he needs a clean-up," Dominic finished with a grunt. "He's stinking the vicarage out."

"There's the problem with Celia's jewels, my love. She was insistent Dick must have snatched them while in her bedroom. But he couldn't possibly have, his head appeared out of the broken window within a second or two of flying through it."

"I agree, Jane. She's picking on the first person she felt might have had the chance, but he didn't, I'm sure. The police will be involved again, which means him being suspect number one, you know what Bracknell's like," Dominic groaned.

And that ended the first village fete attended by me. Let's hope they would not all be like this!

Word of the Lord

*T*he following day the excitement of the fete died down, even the fight between Jack and the Count averted, although it had been a very close thing. Had it not been for poor Dominic's untoward balloon flight, serious injury could have been inflicted. However, the underlying situation remained explosive.

Lady Celia had persuaded the Count into the Manor for light refreshments with wine, while Dominic, after a brief rest to gather his wits, got the wayward pair to the vicarage, so well away from another bout of likely fisticuffs.

"Really Jack," Dominic snapped irritably as we met the pair outside the inn, "what on earth possessed you to go off half-cocked like that?"

"He's taking over Olga, a bloody newcomer throwing his weight around," Jack grumbled. "I was only trying to look out for her."

"You don't own her, in fact as far as I'm aware, you have never even asked her out anywhere or for a date. She has a right to go out with who she likes until you change that situation," Dominic pointed out.

"Come on, I'll treat you to a beer. Let's pop to the inn." I hoped it might head a row off.

"Never mind about that, our Jack, what am oi a-goin' to do now oi've lost moi job? Moi diary's right empty," Dick complained as we walked.

"Your diary's always been empty," Jack snorted. "Just don't come that nonsense with me."

"Maybe so," Dick grudgingly replied, "but now oi b'ain't got no work and Maggie will be on at oi a-cause we ain't got any social life, neither. Oi don't know what oi'm a-gonna do," he muttered, throwing the little book down onto the table in disgust, then sat staring at the nearly empty ale glass the contents of which, had vanished with remarkable speed. "Oi never took her silly old jewels."

"You've always been hard up, you might have taken them for a rainy day," Jack retorted.

"Now look here, our Jack, oi knows oi haven't done much work since you came here, but that bit of money came in handy for a few extras."

"Not to mention a few ales here or there," Jack added with a nod.

"Look here you two," Dominic snapped, "you promised me to go easy on the drink. Don't you dare break your words?"

"Moi names been all a-smirched up again now, revrund. Oi thought oi'd got over that sort of thing after being cleared of the fire."

Dominic nodded, softening a little. "It seems so, Dick. I hope you didn't take them, you are telling the truth, aren't you?"

"Oi would never do a thing like that, revrund, as oi never did the things old mother Sharpe were accusin' oi of. Who made those muddy footprints through her house, that's what oi'd like to know?"

"That is a puzzle," Dominic agreed. "The police didn't seem interested in finding out when I mentioned it, said they were the gardeners. Can't see him wandering about the house in the middle of the day with muddy boots on, CHS would never allow it."

"You're in a tight spot again, my old china," Jack said in agreement, "that's no mistake."

"You've lost your job as well, our Jack" Dick returned quickly, "although not for the same thing."

"That's true. At the moment I can't see a way of getting either of your jobs back," Dominic stated.

"Perhaps I can put in a good word? We often meet at the WI meetings."

"That be a good idea, Missus revrund, else oi can't see any way to a-clear moi name, or us getting work around here ever again."

Dominic cast a stern look my way. "Be very careful how you approach CHS my dear. She's really put out over the way the Count has been treated and the damage to the window."

"If she won't let us back, there's no way of proving who did nick her jewels, is there, revrund. Us won't be able to find any clues."

"I can only try, Dick, we are still on friendly terms."

The inn door groaned as it swung slowly open, a noise that sounded as if it was guiltily undertaking the act, drawing all our attentions in that direction.

A scruffy, unkempt individual stood within its frame, together with the stale smell of a long unwashed human starting to overpower us.

"Gordon Bennett, cop the state of him," Jack exclaimed.

Dick laughed. "And you reckons oi ain't up to scratch. He leaves oi a-standing with that filthy old Macintosh and grubby trousers full of holes."

Jack chuckled. "He's wringing his hands like bloody Fagin. Fair gives me the creeps. Don't go anywhere near him Missus reverend."

"I have no intention of doing such a thing, Jack. He gives me the creeps, too. Please call me Jane." Yet, at the back of my mind, there was something about his appearance that was strangely familiar, but I couldn't place it.

The tramp cast around the pub at the patrons, finally moving towards our group.

"Gawd bless yers, my dears," he said. "You all seem kindly folk."

"There be only one person around here that blesses

people, that be the revrund here," Dick pointed out tartly.

"What do you want," Jack snapped, "apart from a bloody good bath?"

"The name's Isiah Bono."

"I never asked who you are, what's your pitch?" Jack replied, guardedly.

"I just come to preach the gospel, then maybe sell a bible or two," the apparition replied.

"Bibles!" Dick snapped out. "You b'ain't no preacher for a start, and secondly, we have one right here, thanks very much."

"That don't stop a man from spreading the word of the Lord, does it? You seem a good sort, won't you buy one?" A hand reached to Dick's shoulder, fingers poking through the ends of the woollen glove that partly covered it.

"Keep away from oi."

"Let me see one," Dominic demanded.

The filthy individual backed away.

"Hey You?" Charlie bellowed as he quickly came from behind the bar, preventing Dominic's inspection.

The tramp's body stiffened into a crouching position, as a cat might if readying to go on the defensive, plainly a well-rehearsed and automatic reaction when sensing trouble. "Who me?"

"Yes you, you're scrounging again," Charlie snapped. "I told you a couple of days ago not to come in here unless you smartened yourself up. All you do is stink the bloody place out making a nuisance of yourself. Out, now!"

"But I'm just giving out the written word of the Lord," Isiah said, feigning an innocence that wouldn't have fooled a five-year-old.

"He nicked those from the lower village chapel, reverend," Charlie snarled at the man. "That's not a very Godly thing to do, is it? This is the last time I'll tell you, don't come in here pestering my customers, else I'll call the police. Now out!"

"All right, all right, I'm going."

"Phew!" Jack breathed. "Thank goodness for that. Leave the door open a bit, please, Charlie. Let's get some fresh air in here."

"What was that about stealing those bibles?" Dominic asked.

"Bracknell told me. Reckons they came from the Baptist chapel over there, the door had been forced. That's not the only stuff that went missing, he said. The bibles are standard issue for those places, so the police can't prove anything. They turned his shack over, found nothing there, either. Just keep an eye on him and St Mary's locked for now. He's pretty harmless, just a nuisance, people don't want him around here, especially the Colonel."

"Oi knows the bleeding feeling," Dick half groaned.

"You've not sunk that low mate. You have a nice wife and home now."

"Oi b'ain't got a job though, have oi?" Dick pointed out. "CHS has seen to that. Oi'll have to pinch the lead off the church roof to make ends meet."

"WHAT!" Bellowed Jack.

"Only kidding," Dick said with a nervous laugh. "You take oi too serious at times, our Jack."

His outburst at not having a job must have taken Dominic aback as much as me. To hear Dick, complain about being out of work was something never heard before. He had always studiously avoided it.

"You shouldn't crack jokes about things like that, it's sacrilegious," Jack said as he banged the table with a fist.

"Jack's right," Charlie put in. "Many a true word spoken in jest."

"Oi wouldn't do a terrible thing like that. Lost moi job, but it ain't the end of the world."

"It is for me and Olga. How am I going to make any headway with her now that Count's got his clutches on her," Jack growled. "She'll not be interested in me with this cloud hanging over the pair of us. He's well off, I'm broke, no contest, is there?"

"Oh, that's why you're a-looking so down-in-the-mouth, is it? What about us and CHS? Oi expect that copper'll be round asking a load of daft questions again, and that'll go down like a lead balloon with the girls."

"If you're innocent, you have nothing to fear," Dominic put in. "The police aren't fools, they have access to the crime scene, I expect they'll be forming a case."

"Oi knows you mean well, revrund, but they got it in for oi in the first place, especially after old mother Sharpe did all that accusing last year. Mud sticks, then once they have you in their sights, they never let go."

"There's not much more we can do here," I pointed out. "It's getting late now, best we all go home for some rest. Perhaps things will look better tomorrow?"

Church Lead

We were woken in the early hours. I knew it was early, it was still dark.

As we went downstairs, Dominic picking a poker up on the way. "Who is it?" He called through the closed door.

"Constable Bracknell, revrund. I need to speak to you. Open the door please."

"What on earth is so urgent you wake us at four o'clock in the morning?" Dominic uttered.

"Your roof lead, vicar, it's been stolen. I was doing my nightly rounds when I noticed some broken masonry on the path alongside the nave. There was a set of ladders stood against the guttering, so I shot up to see why. That's when I saw the problem."

"We can't do anything right now, surely? For a start it's too dark to see, best we wait for daylight. Thanks for informing us, constable."

"That's very bad news, my love, isn't it? Lead is expensive, is that right?"

"Yes, it is Jane, that's why it's been stolen, to sell on. Who could have done it though?"

The door thudded again.

"Now what?" Dominic snorted. "I'm still in pyjamas."

"I'll come as well, my love."

Jack's worried face looked back at us. "Can you help, reverend? They'll arrest Dick for this, that's certain."

"Why should they do that?" I asked.

"Because Charlie heard him say he would nick it, in the inn last night. He phoned me, said the police have been round with a load of stupid questions."

"Let us get dressed" Dominic said. "We had better go to see him."

Jack hammered on Dick's door. Nothing happened. He thudded again. "Wake up, it's Jack with the reverends."

The door swung open. "Do you have to thump like that at this daft o'clock in the morning, our Jack? We were all a-bed."

"So was the reverend and Jane when I had to wake them up, so stop moaning."

"Oh ah, mornin' revrunds, didn't see you in the dark. What do you all want?"

"That was a damned fool thing to do. We all know you've got some money problems, but pinching that lead really takes the biscuit."

"Lead? Biscuits? What the hell are you talking about?"

"Don't come the old innocent bit with me, Dick, you know as well as I do what I'm talking about. You've done what you said, nicked the bloody lead from the church roof. Bracknell found CHS's ladders set against the wall, just as you left them."

"OI b'ain't been nowhere near the church, our Maggie and Annie will tell you that. Came straight home from the inn, oi did."

"What time did he get in girls?"

"Let oi think, t'were 'bout eleven, oi suppose," Margaret confirmed.

"There!" Jack exclaimed. "I left you just gone five, you had stacks of time, so your tale won't wash with me, my old china."

"Are there any witnesses that you stayed in the inn?" Dominic asked.

"Charlie'll tell you. Oi played dominoes with old Jake Crowe, the gravedigger, until late."

"When exactly was late?" I asked.

"Not sure exactly, Missus revrund," Dick mused. "Ten'ish, oi s'pect."

"That makes you an hour adrift," Jack snorted. "Where's your diary?" Jack demanded out of the blue.

"In moi pocket, a-corse."

"Let's see it then."

Dick went to the wardrobe door to fumble through his jacket and trouser pockets. "Crikey, Jack, it b'ain't be there."

"No, of course it ain't. It's down at the nick."

"What's it doing there, our Jack?"

"Because it was found beside the ladders, that's what it's doing there. Now get out of that!"

"Oi ain't been near the church, honest. The last time oi had it was in the inn, you remember, when oi were a-talkin' to Charlie."

"That's another thing, he heard you say it," Jack reposted, jabbing Dick in the chest.

"Say what?" Dick looked blankly back.

"That you were going to nick the lead, you twit," Jack snapped.

"Ber… but oi said oi were only a-kidding on, didn't oi?"

"That's as maybe, it won't make much difference now. The copper'll be here in a minute, so you'd best get some clothes on."

"Where are we a-goin'?"

"The bleeding nick, if you don't get a move on. Get cracking."

"Just a minute, oi ain't done nothin' wrong, why should oi run away from moi home. What about moi missus and Annie?"

"The reverends will help me look after them, won't you?" Jack asked, turning to us.

I took a hand of Dick's reassuringly. "Yes, we will. You must call me Jane now, too, as Margaret, Jack and Annabel do. I don't think an hour would have been enough time to shift that amount of heavy metal, then put it somewhere else, anyway. That would take half the night.”

"Well, I don't know that we should be helping a fugitive,” Dominic started...

“Yes, we will, Jack. I believe Dick,” I put in quickly. “He needs a little time, that's all, Dominic, my love. Let's give him that, to clear his name?”

“There, now get a move on. Have I ever let you down?” Jack said.

“No, oi guess not, our Jack.” His big brown eyes swung to Margaret. There was sadness in them, almost a tear. “Oi never did it, you've got to believe oi, moi dear.”

“Oi do, moi love. What are they a-doin' to you again? Why don't they leave you be? Do what Jack says, please. The revrunds will see oi and Annie alright, try not to worry, won't you revrunds?”

“You'll be back before you know it,” Jack put in encouragingly.

“Just hang on, moi love, try not to worry. Give oi a kiss. Oi'll have to be off now.”

They hugged. It was a poignant moment. Margaret desperately tried to stifle her sobs, wiping her tears with a handkerchief. A silence hung in the air.

“Where are we a-goin', our Jack?”

“Rogan's old pigsty.”

“They'll find oi,” Dick wailed.

“Nah, its safe, the ground's open for a good stretch all around, so you won't get surprised. The reverends won't let on, will you?” Jack ended.

“No, we won't,” I said pointedly, in case Dominic wavered. “I'll bring you some food later.”

“Thanks, um, Jane, oi appreciate that. Thank you too, Jack, oi'd be in a mess without you, wouldn't oi?”

“Yes, you would, wouldn't you?” Jack snapped, rounding on him. “You'd better come clean. Don't forget I know how desperate you are to look after your missus, now Annabel lives with you, it's a double responsibility. Your trouble is, you get up to too many stupid pranks, but this is serious, it ain't a prank anymore. The truth now."

"Christ, you don't think oi'd pinch it, oh, sorry revrund, but oi just wouldn't, not stoop that low, not for nothin'. Especially with the revrund and Miss Jane, oi mean missus Jane. Oi've been framed, that's for sure, you've all gotta believe that," Dick pleaded.

"I believe you," I said. "This is a dirty trick to keep the suspicion off of whoever's really taken the stuff."

"Mmm," Jack mused, rubbing his chin. "It doesn't seem like you at all, mate. But if you didn't take it, who the bleeding hell did? That's what we've got to find out, and you can't do that in jail, can you? Proof, we need proof, so I'll have a scout around later, see what I can find out."

"I'll come with you, Jack. Having a vicar's wife along might help."

"Oh, good Lord," Dominic muttered. "My wife's getting mixed up with crooks."

"Only with Dick and Jack, my love, they aren't crooks, are they?"

"Um... no, I guess not. Please take care. I love you."

"I will, Jack will look after me. I love you too. But we must help poor Dick, he needs us all right now."

"I'll keep my eyes on her, reverend, have no fear," Jack replied.

"Crikey, our Jack, that's a tall order, we don't even know where to start."

Wavering flashlights approached in the distance

"Quick, they're coming along the lane. Up into Barham's Wood, we'll cut across East field, there's an old barn there you can hide in for a while."

Dominic gave me a hug. "Please be careful, darling."

A dash out the back door, up into the wood, across a field and there stood the shed.

"Phew, it stinks a bit," Dick muttered.

"Farmer Rogan used to keep pigs here until his new block

was built. Still, the pong will hide your scent," Jack finished with a laugh.

Dick sullenly poked the ground with a bit of stick. "Oi got it," he exclaimed with a seeming flash of inspiration. "What about those gypsies camped farther along the lane. It must be they?"

"Oh Dick," I chided, "Don't try to shift the blame onto them without an ounce of evidence. They are Romanies, real gypsies with a great tradition. They come to church on Sundays, so are also religious."

"Jane's right, they live by a religious code, so it's hardly likely to be them. It might not be a bad idea to go for a chat though, they might know something through the grapevine, sort of thing."

"There b'ain't no grapes around here, our Jack, not that oi've ever known."

"Not real grapes, I mean word of mouth. You're a right banana at times."

"It's all a-getting a bit past oi, grapes or bananas," Dick snapped back in irritation.

"Just keep out of sight, Dick. We'll go to make a few enquiries," I encouraged

"Do as Jane said, stay low, keep your eyes open. If anyone approaches move out, keep them and the shed between you. Once clear, lie down. Come back after they hop it. Alright?"

"Cripes, Jack, oi'm scared."

"Try to keep your spirits up, Dick, we'll be back soon," I said with a hug.

We turned at the doorway. Dick looked very downcast, sitting alone in the corner of the barn, I felt a great deal of pity for him.

"You're a good way from the village," Jack called. "It should be okay to light a fire if you're cold, as long as it's in here."

"Alright, our Jack. Oi'll nip to the wood to find some timber." He seemed more cheerful.

Jack mused over events as we walked. "It's a right old puzzle, Jane. Who could have done such a thing? Those gypsies aren't the usual ragamuffins that come scrounging around. I got some pegs off them and they we well made; they keep themselves to themselves for the most part. They might know if there are any rogues around locally."

Arriving at the field, I sensed Jack's concern and wariness. "They aren't going to bite, are they? Might be suspicious, that's all."

He nodded. "You're right. Here we go then."

As we approached, a thick set, dark haired man stepped out of a caravan, he eyed Jack, then nodded curtly at me.

Jack held a hand out. "Hello, my name's Jack Sweeny, this is Jane, the vicar's wife."

"By the Virgin Mary, we've got permission to camp on here, so we're not breaking any laws."

"Irish, eh," Jack answered in as friendly a tone as he could muster.

"We just came for a friendly chat," I put in, "that's all."

"Oh aye, friendly, is it?" His expression eased. "The vicar's wife, are ye? What can we after be doing for you, this fine morning? We don't have many pals around here since that nitwit went and stole the lead off the church roof. Tis not about dat, is it? By the suffering Jesus, nobody here would dream of doing such a ting. We're all God-fearing folk from the old country, so you be remembering dat."

"You're Romanies, aren't you?" I quickly put in. "We know about your way of life and respect it. Yet in a way, it's because of that we're here, you being religious and honest." I hoped it sounded sincere.

Gypsies

"Well, by the Blessed Virgin Mary, you're not bad sorts at all."

An inward sigh of relief went through me. "We're not accusing you of anything, so you do have some friends here. It's just that we have a problem you might be able to help us with. Jack will explain."

"My mate's in the mire about this as well, he didn't do it, either. We wondered if you had an ear to the ground about it?"

"'Tis your mate they're being after, is it? That wouldn't be him in the hut over the field away?" The man half closed one eye, tilting his head a little to squint at Jack, in an *'I know he's there,'* look, testing Jack to show his hand so put trust in this band of people.

"We'll, I..." Jack stammered.

"Yes, it is," I said. "How do you know?"

The Irishman laughed. "Don't worry, I'll not be giving him away. We smelt the fire he lit." The man slapped Jack's arm. "His name isn't Drummond, is it?"

We were dumbfounded. "Ber... but how do you know that?" Jack fumbled for words.

"Don't fret yourselves, my friends. The local copper was here asking questions, thought we were hiding him and had a good look around, so this place is in the clear. It was him that told us about the stealing and how they're looking for him. I've seen him around the village, by all the saints in heaven, I don't tink he's a one to go stealing from a church. Will you leave it wit' me for a few hours, I've an idea, just might have someting for you later. If your friend wants to come here for a meal, he'll be very welcome. I'm Danny O'Flattery, by the way, nice to meet you two."

"Cheers Danny, that's appreciate," Jack replied. "We're in a tight spot, as you can imagine, any help is a Godsend. I'll have a look around the village, in at the inn, too, see if Charlie's heard any rumours."

"I'll go to get Dick. He won't panic if he sees me going." Leaving the men, then traversing the field, my brain wondered what on earth this man could come up with in a couple of hours. Giving a soft call to let him know who it was.

"Morning Jane. That don't seem right, oi a-calling you by your first name," Dick muttered. "Where be Jack, any news yet?"

"He's going around the village. We've found somewhere for you to hide, better than this."

"Oi can't go home."

"It's with those gypsies. We went to see them. They think you're innocent too, so that's good news, isn't it?"

He looked doubtful. "They'll give oi away."

"No, they won't. They are honest, gave their word about that. Come with me."

He grabbed my arm, pointing across towards the lane. "Look Miss Jane, you were followed. Someone's a-coming."

"No, I was very careful. What now?"

The dark uniform of Constable Bracknell began getting closer.

"Crikey, it's the law. We'll have to go down the field, it slopes, and we'll soon be out of sight if we lie down."

"Lie down! I've got a skirt on," I protested.

"Oi won't look," Dick retorted with a wide grin.

For an instant I was cross with him for being so cheeky. But his grin dissipated that feeling, it was good to see him smile again. "Alright, but promise."

We lay, side-by-side in the young crops, occasionally peering over the ridge of land.

"They must be onto oi," he groaned. "Oi'll go to prison for something oi didn't do, sure as hens lay eggs."

"For goodness sake stop panicking," I uttered quietly, saying it as calmly as possible. "He's just checking places out, making sure you're not there."

"But that means they think oi did it. Oi'll never be free again," he wailed, seeming to sag within.

"He's gone now. Come with me to the gypsies."

At the hedge of the field, we paused awhile. "Wait here, I'll make sure it's clear."

With a light tap on the van door, I called. "Danny?"

A rotund woman opened it, how she managed to get in and out was a mystery. Yet, strangely, she held an air of delicacy with a cherubic face that appeared to make her look a lot younger than she actually was. A cigarette hung from her mouth, flashing the thought through my mind in an instant, that she must have been a larger relative of Margaret's. "Is Danny here?"

"Oh, be a-coming in wit you, sit yerself down."

Danny rested in an armchair with a glass of Guinness in one hand. He smiled. "This is Maureen, an auntie of mine. Reckons she can tell fortunes, as most gypsy women can. Where's your friend?"

"Hiding outside scared out of his wits. Thank you, Maureen, but I don't need my fortune told, it's already mapped out."

"She's the vicar's wife," Danny said, somewhat in my defence.

"It's not just the future I can see," Maureen retorted indignantly, "It'll be the past, too."

I smiled. "His past is all too well known in the village as any of its inhabitants will tell you," said I.

"He was a bit of a scallywag, I'm given to understand," Danny mused.

"No, distant past, of another life long ago, much like reincarnation."

My God, the thought occurred, fancy wanting to go back into Dick's previous lives. Goodness knows what horrors might lurk there.

"Will you two stop the nattering, and by the Mother of Mary, get him in here, he'll be needing a drink."

"You can say that again. Gasping by now, I shouldn't wonder."

Dick made himself comfortable on a chest. "Like nectar," he muttered, putting the glass back on the table as he smacked his lips. "Oi needed that."

"Taut you might. The next ting you'll be needing, is a bart. You stink someting awful."

The snigger that escaped was impossible to stifle.

Just then, Jack knocked

Dick glared at me. "Oi can't help it, oi were a-stuck in that old pigsty all night."

"Tis alright, my friend. Maureen will show you the bartroom. Now Jane, I went for a walk early," Danny continued, "overheard the Colonel talking to the vicar in the lane. Miss Maybrook's house was broken into yesterday afternoon while she went to the store. Whoever did it was looking for money, because they ransacked the drawers, the mattress was pulled out and everyting trown about. Some old ornaments have gone to be sold off somewhere, I reckon."

"Crikey," Dick mumbled. "It gets worse by the minute."

"We don't like dat sort of ting either, Dick, everyone blames us then we get a bad name."

"Not half as bad as mine," Dick snapped back.

"Be patient my friend, tieves like that always hang themselves in the end. There's a tinker camped in Blackthorne Copse that we've known of for some time. When I crept up on his camp, the fool never knew anybody was there," Danny explained, grinning.

"You would make a good poacher," Jack said.

"He's sleeping rough in a shack made of old car parts held togeter with bits of timber, cooking over an open fire. By the suffering Jesus, tis a mess down there. About a hundred yards away there's a heap well covered with old sacking and branches. That's where he's stowed the stuff that's gone missing, the police missed it when they searched."

"You're probably right, Danny, the trouble is proving it. That heap has to be connected to him, else he'll deny any knowledge, claiming somebody put it there to incriminate him." Maureen pointed out. "Dat'll be us, most likely."

"By the Blessed Virgin Mary, you're right, Maureen. One sniff of anyone approaching and he'll be away faster than a leprechaun, dat won't help Dick."

"Mmm," mused Jack. "In that case we've got to catch that sly old fox in his den, red handed with the loot, with witnesses."

"Goodness Jack, that's a tall order," I pointed out. "Especially as everybody in the village are bound to be on the lookout for Dick after that burglary, so it will be difficult moving him in daylight."

"You and me had better reconnoitre the place, see what's going on, Jane. Dick can stay here until we get back."

A short walk took us to Dominic talking to Margaret.

"Good day, Vicar," Jack said as innocently as he could.

"Where on earth have you been, my love?" Dominic asked."

"Doing what I said I would, looking out for Dick, now we're trying to find out who is behind this trouble."

"He's in a lot more trouble now, my love, you should leave it to the police."

"Get real, reverend, you know as well as we do, Dick never had anything to do with those thefts, he wouldn't harm a fly," Jack retorted. "Bracknell has it in for him as it is, the slightest thing, Dick gets blamed."

"Why has he run off then? If he's not guilty he'll be cleared, just as he was over that Briskett business."

"Moi Dick never did it," Margaret stated vehemently.

"Somebody did it. It's either him or those gypsies," Dominic snapped back. "Why has he stopped trusting us?"

"Trust works both ways. Whatever happened to faith, my love?"

"Jane's right, reverend. He's scared stiff, and after all the time you've known him, I'd have expected you of all people, to believe him. It's not the gypsies, either," Jack added.

"How do you know that?"

"We went for a chat. They are a decent lot, they're as angry about the thefts as we are."

"How can anybody help him if he won't help himself? Let me talk to him."

There was a silence as both men looked at each other.

"You must promise not to inform on him, my love. Give him a fair hearing, too, don't just jump to conclusions, as everybody seems to be doing here, especially Bracknell. We need time to sort a few things out. There's a lot more to this than meets the eye. If our plan fails, Jack will do whatever you say, darling." It put Jack on the spot with me having a lot of faith in whatever he had up his sleeve.

Dominic nodded. "Very well, I'll agree. Where is he?"

"Is he alright, our Jack?" Margaret asked.

"Don't fret, gel, he's fine."

"Can oi see him, too?"

"Reckon so. But with us going mob handed, we'll need to keep our eyes peeled."

"Lead on, Jack," Dominic said.

"You promised," Jack pointed out.

"I'll keep my word, don't worry."

"Okay, I'll trust you, after all, you did stand by him all through that boat business when everyone here wanted his skin hung up to dry from the nearest tree."

"I'm putting my faith in Dick's innocence and sticking my neck out for him now," Dominic pointed out.

"You're a real decent chap, reverend."

Jack tapped on the van door.

Danny's head poked out. "By the suffering Jesus, who are all these folks? Oh, I see, it's the vicar man. You'd all better come in out of sight."

"Oi never did any of it," Dick remonstrated. "Oi'm a-being hung out like a scrapegoat again, revrund. You know oi wouldn't touch a single stone of your church, so it be all lies."

Dominic gave him a long look. "Very well, I believe you. It's scapegoat, Dick."

"By the Mother of Mary, that's a lot in your favour, my friend. Here, have a Guinness."

"That's not all of it, moi Dick, not only the lead and the Maybrook stuff. Master William hasn't been seen about the village and CHS is acting very odd, hardly speakin' to anybody, nor a-comin' to the WI meetings. The Colonel's been a-toing and a-froing to the Manor a lot as well, more than ever he has before."

"Do you think that has any bearing on these thefts?" Dominic asked.

"Oi dunno, revrund, but it be mighty funny goings on, in moi book," Margaret replied earnestly.

"Alright, Margaret, but we must go one step at a time. Let's clear Dick's name first."

Skulduggery

"*T*here's only one way I can see of doing this," Danny said.

"What's that?" Dominic asked.

"We'll be after setting a trap for that tramp. It'll be a big risk for Dick, but if tings set right, it should work. The crafty old devil will be looking in the one direction, so won't be seeing what's coming from t'other. By the sufferin' Jesus, we'll teach him a lesson or two."

"Really, what have you in mind, Danny" I put in.

"To get the tramp going to save his ill-gotten gains with the police in sight. To do that we need a distraction."

"Oh, one of those again."

"To be sure, my dear. We must get Dick to that inn witout being seen. Perhaps that blacksmith chap would help?"

"HIM! No chance, he hates my old mate since the fete and the accident with the horse and cart," Jack snorted.

"Yeah, let's go there, oi'm about ready for a punch-up."

"Hang on, you," Jack snapped. "This isn't the time nor the place, for you to go get slaughtered."

"Mmm, that could work to our advantage," Dominic added. "If he goes after Dick, the rest of the village will follow to see the fight. That will provide our witnesses."

"By the suffering Jesus, this is some vicar you have here. He tinks like an Irishman!"

"First, a plan," Jack said.

"Right, I'll go have a quiet look around," Danny replied

thoughtfully. "In the meantime, Dick must be moved to a safer hiding place. No offence, vicar, but a slip of the tongue and all our plans will be lost."

"Yes, that's sensible," I cut in, before Dominic could open his mouth. "My husband can go back to the vicarage, which would seem normal if anybody calls. Be off now, my dear, leave us to it."

"Are you sure, I don't want you hurt."

"By the sacred cross, she'll be fine wit us, not a hair on her head will be even ruffled," Danny added confidently.

"While we're waiting for the menfolk to make their minds up, I'll tell your fortune, Dick," Maureen stated. "Sit next to me."

Dick sat. Maureen was not a person one argued with.

"Be putting your right hand between mine," she ordered. Within a moment her eyes closed as she began concentrating, her face taking on a blank expression as a trance deepened.

Dick cast a nervous glance at Margaret and me. "Be she alright?"

"Shss, don't talk," Margaret whispered.

"Ohhhh," Maureen wailed. "There's a ship at sea, guns blazing, men dying." A pause ensued. "There's a church and a young man dressed in rags, a military man, too, an officer. There's a cave, dark and deep with the smell of death, yet the glitter of riches, a man on a horse, a gilded frame."

Margaret stared at Dick, who shrugged his shoulders.

Maureen sprung into words again. "A slow, suffering death. Now the cold walls of a room surround me, then death again. Ahhh," she moaned, slumping into the chair.

"Cripes," Dick hooted, "she's passed out."

"Quick, here's a glass and a bottle of brandy, give her a sip," I cried, handing Dick the objects.

"BRANDY! Oi think oi'd best taste it first to be sure it's alright." He grabbed the bottle, taking a long slug. "Oh ah, that be fine, a nice drop of stuff, too."

"Give it to her, you idiot," Margaret yelled, snatching it

back.

Maureen's eyes opened. She looked long and hard at Dick. "Beware, young man, there's dark deeds afoot, by the suffering Jesus, dark deeds to be sure."

"Will you stop putting the fear of Christ up him, Maureen," Danny snapped as he came from the other room. "You do talk a load of blarney at times."

"T'was seen, as plain as Cork Castle."

"It's the cork that you can see is in that brandy bottle," Danny retorted sarcastically.

"Don't go mocking fate, I've never seen wrong before, Danny, you know dat, neither has any drink passed my lips," she ended, indignantly.

"She's right, to be sure," Danny grudgingly admitted with a nod.

"We've found a place for you to hide, it's an old cave at Smuggler's Cove."

"There!" Maureen screamed in exclamation. "I said there would be a cave."

"Away wit you, woman. You probably heard us talking in the next room."

"I saw," Maureen insisted, glowering around the room. "I saw, and it's always right."

"Jesus, Mary and Joseph, let's hope you've not been frightening him with the death message?"

"It might have slipped in," Maureen pouted."

"At least twice," Margaret confirmed. "She said it a few times."

"Oi don't wanna go in no cave if oi'm a-going to die," Dick hooted, fear in both his face and voice.

"You're not going to die." Danny spun on Maureen. "For God's sake, you see what you've done now?"

"I'm sure it wasn't him. It was distant, somebody else, perhaps in another time or life. Do you believe in reincarnation?"

"Reincarnation?" Dick muttered. "What are they,

flowers?"

"By the holy Mother of Mary, don't you know anyting? That means having lived years ago, then coming back as you are now."

"You mean oi b'ain't a-going to die?" There was a note of relief in his voice.

"It's not very likely," Danny put in sarcastically, "unless it's from boredom."

"Phew, thank goodness for that," Dick groaned. "Gave oi quite a fright. Can oi have another shot of that brandy?"

Our group, comprising Dick, Danny, Jack, Dominic and me, managed to fit into the vicar's car somehow. It took about ten minutes to drive to the clifftops above the wide cove.

The wind blew gently across, causing a myriad of ripples on the water that reflected the setting sun, like golden nymphs dancing joyously on the sea. A distance offshore, a yacht bobbed at anchor.

"Peaceful, isn't it?"

"I hope it stays that way, Miss Jane," Dick mumbled.

"Get going," Jack ordered. "It's the first cave you come to."

"Not full of bleedin' bats, is it?" Dick questioned, a definite edge to his voice.

"Do you want Squeaky to test it out first," Jack snapped irritably.

"No need to get like that. Oi'm a-goin'."

"Here, this bag has a few bits to help, a sleeping back, small stove, some grub and a couple of cans to keep body and soul together. It's not cold, so you'll be okay and nobody will find you," Jack added.

"Shss, two cars have stopped over there," Danny warned.

Dick peered through the gloom. "That's Sid Slimebucket's

car, oi'd know it anywhere, big flashy Yankee thing, just like him."

"By the sacred Mother of Mary, who's Sid Slimebucket?" Danny queried.

"A shady car dealer from the next town," Jack answered. "Always into some deal or other that's usually on the wrong side of the law. His name's not Slimebucket, that's what Dick calls him, it's Sandcastle."

"The other car is that big black limousine we saw in the village," Dick muttered.

"Look, it's that galoot from Briar Cottage. How the hell does he know Sid?"

"Beats oi, our Jack. He'd be the last person oi'd expect those strangers to take up with, especially if it's underhand."

Danny shook my sleeve. "Look Jane, there's a dinghy coming in from the yacht. See, Sid is signalling wit a torch, now there's a ting for you. Can they land here?"

"A-course they can," Dick said, assuming an air of authority on the matter. "There's a nice sandy beach that were used in years gone by for a-bringin' smuggled goods ashore."

"Bleeding know-it-all," Jack replied.

"That's right, our Jack. T'were said they smugglers stored it in one of the caves here, cut into the rocks by the sea and storms, some so fierce, long tunnels were dug deep under the headland. It's rumoured there's a secret passage the other end of one, that goes to a cottage atop the cliffs. On many a dark night the Revenue Officers would lie a-waitin' at these here cliffs to capture them."

Jack gave Danny a roll-eyes look. "Comes out with a load of old cobblers at times, doesn't he? Still, we can't say we don't get our money's worth when he spins a tale."

"B'ain't a tale," Dick argued. "It is the truth."

"You said that about Melissa, and look how that turned out," Jack countered.

"'Tis, Danny, oi swear it."

"We'll not be having any swearing, the vicar and his lady

are present," Danny said, pointedly.

"Stop arguing," Jack whispered. "I'm for getting nearer. See if we can hear anything."

"Count me in." Danny came back, enthusiastically.

"Us too. We must find out what's going on here," I agreed.

"Mind your footing, my love, it's slippery along here," Dominic warned.

Jack held a hand up. "Listen, their voices carry well."

"…rugs in crates," Sid Sandcastle's voice filtered through the night… "Take care… the stones…" came brief snatches of a reply.

Plainly Sid was impatient. "How bloody long have I got to wait?" he snapped. "I've a business to run."

"We can't move yet," a stranger's voice replied. "After those robberies the local police are on an alert. Please be patient."

"It stinks and I don't like it," Sid retorted. "It's a thirty-year spell in the nick if we're collared, I'm sticking my neck out for a townie."

"The boss is not a townie, so if he says wait, we wait. The merchandise will have to stay where it is for at least another week."

"Another bloody week! Shit, that's ages with the old Bill snooping about," Sid rapped.

"Shut up! You're in this up to your neck. The only way anybody leaves the bosses organisation is feet first."

"Are you threatening me?" Sid snarled. "I've my own heavyweights, just be careful."

"The organisation takes care of things, so I don't need to threaten you or anybody else. Do I make myself clear?"

Even in the dark Jack's concerned face was clear to see. "That doesn't sound very good, bloody dangerous if you ask me."

"Shss," I whispered. "They might hear us, then what? They would want to silence any witnesses."

The second man spoke again. "Don't try to contact me in the village, it's too dangerous. I'll be in touch when the time's right. Remember, the boss likes things done his way, and you," the man went on, turning to a sailor from the yacht, "Threat the merchandise with proper care, we don't want an accident, not yet, anyway, do we?" An evil laugh followed that statement.

They each went to their cars and drove away. The dinghy left for the yacht.

"Crikey," Jack muttered. "They sound like a pretty heavy mob to me, gave my skin goose bumps on my goose bumps."

"Oi wonder what this merchandise is?" Dick said. "Must be pretty important if it means thirty years inside."

"By the Holy Crucifix, what a to-do," Danny mused. "He mentioned the organisation, whatever that is, then rugs in crates and stones. Was that a load of blarney or not?"

"Deadly serious, I'd say," Jack answered. "Let's put our heads together for a think. Rugs, stones and crates, maybe they have them at Briar Cottage? Furthermore, who's the boss guy? First, let's get you settled in the cave out of the way, me old china," Jack said, giving Dick an encouraging shove. "You can keep an eye on that yacht and anything else that goes on."

"Oi! Stuck here all on moi own with a band of cutthroats hanging about?"

"Dick's right," I stated. "He shouldn't be here alone, it's too dangerous. I'll stay with him."

"My God," Dominic spluttered, "I can't allow that, a vicar's wife taking on crooks."

"Don't worry, Dick wouldn't lay a finger on me, would you?"

"I didn't mean that, darling, it's the thugs I'm worried about. We'll both stay."

Dick cheered up. "You can count on oi. It'll be better with company and something to do."

"Rugs, crates and stones," Dominic repeated Jack's information out loud, doubt in his words. "What do you think, Jane?"

"You all know how impossible it is to keep a secret in the village. There's no way anything could have been moved without Miss Maybrook seeing that activity, you know how she notices things. In that case, there probably isn't anything at the cottage."

"She's a nosy old cow, that be right enough," Dick confirmed.

"Don't say that, she's a sweet old lady, just perceptive, that's all. But I can't see what could possibly be worth a thirty-year sentence, especially for smuggling rugs and stones, it baffles me," I pondered.

"Mmm, it depends on what sort of rugs and stones they are," Dominic added. "If it's illegal and worth taking these kinds of chances for, they must be very valuable."

"Pah," Dick scoffed. "That be going from the sublimical to the daft."

"You mean, the sublime to the ridiculous," Dominic snapped back.

"Oi reckon that count is involved," Dick replied. "He seemed a fishy bloke to our Jack."

Dominic snorted. "That's because you're sticking up for Jack after he stepped in between him and Olga, and for no other reason. If CHS could hear this, she'd go mad. He's been a model guest so far, even paid for the balloon show then donated a crate of his own wine from his chateau. We shouldn't make wild accusations regarding a matter we know nothing about. Proof, we need proof," he finally pointed out.

"Oi reckons she be mad alright, a-goin' on the way she be," Dick muttered.

"True, my love," I put in, ignoring Dick. "There was a chateau label on them, I looked, but can't recall the name in the Macon region, and I've travelled all over it."

"If you wants proof, oi'll get it," Dick snorted. "Just you wait and see."

"Take it easy, Dick, you can't go into the village at the

moment, remember? I'm not against you, just pointing out what will happen if you go off half-cocked," Dominic said.

"Sorry, revrund. We will get that proof, won't we?"

"Yes, Dick. You're speaking the truth now, absolutely. There's a lot of skulduggery going on here which we need to get to the bottom of."

The Bait

*T*he night passed quietly. It had been a bit chilly though, so we cuddled together for warmth.

"Goodness knows what time it is," I said in Dominic's ear softly. "It's getting light."

A voice drifted down from above. It was Jack calling. "Are you awake?"

"Yes, Jack," Dominic replied. "Come on down."

Bits of cliff tumbled onto the sand, then Jack appeared, a grin on his face. "You look cosy. Anything happened?"

"Nah," Dick replied. "Been quiet all the toime. It's odd though, they kept the lights on the yacht all night long, bit unusual, b'ain't it, don't they ever sleep?

"You're right. Maybe they have something to guard or stand a watch over."

"We had a look around last night, too. The next cave over is a lot bigger, goes back as far as you can see and then some," Dominic said.

"How far?"

"Oi don't know," Dick muttered. "None of us felt like a-lookin' into pitch black caves after midnight. All we did was poke around near the entrance. After what Maureen told oi, you'll not catch oi inside any cave on moi own."

"And?"

"For starters, oi'd say it b'ain't been used for years, not 'till recently, that is, a-corse there be fresh footprints a-goin' inside."

Another scrambling brought a shower of small rocks down. Danny stood after he fell. "Begorrah, it's slippery. The top of the morning to you all. Mighty pleased to see you again."

"Did you hear what Dick said?" Jack asked.

"No."

"Tell him," Jack commanded.

"Mmm," Danny mused. "By the Jack. Son, ter Fater and der Holy Ghost, that's most likely where they've stashed the goods."

"Let's go and find out," Jack said in determination. "Where's the torch?"

"Dick dropped it on a rock last night," I said. "It's not working."

"You eejut, can't you be trusted wit a simple ting like a torch?" Danny cried. "Now how are we to see what's in the place?"

I was waiting for Dick to state, 'It t'were an accident,' but he didn't.

"We can feel our way in," Dominic volunteered. "Or at least Dick can, he's the one that broke the torch. Its light now, you'll be able to see."

"How come oi got elected?"

"We'll be right behind you," my comforting words went to him.

"In you go then," Jack said, giving him a helping shove.

"Crikey, our Jack, a bit nippy in here." Dick gave a noticeable shiver.

Taking a hand. "Come on, my brave cave dweller, I'll come with you."

"Thank you, Miss Jane."

The deeper we went, the colder and darker it became.

"Oi can't see much. Perhaps we should come back later, Miss Jane," Dick muttered with an obvious lack of enthusiasm.

"Now's your chance to clear your name, Dick. Whatever's

going on may be in here somewhere. Remember how brave you were on the Manor green with the raiders and ducks. You can do it, I'm sure. Please stop calling me Miss, a simple Jane is fine, Dick," I whispered.

"Why are you a-whispering? There b'ain't nobody else in here."

"I don't know, just felt it was the right thing to do. It's very cold, can hardly feel my fingers. Let's get on and find out whatever it is, so we can go back."

"It's a-givin' oi the creeps, too, and it's a-comin' too close to Maureen's predictions for moi likin'. Can't see a hand in front of moi face, neither. Yar!" Dick hooted.

"What's the matter?"

"Oi just fell over a box, nearly broke moi foot. Oi said we should have come back later with a torch."

"Where is it?"

"On the end of moi leg, a-corse, Miss."

"The box, I mean, not your foot."

"Oh ah, that. Almost under moi feet. T'ain't very big, hardly worth all the fuss."

"Let me see." I groped with my hands.

"That be moi leg, Miss."

"Sorry. Ah, here it is. Can't open it, the lid seems stuck tight? There's a funny smell."

"They hardly be a-smugglin' smells, are they, Miss Jane?"

"You're right Dick. We'll have to get some expert advice."

"The only way is to open it."

"That might ruin evidence, we dare not do that, even if we could. Let's go back."

"Well?" Jack asked as we stepped out.

"Just an old box," Dick said, disappointedly.

"What was in it?"

"Don't know, Jack, the lids stuck fast and we didn't have a torch."

Jack gave Dick a glare. "I wonder why?"

"Maybe for the best," I put in quickly.

"Yes, Jane," Jack agreed with a nod. "If they planted it in there, then find it disturbed when they go back, it might set the fox among the chickens, upsetting our plan. After all, none of the villagers would ever imagine anything criminal going on here, right under their noses, nor are they hardly likely to take our words for it, are they?"

"S'pose not," Dick agreed. "Best get back to Danny's then."

Arrested

*B*ack in Danny's caravan, Dick sat looking miserable. "Oi can't see how moi names' a-going to be cleared," he grumbled.

"By the suffering Jesus, cheer up. Tis easy. First, we sort out that tramp, he's giving us all a bad name, so you're the bait."

"Oi, why oi?" Dick cried in panic.

"Because you're the one everybody will follow without any persuasion. They won't come haring after us, will they?" Jack pointed out with a fair degree of clarity.

"Don't be fretting, me darlin'," Danny added. "We'll get your courage up wit one or two of these," he went on, waving a bottle of Guinness in front of Dick. "I tink they'll help you make your mind up."

"You're right there, our Danny. "Oi need some bottled courage afore oi go anywhere near the village," he gasped. "You're all a-puttin' moi life on the line."

"Jesus, Mary and Joseph, he drinks like a lake trout and full of blarney wit it, that's for sure. Here you are, remember, don't get drunk, oterwise you'll be getting caught."

"Have a heart, Danny boy," Dick said, looking reproachfully at his host. "What if oi falls over, twists moi ankle or somethin'?"

"You'll just have to be sure you run as hard, fast and as straight as you can, in that case," Dominic snapped. "You do it when it's opening time at the inn well enough. With luck, the whole village will be hard on your heels, so you won't need a lot of encouragement."

"Hard on moi heels! Oi'd best have another one of they cans, Danny."

"Come on," Danny said. "We had better get moving. I'll go with Jack to the field, Jane wit you and Maggie to the bridge, the reverend stays wit you, then we'll be well spread out. We may have to shout a bit when Dick appears. May the Father, the Son and the Holy Ghost, look kindly upon us."

"Amen to that," Jack said under his breath.

Our group moved to the rear of the inn.

"It's clear," Danny grunted after a check, waving us to him.

"Stand up!" Jack said to Dick. "He should never have had the last Guinness, Danny. Look at him, wobbling all over the place."

"Don't be worrying, he'll be doing fine."

"Done in, more like, blooming twit getting sozzled," Jack snorted back.

"Hic," went Dick

"Danny and me are off now, me old china. Give us half an hour, then move out into the open. For goodness sake, try to keep on your feet."

"Oi got it, our Jack, on moi skates."

"Plates, not skates, plates of meat, rhymes with feet. Ye Gods, this ain't gonna work."

"I'll stay with him," I snapped, volunteering. "Dominic can do the halfway bit with the sisters then go to the bridge in case he needs help."

"Can you run?" Dominic asked, unsure.

"Of course I can, darling, certainly as fast as Dick in his present state. Don't worry."

The wait seemed an eternity to Dick, who was getting ever more nervous as minutes ticked past.

"Oi tells you Miss Jane, oi'm none too keen on being chased all that way, then past the Manor Green by a bloodcurdlin' mob."

It was a risky manoeuvre, so couldn't say I blamed him. There was no guarantee this mad hat scheme hatched by Jack and Danny, would work. Dick probably had visions of being incarcerated in some awful prison breaking rocks with a toffee hammer, followed by years being made to sew mailbags for not gaining his rock quota.

Looking at my watch, it said, "It's time to go, Dick."

A heavy sigh took him, a pair of pleading eyes cast my way. "Oi'm scared, Miss Jane."

"I'm coming with you Dick, we'll do it together. There's a lot of support out there, just have faith." He looked so miserable a cuddle was given. "Ready?"

He sighed again, then nodded, moving along past the forge, making sure he knocked a stack of shovels over in the process that went clattering down, then, before any reaction came, we walked into the roadway leading to the Manor and Moody's bridge.

Two things happened immediately. Bert Rudge dashed out of the inn to see what the noise was while a group walking down from Barnham's wood consisting of the Colonel, the Major and Constable Bracknell, caught sight of us.

"Oi, Drummond," Bert Rudge yelled. "You're wanted by the police."

"Ya phooey, can't catch me," Dick shouted back.

"Moi Dick," Margaret hooted from the bridge, as only she could.

The Colonel's voice added to the cacophony as he joined in. "My God, Bragshawe, there's that damned thief Drummond!"

"He b'ain't no thief, you leave him alone," Annabel screamed, promptly sticking up for Dick, completely forgetting her role in the chase.

"Shut up, you stupid woman," the Colonel snapped. "Come on Bragshawe, up and after him. Tallyho!" he went on, waving his stick in the air.

Acting on impulse, nor liking being called stupid, Annabel grabbed hold of the Colonel's jacket.

"Let go of me! Have you gone mad?" he hooted.

"No, oi won't, you were rude to oi, you rotten old Colonel."

"Let go… you… you…" the military man blustered, frantically flailing his arms about, desperately trying to free himself of Annabel's iron grip.

Around and around they spun…

"Annabel!" Constable Bracknell shouted. "Control yourself, otherwise I'll have to arrest you."

She glared at him, but maintained her hold.

"Annabel," warned the policeman."

She let go at last.

This kerfuffle had given Dick and me, a decent head start. "Run Dick, to Moody's bridge, come on, follow me."

Suddenly free, the Colonel shot forward, colliding with the Constable. The pair fell over in a heap of arms and legs.

"Get off of me, you're impeding justice."

"Good heavens man, it was an accident."

Dick had shot off on an erratic course for the bridge.

In my judgement, he wasn't going to make it. The Colonel was on his feet by now, he and Bracknell were gaining ground fast. My heart sank, the plan was going badly awry.

To my surprise, Dick made the crest of the bridge, but the Colonel was only feet away. It was amazing how fit he was, fitter than the policeman, who had given up the chase, puffed out.

Just as the Colonel's hand reached out to collar Dick, young Gordon Rogan came over the hill on his skateboard, deftly balancing himself by swaying this or that way to stay mobile.

Horror took his face as he desperately tried to avoid the Colonel, running smack bang into Dick.

Whump! The collision was solidly audible.

Dick screeched like a stuck pig, shot both arms out to steady himself, leaping into the air to inadvertently catch young Gordon in an ear with his elbow. The lad fell headlong.

Whatever goes up, must come down…

Boing…Dick's feet somehow found the skateboard, his forward momentum reversing its direction. The complete manoeuvre taking just a twinkling of an eye.

"Yikes," came Dick's wail as he was propelled downhill at breakneck speed on the other side of the bridge's slope.

"Good grief, he's making a getaway," the Colonel snapped. "He knocked that poor little lad off his board to do it. He's a damned scoundrel." The tallyho brigade stopped to pick up Gordon Rogan.

"My God," muttered the Major, having miraculously managed to join the group. "He's actually going to stand on that blasted contraption."

"It's a well-known statistic, Bragshawe." Colonel Masterson postulated, "that while under the influence, people do things they would never have dreamed of achieving while stone cold sober. Drummond wouldn't normally get near one of those damned contraptions, whatever the circumstances."

"Well, Mister Clever Clogs," Margaret sneered, "there he be, a-doin' alright, too."

My heart went out to him, knowing Dick hated fast transport of any kind, yet he went along the road with a deftness not unbecoming of Nureyev himself, flashing along the lane in a blur while somehow using the down-gradient to the Manor Green to good effect. However, it had to be said, impetus was gaining.

Dominic had been waiting patiently by the Manor Green with Margaret, the idea being to enact that part of the plan

"What the…"

Dominic's startled cry wafted through the ether as Dick closed the gap between them at breakneck speed.

The collision was brutal, both men went spinning in different directions.

"Good Lord, what are you doing," Dominic gasped, sitting up on the tarmac.

"S'cuse oi, revrund. Oi got that little job to do, hic."

"Just a minute, why has the plan changed, and why are you on young Rogan's skateboard?"

"Oi gotta see a man about some cows," Dick muttered back, found terra firma to go dashing off.

Having caught up, the policeman helped Dominic to his feet.

"Are you alright, Reverend?" Bracknell asked.

"Yes, thanks, Constable."

"Right, Chantril, let's get that damned rogue," Masterson snapped irritably. "After him, after him."

"What are you talking about, Colonel?" Dominic demanded. "You're nearly finished. We all should go in a more organised way."

"Oi agrees, revrund," Margaret added.

"Thank you, Margaret, at least you have some sense."

The Colonel nodded. "You're right, vicar, not as young as I used to be, don't'cher know."

"Go on," encouraged Margaret, pushing the Colonel in his back. "He may need help."

"Help! Why on earth would that scoundrel need help? What's she on about, Chantril?"

"Let's go and see, shall we?" Dominic answered, giving Margaret a wink.

"I'll need to arrest Drummond," Bracknell muttered angrily. "Let's get after him."

"He went through the hedge towards the copse," I put in.

"Thank you, Jane," the Colonel replied. "At least you're being helpful."

The mass of people moved through a gap in the hedge. As we emerged, a commotion drew everybody's attention to our left.

In the near distance a herd of cows thundered across the field our way, a couple of people behind shouting blue murder with waving arms.

Bang!

"Hey, stop firing that shotgun," Constable Bracknell ordered at the top of his voice. "You could hurt somebody."

"That's the general idea, bloody rustlers stealing my herd," farmer Rogan retaliated.

"We'd all better get out of the way, they're not stopping," Dominic cried a warning.

Isiah rushed out shouting his head off. "Keep those cows out of here, you lunatics. They'll bust my place up."

Danny appeared. "What? Hotel rubbish tip! It needs taking down. By the suffering Jesus, I'm as sure as I'm Danny O'Flattery, you have no permission to camp in here."

"Yes, I have, the farmer gave it."

"No, I didn't," farmer Rogan snapped. "You're trespassing."

The herd calmed once Danny and Jack stopped chasing them. One leant against a tree, pinning the tramp under it.

"Well, Begorrah, they like him," Danny quipped. "That one's licking his coat. Must be the smell that's attracting it."

"Get this beast off me," Isiah screamed.

Dick's battered hat hove into view above the cow's backs. "Whey hey, round 'em up, cowboy."

"Jesus, he's drunk, now how do you tink he managed that," Danny said with a grin.

"He had a lot of help from you, that's how," Jack pointed out.

"Look mate, give me a hand get these cows out of my camp, I'll make it worth your while. I've valuables over there I don't want disturbed," Isiah said, hoping Dick might be his salvation.

"Something for moi troubles, eh," Dick retorted, moving towards him while rolling a sleeve up in a meaningful way. "It'll be a fist in your teeth for all the trouble you've a-caused oi."

"Gotcha!" hooted Constable Bracknell, slapping a hand

on Dick's shoulder.

"Yikes, it's the arm of the law," Dick cried, then with a deft duck and weave, made a bolt for freedom.

The Colonel stood in his way. "You're under arrest, Drummond."

"That's my job," Bracknell snapped in annoyance.

"Go for the field," Danny cried out. "There's something interesting there."

With an agility I had never before seen him execute, Dick was out of the crush of people heading for wide open spaces.

There was a yell, Dick vanished from sight. We found him lying in a heap of rubbish, face down.

"Do you mean this, Danny boy?"

"You're under arrest," Bracknell yelled in triumph, grabbing Dick by the collar. "Come along with me, Drummond."

"Hang on copper. While we're here, let's see what's in this heap, it might be interesting. Danny put a foot under the edge of the canvas sheet, flipping it over. "There you are, copper, all the stolen goods from these here parts, nicked by this wretched creature," he ended, grabbing Isiah by the scruff of his neck. "He just tried to bribe Dick, saying he had valuables here, this is what he meant."

"Well, I'll be… it's the lead sheeting and ornaments from Miss Maybrook's house. Don't let go of him, gypsy, I want a word or two with him."

The name's O'Flattery," Danny retorted. "We're all good God-fearing folk, copper. See over there, it's the scout's handcart he used to move the lead with."

"It wasn't me, no, it wasn't me," the tramp blustered.

"Oh, somebody planted it here right beside your camp without you realising they were doing it, is that right?"

"That's right. That's exactly what must have happened. I'm a heavy sleeper."

"Pull the other one, it's got bells on it. You're nicked."

"All's well that ends well," Dominic said, "You're in the

clear with this business now, Dick, he's the culprit right enough."

"Well Drummond, it seems I owe you an apology. I was wrong about this. I'm sorry for any inconvenience caused. Will you shake on it?" Bracknell asked.

"Moi name's Mister Drummond," Dick cut back harshly.

"Yes, right, Mister Drummond. Will you?"

"Go on Dick. He was only doing his job."

"A-doin' it with a bit too much enthusiasm, if you asks oi, revrund. All his evidence was circumferal."

"You mean circumstantial, Dick," Dominic corrected. "It takes a brave man to admit he's wrong and say sorry, braver by far than one who'll deny a mistake, it's also a wise man who can accept the apology."

"Oi s'pect so, revrund, you're usually right about those things. But oi had you on the go, didn't oi, copper?"

Bracknell glowered back. "There's still the matter of the jewellery, reverend."

"Oh, isn't that here?"

"No, it isn't, so Drummond's still under a cloud over that. I've no proof of anything, so can't arrest you. Don't leave the area and report to me every morning," he ended, wagging a menacing finger at Dick.

"At least you're in the clear about the lead. In my book, you are about the rest of it. Now for the love of Mary, leave Dick and us alone," Danny snapped, glaring at the Colonel's group. "Next time get some facts before you start accusing folks."

"I'll lay odds this tramp has stashed the tomfoolery somewhere here, we just haven't found it yet," Jack snorted.

"Tomfoolery?" Colonel Masterson queried. "What's the blazes is that?"

Jack gave a condescending glance. "Slang for jewellery."

The Colonel humphed. "I'm still unconvinced he's not a jewel thief. We've had a thorough search here, yet found nothing."

"You're as bad as the copper," Dick snarled, squaring on the Colonel. "No proof of anything yet willin' to accuse oi of it all the toime."

"I don't think you did that, Dick," I stated firmly. "We'll stand by you, won't we, darling?"

Dominic looked at me, confused momentarily. "Yes, I'm sure we all will, considering these as well as the events at the Manor that day. Dick hadn't the time for searching drawers to steal anything."

"Moi hero," Margaret cried, throwing her arms around Dick's neck.

"Put oi down, Maggy."

"Maggy, that's not a bad name," Danny said approvingly.

"Can oi call you that?"

"It's a lot better than some of the things you've called oi," she answered, giving Dick a peck on a cheek.

"Ahem!" the Colonel cleared his throat. "Seems we all went off a bit half cocked."

"T'weren't oi that solved this crime, Colonel. It was Jack and Danny."

"Oh Jack, you saved moi Dick," Maggy said.

Jack took a hasty step back. "No luv, it was Danny."

Danny stood grinning. "Tanks for the vote, but we all did our bit. Dick was the bravest, taking all the risks."

"You'll see," Dick said, turning on the Colonel to stab his chest with a finger, "we'll solve the other one as well."

"That remains to be seen," the Colonel retorted sourly.

"Really, Colonel, that's not being reasonable," Dominic snapped.

It was such a sharp reply, the Colonel took a pace back. "Humph," he went. "I expect your right, Vicar, time will tell. Perhaps we can shake on it? As for you, Rudge, it's high time the animosity between you two was buried, so you can shake Drummond's hand as well. Then I'm going to take us all to the inn to buy drinks all round."

"Crikey," Dick whispered in my ear, "If he's a-goin' to

open his wallet, look out for low flyin' moths, Miss."

"I'll not touch his hand, not ever," Rudge hissed, spoiling the opportunity. "I've hated him ever since our families were together at Sharpe's farm."

"Why you…" Dick growled, taking a step toward the man.

"Leave him alone mate, he's not worth it," Jack snapped, grabbing Dick's arm.

"Perhaps you'll be able to resume your work at the Manor now," Dominic added.

"Do you think so, that she'll see it your way, revrund? Oi know oi've been a layabout for years, but that job was interesting and made oi feel more a part of this community, if you knows what oi mean."

"Independence, Dick. It gave you some independence and Margaret security."

"That be right, revrund, you knew all the toime. See our Jack, it's like oi've always said, the revrund's got a direct line to his boss, how else could he know how oi feels?"

Dominic laughed. "If I had that, I would be head of the church. No, Dick, it's just knowing how people react while being involved with people."

"Will you come and see CHS with us, please, revrund? Oi'm a bit nervous about meetin' her after all the misunderstandings."

"Of course, Jane as well, I am sure."

Spying

"*T*he Colonel took Dominic's sleeve. "I'm not sure now is a good time, Chantril, even with Jane along. She's under a lot of pressure at the moment."

"Pressure? What's the matter, has she a horse sick?" I asked.

"Um, no, not quite like that. Family matters, don't'cher know," the Colonel replied vaguely.

"Family matters?" How odd. As far as I knew, she had no relatives, only Master William.

Our small deputation began walking up the Manor drive, at about halfway Celia opened the main door, waiting.

"Good morning to you, Lady Hornby-Smythe," Dominic greeted. "Might we have a word privately?"

"Certainly, Vicar, but only you and Jane, nobody else," she ended, casting a disparaging look at Dick and Jack.

Dominic shrugged his shoulders at the pair. "Sorry, perhaps it's best."

As the door closed behind us our feet sunk into the deep pile of the carpet, an instinctive feeling hit me something was wrong within these walls, very wrong indeed. The atmosphere was very different to Celia's usual welcome. There hung a formality. "Where's Olga with the usual tray of tea?" I whispered.

"It is a bit strange."

"Well?" Celia demanded abruptly.

"It's about Mr Drummond," Dominic began. "We

wonder if…"

Celia held a hand up, palm out. "I'm aware what it's about," Celia snapped, before Dominic had a chance to continue. "It is out of the question to offer them their positions back, Vicar, it's beyond my control."

"But they've been exonerated," Dominic stuttered, aghast. "There's no reason for taking that attitude. They would very much like to work again, here if possible, and you must agree, Lady Hornby-Smythe, Dick has tamed down since you took him on. It's what he needed, responsibility."

"I hear what you're saying, Vicar, but my mind is made up. Besides, there are some very important business details in London to attend to, so I dare not trust those two here without supervision. Oh, while you're here, vicar, I won't be attending any Parish Council or Women's Institute meetings, either."

"What!" Dominic exclaimed.

It was plain from the look of shock on his face, her statement was a bombshell. From my brief time here, knew Celia was a driving force in the village, indeed the hub of the WI. Life there would be difficult without her.

"The WI has little to do with me," Dominic said after a pause, "It's all rather a pity you have decided to take such a negative interest. Are you alright? Is there something we may be able to help with?"

"I'm fine Vicar. Now, if you'll excuse me, there are things to attend, Sorry to spring it on you, that's just the way it is right now."

"Perhaps, Master William would like to join in with the scouts, while he's home?" Dominic offered.

"Oh," Celia gasped loudly. "See to them, Olga." With that bald statement, she fled from the hall into the depths of the Manor, a hankie clasped to her face.

Dominic gaped at me in disbelief. In fact, I had never seen the woman act in such a strange way before, no matter what sort of emergency had arisen.

"My am so sorry beinks, you must leavinks be now, pleases," Olga said softly, as she ushered us out.

"I was sure she would have given them their jobs back without question," Dominic muttered as he stood outside, dumbfounded.

"Something is very wrong," I replied tersely. "I've never known her act like that. It must be to do with Master William."

"Goodness knows what it is. The lads had better keep a low profile with her in that mood."

We found them outside the inn.

"What's the matter, revrund? You look a bit shaken up, to oi."

Dominic made no effort to reply.

"It's your jobs," I put in, hoping to get Dominic motivated.

"She's given us the thumbs down, hasn't she?" Jack said flatly.

"Has she, revrund, why?"

"Celia's in trouble somehow, we don't know how, it's a puzzle," I went on.

"Oh, is that all," Jack retorted. "I've got no sympathy for her. It's her fault Dick's in this mess right now. The least she could have done was let him work again."

Dominic heaved a sigh. "Jane is right. I've never known CHS act like this before. She left us in tears for no apparent reason, didn't she," he asked of me.

"Yes, just dashed off crying with a hankie, now that's not like her, is it? We both know how much this meant to the pair of you. Bear with us for a day or two, please. Perhaps whatever is troubling her will pass?"

"What's the matter with the old cow, Jane," Margaret asked.

"She seems broken, Margaret, very quietly spoken, not her usual brash and confident self. She's dropped out of the village life, as well."

"Ha," Jack snorted. "Typical, that is, the slightest thing wrong, then everybody's given the elbow."

"No, Jack. There's something else. For goodness sake, you should know her as well as anybody, better possibly. She's well respected here for her liberal views, so it's unfair to say 'the slightest thing,' is it? She gave Dick her support all through that dreadful business with the police along the fire at Sharpe's house, and still gave you both work."

"S'pect you're right, Jane," Jack muttered apologetically.

Dick looked miserable. "What am oi and moi missus a-goin' to do now in the village? We'll be sent to Blackpool with a stagnant on our characters, that's what. Marked out for life."

"You mean sent to Coventry with a stigma," Dominic corrected automatically. "I'm sure it's nothing to do with the theft. She would never have employed you if she thought that of you."

"What then?" Jack demanded. "What are we supposed to have done?"

"Nothing, as far as I can see," Dominic answered calmly. "Whatever the problem is, has nothing to do with the last business at all. She was on edge the whole time, as if anxious for us to leave, even as though we were in the way of something. Then, when Master William was mentioned, well… that just about did it."

"Look, there goes the Colonel, on his way to the Manor, I bet," Jack cried.

"I hope he gets a warmer reception than we did," I observed.

"That's a good point, Jane," Jack agreed. "Maggy, nip back along the hedge line to have an earwig. Make sure you're not seen, otherwise it'll put them on their guard. Go girl, quick, don't lose him."

"That's a dreadful thing to do," Dominic spluttered. "It's tantamount to spying."

"Yes, my love, but it's the only way of getting behind this smoke screen Celia's putting up. It could be for her own good."

We waited an age. "I hope Margaret's alright," Dominic uttered aloud eventually.

"She knows her way along there like the back of her hand, revrund," Dick grinned back. "Remember how she did that callin' into the pipe at the stables. Moi Maggy will be fine."

"Here she comes," Danny shouted. "Well done girl, the saints must have been watching over you."

"Well?" asked Dominic.

"Give oi a chance to get moi breath back, revrund. It t'were like this, the Colonel said to CHS, *'You've got to pull yourself together, I know this ordeal is pushing you to breaking point, but you must keep a stiff upper lip, don'tcher know.'*

'That's all very well for you, Colonel, but you're not in moi position. I just can't bring moiself to see village people or attend meetings.' "Oi suppose she meant the WI ones," Margaret added. "Then the Colonel said…

'Behavin' like this will only attract attention, old gel, and that's exactly what we don't want. Look, oi'm due to see them this evenin', perhaps they'll relent a little, letting you speak?'

"CHS, cried then, oi'd never seen her do that afore. Then she went on…"

'Oi do hope so, Colonel, oi can't bear to be parted from my…'

"Just then a crow made a dreadful cawin' noise so oi didn't hear for a bit until it stopped, just in time to hear her say,

'For much longer.'

"The colonel suggested getting the police, but CHS refused that, said it was too soon and might be disastrous if it went wrong. He made that funny noise he does, and left. So, oi came back here," Margaret finished.

"Crikey," Jack muttered. "What a turn up for the books. Wonder it is she couldn't bear to be parted from? Now there's a thing."

"Oi dunno, Jack, a bloomin' bird made that row right beside moi ear, so oi couldn't hear that bit. P'raps it be an horse, you knows how much she loves the animals."

"No, it can't be a horse," Dominic said. "She seems terrified about it. Who are these people and what are they likely to do, well… whatever it is?"

"The revrund's right," Dick pointed out. "Whoever would get into a paddy about an horse?"

"You be watching your tongue," Danny snapped. "We love our horses as one of the family."

"She might if she thought they were going to ill-treat it," Margaret said.

"Nah, not a strong enough motive," Jack answered.

"Just a minute. You hit the nail on the head, Danny, like one of the family, you said. Where's Master William? He's not been seen for ages."

"Jane's right," Danny almost shouted in excitement. "You said you haven't seen him since before the fete, Dick, is that right?"

"Yes, he's been mysteriously absent ever then in fact. I bet that bloody Count's mixed up in this somehow." Jack gave what I thought was a growl.

"Don't be ridiculous," Dominic came back sharply. "You're being prejudiced, just jumping to conclusions again because he's courting Olga so strongly. Remember what happened when we decided without proof, that Dick had stolen the jewellery and how much anguish that caused him."

Jack glowered back. "He's a shady character, if ever I saw one."

"All he's done so far, is give," Dominic retorted.

"What about him down at the cove," Dick added. "The one from Briar Cottage?"

"That's all circumstantial as well," Dominic said with a scowl. "However, it's more probably them than the Count. At least they're more likely to have a direct connection."

"You're right there, revrund. He's in Cahoots with Sid Slimebucket, he knows loads of villains. Them at the bay be up to no good, too, so they are bound to be involved," Dick confirmed.

"How do you know they're villains?" Dominic demanded.

"Stands to reason, revrund," Dick stated. "If Sid's in on the deal that proves it, he's been done more times that oi've had hot dinners."

"Done?" I asked.

"Nicked, put inside."

"Oh, I see. Thank you, Dick."

"Any word from that French policemen of yours?" Dominic asked.

"No, my love. He's a very busy person, this may not seem so important in Macon."

"Alright. Let's assume the Count's in the clear. We can follow the Colonel later, see what he does and where he goes. That may shed a little more light on this mystery."

"Done!" Dick exclaimed.

"We may well be if we get caught," Jack pointed out.

"What I don't understand, is why go to these lengths with young William and Celia? There has to be a reason behind it? Blackmail is a very serious crime, as is abduction," I pointed out.

"She's loaded, has to be, running a place like that Manor. So, it's probably money," Jack put in.

"There must be lots of other, far more substantial people to blackmail for cash, surely, Jack?"

"Can't imagine what else, then, Jane," he mused.

"Maybe she's seen something or has stumbled on the real cause of the crime?" Dominic said.

I nodded agreement. "That makes more sense. Grab William and threaten all sorts of things will happen to him if she tells on them."

Jack stood scratching his head. "But what? It has to be something dramatic to warrant years in jail."

Danny pursed his lips, sucking in. "Begorroh, kidnapping will bring a long term inside on its own, so whatever it is they're protecting, must be mighty valuable."

A White Face

*T*he evening was getting on when we noticed the Colonel drive past the vicarage at his steady fifteen mikes an hour.

"Quick, into my car," Dominic cried. "Don't want to lose him."

Danny roared out laughing. "You'll have to be driving like an eejut to lose him at that speed, Vicar."

We piled in, a kind of miracle getting five of us in this tiny car, because neither Danny nor Jack were small men. We decided Danny in the front, Dominic driving, with Jack, Dick and me in the back.

Dick gave me a sheepish grin. "Oi'm sorry Miss Jane, bein' all a-squashed up like this," he said apologetically.

"Never mind, we can't help it, soon be there."

However, it was just by luck Dominic had a car at all. The Colonel had bought a new one and kindly given the vicar the old motor, so I mused, although a bit of a stickler, he wasn't such a bad old stick, after all.

We followed at a respectable distance.

"Lucky it's not too dark," Dominic said. "Otherwise, I would have to put my headlights on and he would see us."

"Why not take the short cut by the ruined priory, revrund? He won't see us then at all."

"Neither would we see him," Jack snapped.

"Oh ah," Dick muttered. "Neither we will, you're right there, Jack."

"We'll keep that in mind, Dick," I added, hoping to cheer

him up. "A short cut might come in handy."

"The Colonel's gone to the far side," Jack said. "Stop here, reverend, we can go down the path. Look, the yacht's still lying offshore, lights on too, just like the other night."

"Don't close any doors, the bangs will alert them," Dominic ordered. "Leave them ajar."

"Look revrund, the Colonel's signalling with a torch, just like Sid did, last time."

Touching Dominic's sleeve to draw attention. "There's activity aboard, the dinghy has left for the shore, although there's still a person on board. Is that a cane or gun they're holding?"

"Hard to say from this distance, my love. You had better stay here, just in case."

"In case of what? I'm not standing on my own for ages with shady goings on all around, I'm coming with you."

"Here's a big bush for cover, its close enough to hear," Jack whispered as we crept along the edge of the sand.

The sound of the dinghy grinding onto the beach came to us, followed by a crunch as someone jumped out, to begin walking toward the Colonel. "I'm armed, don't try anything," whoever it was, warned.

The Colonel humphed a bit as a reply.

"Will she play ball?"

"Has she much option?" Masterson snapped back.

"It's unlucky for her she saw anything in the first place, snooping around here."

"She wasn't snooping at all, just brought her son here for an afternoon out. You're the ones that are snooping."

"Shut up! Lest it'll be the worse for him. Now, to business, we must start moving the stuff inland soon. Have the arrangements been made?"

"Not yet. The woman's too upset to put a show on like that."

"The Boss gives her seven days, otherwise…" words trailed of threateningly as he slid a finger across his throat.

Jack's eyebrows shot up about a foot in disbelief, well, perhaps an inch anyway.

"They're crooks right enough, reverend, and this is pretty heavy stuff by the sound of it."

"Christ," Dick muttered. "Oh, sorry revrund, it just popped out."

"Shss, just listen," Dominic whispered.

"You damned cad! You wouldn't dare," the Colonel snarled tersely.

"I might not, but the Boss would, he's done it before."

"What happens if, God forbid, not everybody goes to this ball? You say it's vital the area around Briar Cottage is totally clear."

"Then the Boss will be very unhappy, won't he, get my drift? When he ain't pleased he does horrible things. He's at the top of the organisation so won't stand any nonsense, got it?"

"I understand. Can she speak to him?"

"No, bringing people here means they might be followed. No police either, otherwise…"

We all noted the inference of the trailed-out words again.

"Humph," went the Colonel, turned away striding to his car.

"Gordon bleedin' Bennet," Jack cried. "No wonder they said thirty years, sounds like kidnapping and smuggling to me."

"I wonder who Mr Big is." Dominic mused. "Perhaps you're right, Jane, it is that smarmy character who asked where Briar Cottage was from the car, that day?"

"Yes, he was a nasty piece of work if ever I saw one."

"I still say the Count's involved somehow," Jack muttered. "That feeling sticks in my gut, reverend."

"I can't see how he is. Maybe he's helping CHS, Jack, like the Colonel? The boats left, now we have a torch, let's go and see what's in the box. Show us where it is, Jane."

"Down in that cave," I replied, pointing.

"Are you sure you oughter be a-doin' this revrund, t'ain't work for an holy man," Dick muttered.

"It's a work of love and caring, so is the work of God, Dick. I'm sure we all care for Master William, I'm sure, even though he may not be very popular at times."

We had barely entered the gloom of the cave, when the noise of an outboard motor drifted in.

"One's coming back," I said, tugging at Dominic's arm.

"Shss, the boat's landed, somebody's walking this way whistling to themselves. "Cripes, they're coming in here!" Jack exclaimed.

"Go farther in," Dominic gasped urgently, giving Dick a shove. "You know the way."

"Rightyo, revrund, but feel your way, oi daren't put the torch on, they'll see it. Mind the crate, we're passing it."

"Stop," hissed Jack, after what seemed a mile hike. "Listen for a mo, no more noise."

"Keep very still, they may be doing something and still here," Danny put in.

Waiting seemed interminable.

"I think it's okay," Jack said. "Let's have a look at that crate."

"Alright," Dominic said. "Be quiet about it, though."

"What do you tink, vicar," Danny asked. "It's heavy, I just tried lifting a corner. There's an odd smell when close to it, maybe something's bust inside?"

"Put it down."

A clink sounded as Danny did that. "If it's full of wine bottles, which would make it heavy. But wine doesn't normally smell sweet, does it?"

"Crikey, Miss Jane, wine! Let's open it and try some," Dick cried eagerly.

"No Dick. It could have been put in here from the boat on these warm nights to keep cool. Breaking into it will show them somebody's been here so knows of it. Then, that could easily endanger young William," Dominic snapped. "Use your brains a little bit, please.”

“Oh, right, let’s go home then,” Dick rattled back, sulkily.

Just before Dominic stepped out, a cough came across the sand. “Mmm, he’s sitting having a smoke, waiting for somebody else, probably. Back into the cave, quickly.”

“Great dung heaps, we’ll be here all night at this rate,” Dick growled unhappily.

“What do you suggest?”

“Well,” Dick mused, “we could go in further, you remember what oi said about a secret passage to the Priory.”

“It’s worth a try,” Dominic admitted. “We’ve nothing to lose with time on our hands. It’s safe to put the torch on now.”

It clicked, but hardly made any difference.

“It be blacker than Blackmire’s heart in here, revrund. Can hardly see an hand in front of moi face.”

“It’s better than nothing, go on,” Jack snapped. “Let’s get out of here.”

The passage got narrower and rockier the more we delved in. Eventually it got too narrow to move, so we were forced into single file.

“Hang on,” Dick muttered. “There’s somethin’ up there, seems stuck in the rocks.”

“What is it?”

“Oi don’t know, revrund. You go and have a look.”

“I can’t get past you, go on a bit further.”

Dick peered into the gloom, waving the torch about.

“Well?” Jack snapped impatiently.

“Give oi half a chance, our Jack, it be bleedin’ dark up there, looks kinda white”

Moments went by…

“Yaaa!” Dick yelled, nearly falling into Dominic’s arms in his fright.

“For goodness sake, be quiet,” Dominic scolded. “What’s the matter now?”

Dick’s teeth were chattering together, he must have been

terrified.

Patting a hand to try helping his nerves I said, "Calm down Dick, we're all here right beside you, don't get in a panic."

"You'd be in a panic, Miss, if you'd seen what oi just did," he declared, a definite tremor in his voice.

"What did you just see, to make that much noise, nearly giving us all away," Jack asked irritably.

"A body up there, our Jack. Horrible it t'were, a-staring back at oi."

"For a start, bodies don't stare," Jack retorted. "Don't start exaggerating again."

"Oh, wonder who the poor soul is?"

"We had better find out, Jane. Let's hope it isn't Master William," Dominic retorted.

"Here, you take the torch, revrund. Oi b'ain't a-goin' back there, not for nothin', not with they starin' eyes."

"There won't be any staring eyes. Not if it's an old body."

"Oi don't know who it is, revrund. It scared the hell out of oi."

By the sufferin' Jesus, let it not be young William," Danny uttered.

A certain amount of scuffling went on as Dominic worked his way forward. "It's not William, Danny, thank goodness," Dominic called back, relief in his voice.

"Now there's a ting. Be they knocking people off and putting them up her?" Danny went on.

"A skull and bones in period costume, by the look of it."

"Let oi see," Dick asked, gaining a sudden surge of bravery. He took the torch from the vicar. "Well, oi'll be jiggered with a prong, that must be Lord Wymondum, the one from the Manor all they years ago." He continued poking about. "There be a tunnel ahead, revrund. Oi'll go and see."

Dick scrambled over the rocks for a while, until…
"Yaaa!"

"For the Mother in Heaven," Danny cried. "Do you want

us all to end up like that Lord? Stop yelling out, sounds carry in caves.”

“Ber… but there’s a face a-lookin’ at oi,” Dick wailed.

“By the Virgin Mary, how can there be a face up there? Tis plain not a soul has been here for about forever,” Danny growled.

“Give Jack that torch,” Dominic ordered. “Let him have a look. At least he won’t panic or shout out.”

“Perhaps you should go if it’s another body, reverend, being a man of the church…” Jack hedged.

Dominic tut, tutted a few times.

“Give it to me, for heaven’s sake. If anyone can shed light on this, a woman might,” I snapped.

“Be careful, Jane,” Jack muttered.

“Perhaps you can explain what of? A skeleton is hardly likely to harm me, is it?” The rocks were sharp and I was glad to be wearing thick jeans. The light caught the very pretty face of a woman, perhaps Spanish by her dark appearance, although it was covered in dust with damage along one side of the gilded frame. On my return it was explained.

“Mmm,” mused Dominic. “It’s cool and dry this far in, no wonder it’s survived.”

“Let’s go home,” Dick wailed. “Oi’ve gone weak at the knees.”

“To be sure,” Danny said, “We’ve been here a while, whoever was on the beach may have gone by now.”

“We’d better cover our tracks,” Jack pointed out. “Snap a branch off the bush and wipe it over the sand.”

“Oi vote we go get the copper. He can go out to arrest them on that boat,” Dick said.

“Oh, very clever. Getting them to kill the kid and hop it across the sea. Some brilliant idea that is,” Jack snorted.

“Oh, no, s’pose not. Can we go home now?”

“It’s blooming dark in there. We need a better torch to check the place over. That picture could be worth a fair bit, maybe,” Jack pointed out.

"We must free Master William before we think of personal gain," Dominic snapped tartly.

"Oh ah, our Willy, oi'd forgotten about that little perisher… oi mean, person, in the excitement," Dick muttered.

"In any case, the picture will belong to Lady Celia," I pointed out.

"How come," Dick demanded? "Oi found it."

"That doesn't make it your property," Dominic snapped back. "It originally came from the Manor, so rightly belongs to whoever owns the place now. There are most likely no living relatives of the Lord alive after all this time."

"Look, stop arguing," I retorted. "We should return to the vicarage for a conference. Once we've decided on a plan, everything will be clearer." Personally, there was doubt it would, but the bickering wanted to stop.

"Shouldn't we let the police handle this?" Dominic pointed out. "After all, it isn't our job to investigate crooks, is it?"

"That depends on Lady Celia, doesn't it? After all, it's her son that's at risk."

"S'pose you're right missus revrund. You always seem to come up with a sensible answer."

"Thank you, Dick, for a little support."

"That's agreed then," Dominic muttered half-heartedly. "Celia is too emotionally distressed to even consider the police. But do we bring in Bracknell on our own? We can warn him of the dire consequences if anything leaked out, or, do we confront the Colonel?"

"See here," I piped up, "if Bracknell knows anything, he'll have to inform Exeter, then they'll be clumping everywhere with their king-sized feet, the crooks will soon enough get wind of things and then goodness knows what will happen. We don't know who the ringleader is yet, they could kill the boy and escape Scott free."

"To be sure, we need to be collaring him," Danny nodded

in agreement.

"How do we blow his cover?" Jack asked.

Dominic glared at him. "We're not in the secret service. We'll somehow have to eliminate one at a time until he shows his hand."

"Say he never does?" I pointed out. "We can't wait forever, neither can William."

"What about this ball, CHS is supposed to throw, my love?"

"At the Manor, I guess. That would clear the Briar Cottage end of the village nicely, allowing these crooks to do whatever is so important to them," I answered.

"That's it then," Dick broke in. "We'll have to wait in hiding until they make their move."

"Then bloody what?" Jack snapped at him. "Are you willing to take on a load of armed and desperate villains?"

"Try not to swear in the vicarage, Jack."

"Sorry Jane, but he's such a prawn at times. It's obvious we can't tackle that lot, not just us few."

"Jack has a good point," Dominic added. "Any other suggestions?"

"Let's go and have a pint, oi reckons that's good suggestion," Dick piped up. "You can have a sherry or something, revrund."

"That's not a bad idea, Dick. We all need something to steady our nerves after the discoveries tonight."

"Is it, revrund? Wow, oi never thought you'd agree to that."

As we made our way there, the Colonel came out of a small lane, plainly deep in thought, head down, a scowl on his face.

Bump! He walked straight into me.

"Goodness, Colonel, what's got into you? You normally look where you're going?" I asked.

He looked, startled. "Oh, I'm very sorry, m'dear, didn't notice you. Things on my mind, don'tcher know. Many things on my mind," he went on, vaguely. After excusing himself, he set off in the direction of the Manor.

"Someone had better follow him again," Dominic said. "Perhaps you, Margaret, you did it very well last time."

"Yes, Maggy," Dick agreed, "Jack'll go through the bushes like a Sherman tank a-givin' the game away. We'll go to the inn as normal, meet us there when you comes back. Be careful," Dick added softly.

Margaret smiled at him. "Oi will, moi love." With that, she set off after the rapidly vanishing Colonel.

Colonel in Command

She was an age again; Dick was getting worried. "Say they've a-cottoned on to her, God knows what they'll do. Oi shoulda gone."

"She'll be fine," Danny cut in. "That's a smart colleen you've got there."

"I'll get another round in," Jack offered.

It was more to break the tension, more than anything.

The door swung open and in walked Margaret, grinning all over her face. "Oi did it fine," she said, looking at all our worried faces. "Don't oi get a drink for a-bein' so clever, then?"

"I'll be getting it, you tell what happened," Danny replied.

Margaret sat down, waving us nearer conspiratorially, to speak in hushed tones. "Oi got through the hedges where oi did last time, hidin' in the same bush. The Colonel knocked at the door, stood a while makin' them funny noises he do. Finally, CHS opened it. She looked awful, poor woman, oi felt sorry for her.

'Oh, it be you, Colonel,' she said. 'Oi thought you weren't a-going to come unless it was vitally important?'

'We needed to wait until the coast was clear, Celia,' he said. 'They demand you go ahead with the ball, otherwise...'

"He kinda paused there."

'I haven't very much choice in the matter, have I, Colonel?' Celia muttered.

'I'm afraid not. Look here, m'dear, why not let me inform the police, *they will be extremely cautious, I'm sure.'*

'No, absolutely not,' CHS snapped back. *'I'll send out invitations for this Friday. It's usually at this time of year, so people will be half expecting them, anyway.'*

'Time it to start at 19:30 hours, m'dear.'

"That's what old stuffy boots said, whatever that is," Margaret went on.

'Very well,' CHS replied.

'Keep a cool head, m'dear, everything will turn out alright in the end.'

"CHS started cryin', the poor love, then she went back in, shuttin' the door. The Colonel stood for a few moments, a-shakin' his head, then left for the Court."

"So," Dominic uttered, "It will be happening Friday, whatever it is, we still don't know that yet, though."

"Oi reckon the Colonel's in half a mind to tell Bracknell," Margaret said, nodding her head in confirmation as she spoke. "He's worried, too, although he didn't let on about that to CHS. Maybe we should have a little talk to him?"

"You're right, Margaret," I said, supportively. "We need some help, and whatever anybody says about him, he's good at organising this sort of thing. Let's all go to the Court."

Almost immediately after Dominic had knocked, the porch light came on as the door opened.

"Oh, it's you, vicar." He looked at us all then, a wariness in him like a cornered animal might have. "You seem to have brought a deputation, Chantril." He gave a nervous laugh.

"Look here, Colonel, we all know about the boat in the cove and more or less what's going on. We decided to take the bull by the horns coming here, but something has to be done."

"Know? Know what?" the Colonel blustered.

"With Lady Celia, Colonel. Don't try to deny it,"

"Um, well, yes. You had better come in, vicar."

Dominic paused to look around the group. "We all know."

"Oh, I see. Very well, the others, too. Come through into the sitting room. This isn't something to discuss on my doorstep."

He listened intently as Dominic went over recent events, how we happened upon the plot and grisly discovery in the cave.

"It's a rum old do," he muttered, "that's for sure. Celia won't allow me to go to the authorities. But we can work together, a bit of a relief after doing all the negotiating on my own."

"While I understand how concerned she must be," I added, "we must get proper support, Colonel."

"You're right, Jane. This is no job for amateurs. We must go to the police station."

Constable Bracknell was at the desk, looking over the body of people standing before him.

The Colonel spoke for everybody.

"I know you mean well enough, Colonel, you too, reverend, but you're reading far too much into this, having heard a couple of random broken conversations. Anybody can come ashore from a boat, there's no law against that."

"What about the box?" said I.

"That could just be provisions, or wine like the vicar said. Most likely put in the cave to keep it dry or cool."

"Then why all this secrecy about moving stuff to Briar Cottage," I insisted.

"Mmm, there is that," Bracknell added. "But what proof have you got that it's Master William. You know what a rascal he is, reverend, most likely run off somewhere and they are taking advantage of the fact. She scolded him something terrible about breaking Leggett's store window with his catapult in front of a crowd of people, I was there. He could easily be camping out somewhere, he's done it before. I've had no complaints about blackmail, threats or violence, no thefts or burglaries since that tramp were arrested. So, what exactly do you want me to say to CHS, I have to be careful, she holds a lot of sway in these parts? If she takes it into her mind to get awkward, I'll get thrown out of the force?"

"Margaret heard one say, merchandise," Jack muttered half-heartedly.

"Do me a favour, merchandise can mean anything? You lot are acting like a lot of schoolboy detectives. My advice is to leave it well alone, CHS too, otherwise you could end up getting a summons. As for you, Drummond, leave the ale alone, it'll be your downfall."

"Look here, copper," Dick snapped back indignantly, "Oi don't reckon…"

Jack's hand grabbed Dick's arm, giving him a meaningful look with a shake of his head. "Okay, we get your drift."

Outside, the mood was sombre.

"He was being very high-handed about it," I said. "He could have gone over our views a lot more."

"That means we're back where we started," the Colonel snarled through his moustache. "Risking tipping Celia and those crooks off into the bargain. I'm very surprised at Bracknell, thought he would have believed me."

"He accused oi of bein' drunk," Dick yelled.

"He's wrong there, we know you're not," Jack soothed.

"Jack be right," Margaret hollered. "Bloomin' cheek castin' nasturtiums on moi beloved. Oi'm a-goin' in there to sock him in the eye," she stated, turning ready to execute the act.

Dominic grabbed her. "Calm down, please. We need you to help us solve this puzzle. You mean aspersions, nasturtiums are plants."

"S'pose you're right, revrund," Margaret replied sulkily. "That silly old copper knows nothin'."

"Well done, Margaret. We can do without having you locked up for assault."

"I don't care what Bracknell thinks, I've a horrible feeling about this," I added.

"I agree," Dominic said. "What we need is a plan.

Colonel, that is more up your street, would you take command?"

It was almost imperceptible, but I was sure the Colonel's six-foot frame grew another few inches.

"I accept, Chantril. Back to The Court, we can have a council of war there in comfort, using that as our HQ."

"What's a council of war, and HQ?" Dick butted in. "Oi thought that were a sauce you put on chips?"

"Nah, that's HP. An HQ means a headquarters," Jack explained.

"Oh, right. What be the plan then?"

"I've no idea, the Colonel's taking charge. We have to pool our ideas," Dominic pointed out.

"We need more help," Masterson said. "I'll see the Major. It's only Sunday, we have a few days to get a team together."

"It's the boss bloke that's going to be the hardest to nail," Jack said. "Wish we could tap the phone lines."

"A good idea, Sweeny," the Colonel said. "Need some expertise for that, though."

"Are we allowed to do that?" Dominic pointed out.

"Actually, no. But desperate times, need desperate measures, vicar."

"Are we in desperate times?" Dominic asked.

"Obviously, Chantril. Celia is almost a broken woman. William is now in the clutches of violent criminals and we have little to combat them with. If that isn't desperate, I don't know what is?" The Colonel ended by humphing a couple of times to show impatience at Dominic.

"As you said, it's only Sunday, Colonel," Dominic countered. "We have several days to wait."

"True vicar, but we can muster our forces ready, there's nothing wrong with being prepared, is there?"

That put the seal to any further discussions on that point.

"Oi'll have a chat to our Fred. He's got a load of army surplus stuff at his place."

"That's not a bad plan. Please do that, Drummond. Now

we're marching," the Colonel cried excitedly.

"I'm going to have a chat with Danny, he might be able to help," Jack offered. "He knows you, Jane, will you come, please?"

Danny listened, nodding now and then as he grasped the points Jack made, also the urgency of it all. "By the suffering Jesus, I can muster a few good men, right enough, there's Paddy, Sean and Pat, they're all great in a scrap," he grinned, waving a huge fist in the air. "Will be just like old times, so it will."

"Well done. There'll be a meeting at the Colonel's house, six o'clock on Thursday. Don't come as a group, you know what to do," Jack said.

"Begorrah, we do, too."

Invasion

*T*he morning was fine and bright, I noted. "Shall we walk to the bottom of the hill for some exercise, my love?"

Dominic nodded. "A great idea, let the sun on our faces, we've been creeping around too much in the dark lately."

"Let's hope this trap goes off as is expected," I muttered. "It's all up in the air and days to go yet, anything can happen in the meantime."

"We had better see if Dick or Jack are at the inn to warn them not to go off alone, that would ruin everything."

The lads had settled in their chairs for a lunchtime drink and were happily sitting with their favourite tipple.

"Morning revrund, Missus revrund," Dick chirruped, seemingly in a good mood.

"It's Jane, Dick. How many times have I got to remind you what to call me?"

"Oh ah, sorry Missus R. Oi must try to remember."

"He's been moaning about not getting our jobs back, Jane," Jack said.

"Oi felt sure she would, now," Dick muttered.

"I admit her refusal was harsh after being cleared of all the other things," Dominic agreed.

Jack sighed. "That's it, I'm out of funds, mate."

"Charlie, bring the lads a drink each please, I'll treat them."

"Thank you, Miss Jane, oh, um, oi means Jane," Dick said, embarrassed at his mistake.

"You both did well so truly earned one. Never mind the look Dominic just gave me, he should agree."

The door opened and in walked farmer Josh Rogan. His eyes searched the inn, settling on our group.

"Ah, Drummond, just the man I'm looking for."

That anybody wanted to see Dick at all, came as a surprise to me, most avoided him like the plague, him being about the most unreliable character in the village.

"Oi!" Plainly he was as startled. "What for, oi b'ain't done nothin' wrong?"

"I know you haven't young Drummond, so you can stop getting into a panic."

We all heaved a collective sigh of relief.

"What then, a-comin' in here upsettin' oi?"

"The Colonel told me you're looking for a job?"

"Oh ah, that be true. Jack'n oi had jobs at the Manor a-doin' her gardens, until that went balloon shaped."

"Pear shaped," Jack put in. "Things go pear shaped when wrong."

"Do they? What's a pear got to do with it?"

"Not perfectly round, wrong shape in other words," Jack explained.

From my associations with them, I knew Jack had a tremendous amount of patience with Dick, which was just as well, because he needed it. He always tried to guide him through life as best he could, usually succeeding, but not always. Then sparks could fly. "Have you work, Josh?" I enquired.

"It's harvest time, Jane."

"But you've got a full complement," Jack pointed out.

"Not now, Jack. Old Bill's gone down with something horrible and George Marbey's bust a leg cleaning his chimney."

Dick burst out laughing. "How the hell did our George manage that?"

"You know George, our Dick, has to do everything the

hard way arse-uppards, much like you. Couldn't get the brush up, so went up on the roof trying to shove it down, lost his footing and fell off the roof."

"That's a good'un," Jack grinned. "What's up then?"

"We were in the middle of harvest, so I can only offer a few days, just to finish off the last two fields, then get it in the bins before it rains."

Dick pursed his lips taking a sharp intake of breath. "Dunno about that, Josh, it be heavy work and moi back goes right quick if oi b'ain't careful."

"I've got to keep my bowling arm in shape for the village cricket match," Jack said, doubtfully.

"It's not lifting that's needed, just driving the combine and tractor, a piece of cake for the pair of you."

"Oi b'ain't driven a combine since… let oi think… since…" his eyes drifted to the ceiling…

"Since your dad worked at Sharpe's farm years ago," Josh Rogan cut in. "You weren't bad at it, as I recall. You'll get paid for it," he added as encouragement.

"At Sharpe's… yes, oi remember now," Dick replied, an absent look on his face.

"We'll get paid, mate," Jack said, pulling Dick out of his reverie. "How much?"

"The going rate for the job, of course."

"You're on," Dick snapped. "When do we start?"

"Tomorrow, half past five."

"Bit late, ain't it, it will be nearly' dark by then," Dick came back.

"In the morning, you great hayrick," Josh replied. "You look like one, too. Tidy yourself up a bit. What have you been doing these last few days?"

"Helping us," I put in quickly. "Some late nights, I'm afraid, Josh."

"I see, okay, helping the reverends good. I'll pay for a pint each before I'm off. See you in the morning." He left.

"What about the cove and Master William," Dick said.

"There's only six days left."

"It won't take long getting a couple of small fields in, be done in four at most," Jack added. "It'll keep us out of the way at the same time."

"The Colonel's organising that," I assured. "There's nothing we can do until he gives the word. Remember, if you're working fields, it will make things look normal."

For some reason, sleep evaded me, so I got up, leaving Dominic quietly snoring lightly. Pulling the curtains open revealed daylight breaking over the far hills, so got washed and dressed. Being an early riser, this wasn't unusual for me, but I was a little worried about Dick and Jack going back into farm work. Dick hadn't done any for simply years, which made him rusty and Jack was a Londoner, so was completely ignorant of it. Not that I was an expert, but many moons ago, had a relative that owned a farm, so had a good grounding, as it were. My heart held a soft spot for Dick Drummond, a scallywag he might be, but relatively harmless, even very brave at times, as we had discovered during the yacht business and recently on the cove beach, where he had really stuck his neck out. Maybe it was a motherly instinct toward him, a thought that brought a smile to my face, perhaps not motherly then, as an aunt might be concerned for his welfare. Goodness, he needed someone to watch over him.

The morning was slightly chilly, which demanded a coat worn for my walk along the lane. This was to keep a weather eye on Briar Cottage. As I was its owner, little suspicion would be aroused in the occupants if I was to wander past. All was quiet there, the black limousine parked outside, so it could be assumed the crooks were still sleeping. It might seem odd if I suddenly turned around to return home, as if spying on them, which I was, of course. As farmer Rogan's place was only a short way farther on, I headed there. The sun was up on arrival.

"Good morning Miss Jane," Dick greeted. "What are you a-doin' out so early in the day?"

"A little spying, Dick."

"Oh ah, the cottage, oi see. All okay, be it?"

"As quiet as a mouse."

"Mice can be bloomin' noisy if cornered, don't believe they can't kick a row up."

"Aren't the fields beautiful?" I mused, walking to the barn doors to look out across them. "See how the corn heads wave so gently in the light breeze, rippling like a golden sea, really magical."

"Crikey! Oi hopes you're not a-goin' all soft on us, Miss Jane, a-startin' spoutin' poetry this time of the day."

"Why ever not, it's a lovely sight, a golden harvest from God."

"Ah, here you are," Josh Rogan said, his voice cutting our conversation short. "Lovely day for it."

"Good morning, Josh. I was just saying the same thing to Dick."

"Is it? Oi b'ain't woke up yet," Dick moaned.

"Come into the next shed. See, there's the combine and tractor," Josh pointed out. "I'll show you the drier before we start, so you've a good idea what to do."

"Go home to bed, that's what oi'd do," Dick groan again.

"For goodness sake stop complaining," Jack snapped irritably. "We'll be out in the fresh air, just like the gardening job, paid for it, too. That should make Maggy happy. Now you've got two women to support. Think how grateful Maggy will be," he ended with a wicked grin.

"Two?"

"Yes, Jane. Annabel as well."

"Oi hadn't thought of it that way, our Jack. Rightyo then, let's start."

"Here's the drier," Josh indicated with a wave of an arm.

"Can you work this great enormous machine?" I

questioned, doubtfully.

"Yes, Miss Jane. Just tip a load into the hopper that leads down into the pit and the elevators lift it up into the storage bins. S'easy. Old Josh will turn the heater on, won't you?"

"It's Jane, I'm not a Miss anymore, Dick." I knew in my heart, it was hopeless. He had it stuck in his woolly head, and that was that.

"I have to milk twice a day, so won't be here all the time. You'll need to keep an eye out to make sure it all works okay. Jack can drive the combine, I'll show him," Josh said.

"Why can't oi drive that?"

"Because you're too much of a hair-brained dumbcluck, that's why. I've struggled hard to buy this farm and don't want it ruined by you. Go on, jump on the tractor."

Chunk, chunk, chunk… clouds of smoke filled the barn.

Rushing out coughing and spluttering, quickly slapping my handkerchief over my face, found Dick had joined me, choking.

"Strewth, the rings are gone," Jack cried.

"Don't worry about that, a bit of residue diesel and oil in the bore, it'll clear."

"On your head be it," Dick retorted. "Don't blame me if it conks out."

Clunk, went the gears, as the ancient machine lurched into the yard. At least the smoke had gone.

Jack jumped in the combine, and off they went. Thrum, thrum, thrum went the flails. Soon a veil of dust obscured them as they began working the field.

"Will they be alright?"

"Yes, safe as houses," Josh replied. "If you want to see the other machinery start, come back in an hour, Jane."

Bidding him adieu, I walked slowly passed the cottage while looking as carefully as possible without making it obvious. All was still. Whatever their intentions entailed, most likely happened after dark.

Dominic grinned when I entered the vicarage. "Where

have you been so early?"

"Checking the cottage, then seeing the pair start work at the farm. Josh said to go back in an hour, the pit will be filling by then and he'll start the elevator. Coming?"

"Yes, get some air in my lungs."

I laughed. "It was more smoke than anything else. Should be clear by the time we get there."

Josh Rogan waved an arm as we entered the yard. "I'll start the elevator now. Might be a bit dusty."

Hummmmm… the electric motor sprang into life, followed by a clang as Josh pulled a lever to start the belts moving.

Something shot across the floor, then another and another…

"Rats!" Dick hollered. "Good job Jack ain't here, he hates the creatures. Oi expects the machinery disturbed them."

"How many are there?" I asked, nervously, looking around.

"Could be hundreds, Miss, nobody knows. They breed over the summer, makin' nests in here where it's quiet and they're not disturbed. They feed off the grain that falls off the elevators."

"Where will they go?"

"All over, oi s'pect. Not back in here until harvest is all in."

Josh came in. "What's up?"

Dick explained.

"Crikey, it's been years since we had this amount. I'll get in touch with that man Smith, he'll cure their hash."

Margaret's dulcet tones wafted in. "Hello Jane. Oi've brung moi boys their lunches." She gave him a hug. "Hello moi love."

"Not in here, Maggy. You knows how oi hates a kissin' and a-cuddlin' in public."

"Public!" There's only three of us here."

"You knows what oi mean, oi get embarrassed."

Margaret snorted. "You weren't so shy behind Josh's hayrick in the summer when you tried to…"

"Oi deny it," Dick snapped.

"Ha," she snorted. "It would take a wagon load of harlots to embarrass you, your hands are everywhere."

"Ahem," Dominic spluttered. "Can you two keep your love lives private, please?"

A giggle was stifled within me.

Jack wandered in. "Hello Maggy, did you bring the tea?"

"Tea!" exclaimed Dick. "Oi needs something a mite stronger than tea. This here's thirsty work."

"You'll have tea and like it," Margaret snapped back. "Ale with farm machinery don't mix. Can oi look in one of they hoppers?"

"A-corse you can, just be careful."

Jack had dipped into the food pack, so about to clench his teeth around a cheese and pickle sandwich when…

"Whaaa…"

"Quick," Jack shouted, leaping up, "she's fallen in the machinery."

"Oi don't want moi missus all a-mangled up," Dick yelled, "turn it off."

"It isn't going," Dominic pointed out. "Josh stopped it when the food came."

"Oh no, neither it b'ain't."

"Help oi," came Margaret's shriek from above.

"What's happen, our Faga… oi mean, moi dear?"

"Oi've fell in the hopper, that's what's happened, you great nitwit. Come and get oi out."

"Look at that," Dick said, "she's even lost her fag."

"Never mind the sarcasm," she snapped angrily as she stood up to her waist in corn. "Just get oi out, moi mouths full of dust and old corn. Oi gave up smokin' last year, as well you know, Dick Drummond."

"You can have that tea then," Dick reposted. "That should wash it down." He burst out laughing.

From Margaret's expression it was abundantly clear being laughed at right now, was not at the top of her 'I want to have things done at me list.

"Dick Drummond," came a steady, menacing voice, "stop actin' the fool and get oi out."

"Not oi," Dick retorted, "not in the mood you're in. Our Jack'll come give an 'and."

"Thanks a lot, mate. I'll get some ladders. Come on girl, walk up those, I'll be right behind you."

"Not on your life, Jack Sweeny. Oi'm not havin' you a-lookin' up moi skirt. Oi'm a married woman."

"Oi told you to be careful," Dick said, most unsympathetically.

"If you'd been a gentleman, you'd have been a-comin' instead of sending Jack." With that, her hand came around like a blur, to catch him under his right ear.

Wallop!

"Ow!" Dick yelped.

"Oi'm off home now. Don't expect any dinner," Margaret snapped in a parting shot as she stormed out.

Dominic shook his head. "You made a really good job of that! Now what are you going to do for food?"

"You had better pop into the vicarage later. Dust yourselves off before you come in, though," my warning went.

"It's nearly dark," Josh remarked. "Better get the tractor and combine in."

"Not seen any more rats," Jack noted. "Wonder where they've gone to?"

"The bleeding moon, oi hopes," Dick uttered.

"They rushed towards the village," Josh said. "Saw them running across the field."

"Best shake this dust off, our Jack. Nip in the inn for a pint, then off to the vicarage."

A Ghost

*O*n entering the village store, Mister Leggett greeted me cheerfully the next day. "Morning Jane, pint of milk, is it?"

"Yes please." I was about to add how well he looked, when Dick came in.

Picking up a paper from the counter, he grinned. "Nice day for it, Miss Jane."

"Haven't you heard?" Mister Leggett asked.

"Heard what, nobody tells oi anythin'?"

"The rats," Miss Maybrook butted in from behind a stand, unusually quick at hearing and even more mysteriously, sociable towards Dick. "Last night it was."

"What was? Can't anybody talk sense this here mornin'?"

"Rats in the church," the old lady snapped back impatiently, fiddling with the controls on her hearing aid. "Tch, tch, blooming new-fangled thing, never works properly when it's needed," she grumbled.

"So?" Dick queried.

"The candles were chewed as well as the fruit for the Harvest Festival," Leggett confirmed.

"Yes, Dominic isn't very happy about it," I returned.

"You've seen him at this time of the mornin'?" Dick gasped incredulously.

"We are married so we live together, remember?"

"Oh ah, a-corse you do, Miss Jane."

I was about to berate him for continually calling me Miss, when Miss Maybrook got in first. "A good thing it wasn't tonight, the bread's going over."

"Is it?" Dick asked.

"Of course, the service is tomorrow," she retorted with a knowing nod of her head.

"Perhaps the ghost got hungry," Dick said with a laugh. "Must have reckoned somebody owed him a bite to eat, it's been a long time since the last festival."

Miss Maybrook gave Dick a scolding look. "Mister Leggett says he saw it walking through the churchyard around nine o'clock last evening," she said, tapping the counter forcibly with the handle of her umbrella.

Dick took a hasty step backwards, perhaps recalling a distant yet painful brush with the implement. "There's many a person hereabouts believes a spirit haunts that there church," he replied. "So far, nothing's ever been proved one way or t'other."

"It must be hard up, starting on the candles," Mister Leggett snorted. "Yet the tales never seem to worry you, young Drummond. Maybe we could persuade you to check it out one dark night?"

"No thanks. Oi done moi share of ghost watchin' at the Manor stables, thank you," Dick retorted quickly.

"We ought to put a proper meal out for it, then," Miss Maybrook suggested. "It's good to keep peace with the spirits."

"You're as bad as the rest," Dick laughed back. "Oi'm off to work. You a-comin' Miss Jane?"

"Yes, it would be a good idea to check on you know what."

"Morning Jane," Jack said as we walked into the shed. "You're just in time, me old china."

"What for?"

"To change the wheel on your tractor, it's got a flat. Fetch a spanner and get the nuts off."

"Rightyo, mate," Dick said, applying the tool and tugging ferociously. "Nothin' happenin'."

"Harder, pull harder."

"Oi think it's a-movin'" Dick gasped through his efforts.

"Do be careful that doesn't slip, Dick," I said. "There doesn't seem to be as much grip as it should have.

Twang!

The nut released, then with nothing to hold him in place, Dick shot backwards, cannoning into Jack.

"Whaaa… that hurt moi hand," he squealed.

A ducked saved me as the implement left the wheel in a graceful arc.

Clang, rattle, rattle…

"You bleeding prawn. What'cher chuck it up there for? It's gone into the top of the old thresher now."

"T'were an accident, our Jack."

"You're the bloody accident. It's your fault, you'll have to get it."

"It's always moi ruddy fault," Dick muttered as he stood up, got some ladders and climbed to the top. "Bloomin' heck, it be high up here."

"Try not to fall then," I encouraged. "Be careful."

"Stop messing about and get the ruddy thing. We've work to do," Jack rapped out, impatiently.

"Can't see it, musta fallen down the hole where the stooks went in," Dick called back. "Too dark in there to see a thing."

"Here, take this torch, don't' drop it like the last one, neither."

"Thank you, Miss Jane." Click.

"There it be, down on the sieve. Oi reckons oi can just reach it."

A silence elapsed as he laid down, stretching an arm out.

"Yikes!" Dick yelped, leaping off the thresher head first into a mound of straw.

"What the hell's the matter now?" Jack demanded, his patience wearing thin with the antics going on.

"Dick sat pointing frantically. "There be a big pair of eyes a-starin' at oi in there. Oi reckons it be a big rat about four feet long, probably the King Rat."

"Are there such things?" I questioned, dubiously.

"In his mind, most likely, Jane," Jack retorted. "His imagination runs away with him at times," he answered with a wistful smile.

"Only at times?"

"That b'ain't fair, Miss. Oi b'ain't a-goin' back up there, not for nothin', oi b'ain't."

"You'll have to, because I can't stand the horrible things," Jack snapped back.

Dick sat shaking his head. "Not for nothin'," he repeated. "It be the King Rat."

"Where's the torch?"

"Oh, up on top still, Miss Jane. Oi dropped it."

"I'll go."

"Are you sure?" Jack muttered. "Say he's right, it is?"

"I've never heard such nonsense, and after all, they are only one of God's little creatures."

"B'ain't no little one, Miss Jane. Got to be enormous, the size of those eyes."

Hiding the fear held in my breast, up I went. Maybe there was something in what Dick said. After all, he had been very brave in the past, so whatever was lurking up here... A shudder took me.

"You okay?" Jack called.

"Fine thanks."

Click... the beam of light sprang out. In it, looking back not a couple of feet away, stood a big farm cat.

"Hello, are you hunting?"

"What are you a-doin' talking to rats, Miss?" Dick asked with a nervous chatter in his voice.

"It's Josh's farm cat," my shout went back. "I've got the spanner, here, I'll throw it down."

Dick stood with a sheepish grin. "Coulda sworn t'were a rat, Miss."

"Well, it wasn't, was it? Now let's get the tyre changed and the field in the dryer," Jack snapped.

◦◦◦

Taking Dominic's arm as we went to the inn to see how the lads had got on, we were surprised to find it full, the hum of talk about a plague of rats infesting the village. The pair sat sipping ale.

"Good evening," Dominic greeted.

"Evenin', revrund. What's up, you a-comin' in here?"

"How's the harvest?"

"About in, now, Jane," Jack confirmed. "We're at a loose end again after we bring the bales in."

"Time's running out and the Colonel's getting impatient," Dominic added.

"Oh ah, he would," Dick snorted. "But it's not his neck that's a-bein' stretched out for the chop, is it?"

"Well, I, err, umm," Dominic stammered.

"Also, what about this church ghost," Jack cut in before Dominic could untangle his tongue. "Been scoffing the church grub, ain't it?"

"Well, yes… but I…"

"S'been seen," Dick said with a derogatory snort. "A-creeping across the graveyard, revrund."

"Look here, you two, there's no ghost," Dominic snapped out, losing patience. "It's most likely the rat population you chased out of farmer Rogan's farm."

"Oi never chased anythin'," Dick came back defensively. "Old Josh started the dryer belts up, oi didn't."

"Had your candles away, I'm told," Charlie Tomlinson said as he approached. "Now the harvest food."

"What do you mean?" Dominic spluttered.

"Come on, reverend. Nobody with any sense believes the ghost story. Maybe that's why Drummond does," he ended with a laugh. "Somebody's having a feast at your expense. Probably those gypsies."

"That's not fair, Charlie" I retorted. "They are okay in our book, aren't they, my love?"

"Yes, I trust them. They come to church, which is a lot more than some others do around here," Dominic parried.

"Keep your shirt on, reverend. I'll look after the Romanies, you see to the church."

"Well, take poor Miss Maybrook…" Dominic began…

"You take her, revrund, as far away as you like, silly old moo," Dick snapped.

He got an icy glare from Dominic. "I was just going to say, that the Major heard her screaming, thought she was being robbed again so burst into her home. He found her standing on a chair waving her brolly at three of the creatures on her kitchen floor."

"Oi'd have thought that one look at her ugly mug, would have been enough to scare them all off."

Dominic ignored Dick's derogatory remark. "The Colonel says it's getting a bit much with rumours running rife, so has called a meeting tomorrow evening at the village hall. Here, Charlie, would you put this poster up, please?"

"That should be educational," Jack said with a wry grin.

"We've gotta load of bales to pick up in the mornin'. Oi'll need to get moi hand back in usin' a prong again."

Jack laughed. "Can't imagine you with a prong, my old china. Just take it steady, bales are heavy chunks to lift up in the air. It should only take a day though, well in time for Friday's hijinks."

"Oi hope they don't get too high or jinky, that's all," Dick muttered.

"Can we have order, please," Dominic called from the Chair person's position in the village hall. "I declare the meeting open. Lady Hornby-Smythe would like to apologise for her absence, she is unwell. Cynthia Wrackham will speak on her behalf."

"Thank you, Mister Chairman. I'm told the plague is wreaking havoc in the stables and Manor grounds. Mainly hay and oats. They chew through sacks and grain goes everywhere."

"It's Olga that's getting her oats," Bert Rudge shouted, from his seat. "The Count's seeing to that."

Jack leaped from his chair, angrily looking around for the location of the voice.

"Sit down, Jack," I whispered. "He's doing it on purpose to get you wild."

Jack slowly sat, glowering across the room.

"One frightened Maude out of her wits," The Colonel cried loudly. "It simply isn't practical having them in the Court."

"With that revealing statement, he sat down.

"Farmer Rogan has contacted Squeaky… I mean, Mister Smith, to come and control them. He's due here early tomorrow morning," Dominic explained. "I hope that helps allay fears."

"What about the Harvest Festival food," Miss Maybrook said. "He can't do much about that ghost, can he?"

"Dominic almost choked on the tea he was about to drink, spluttering into the cup. "Please don't spread wild, unfounded rumours about a ghost. Once Mister Smith has dealt with the rat infestation, I'm sure the so-called apparition will disappear, won't it, Jane?"

"Not half as fast as Olga will to France, with the Count, now he's asked her to marry him," Rudge shouted at the top of his voice.

The jibe was plainly aimed at Jack, intending to make him jealous, which wasn't very difficult and Rudge knew it.

"What! Marry him… that's it, I'll do for the pair of them," Jack shouted, rolling up his sleeves.

"Order, order!" Dominic yelled.

"If you're a-buyin', revrund," Fred Clayburn shouted, "Mine's a pint."

It rankled me. "Fred, be quiet, allow the meeting to continue."

"Thank you, Jane. Now, can we have a show of hands in support of the proposal?"

"Oi don't wear a support, revrund," Rudge interrupted, his voice echoing around the hall." Sweeny might use one though."

"Really," Cynthia Wrackham snorted. "Such rudeness!"

It was plain Dominic was getting hot under the collar while rapidly going that pretty shade of purple. "Call Cynthia," I whispered.

"That be up to you, revrund. But being a man of the cloth and wed as well, I wouldn't do it too often if oi were you," Rudge yelled.

Mister Leggett jumped to his feet. "If you don't shut up, you'll be thrown out, Rudge."

"If you're as fast a-doin' that as you are serving in that joke of a shop of yours, we'll be here all night. It's Drummond and his lot that's a-makin' all the noise."

The crash of chairs rattled around the hall as Dick and Jack departed them at lightning speed, bringing Miss Maybrook out of the nap she had lulled into.

"Now just you hold your horses, a-corse oi b'ain't said a word yet, it's you that's bein' a-doin' all the yelpin'."

A glance at Dominic concerned me, who sat aghast at the turn of events. Lady Celia would never have allowed it to get this far, had she been in the Chair. Sadly, she wasn't.

"Jack and Bert stood face-to-face, jaws jutting like two bulldogs about to tear each other apart in a fury of flesh and fur.

"Did they just growl?" I asked Dominic.

A chair or two was thrown aside as the pair began circling, muscles tensed and ready, gauging each other for the first blow in a clash of wills.

The count stood, a foolish thing to do, taking into consideration the hints that had been expounded here this evening and Jack's escalating anger.

"Please stop, messieurs, this is very silly."

Bop!

"Jack's right jab was faster than Dick at opening time, catching the Count around an ear, knocking him off balance.

Such was the magnetism of the scene, that nobody noticed the Colonel leave his seat to approach the group of antagonists, coming into the fray on Bert's left.

Rudge's right arm drew back in preparation for the second blow of the day.

I stood to call a warning for Rudge to stop, but he ignored me.

The Colonel, in his well-meant endeavour, stupidly stepped in between the two men. "Stop this nonsense," he yelled, at exactly the same instant Rudge unleased his blow.

Thud! The tightly clenched fist hit the military gentleman square in his right eye.

"Ah!" bellowed the Colonel. "What the blue blazes did you do that for?"

"Oh, oi'm sorry Colonel. Oi didn't see you there, it was meant for Sweeny."

"All of you, be silent," Cynthia hollered at them. "Otherwise, the vicar will be forced to take drastic action."

"What's elastic action?" Fred asked. "Does that mean the vicar's stretched to his limits?"

"Out!" the Colonel shouted, making a beeline for Dick and clan whilst holding his damaged eye, his cane waving threateningly in his other hand. He was quickly joined by the Major, Mister Leggett and several members of the Women's Institute.

Loud protestations were heard from Dick and Jack, as each was propelled rapidly towards to doors.

"Out!" repeated the Colonel. "All of you."

"I'll have you," Jack shouted at Rudge across the Colonel's shoulder. "We're not finished this yet, not by a long chalk."

Several more chairs went over as Miss Maybrook joined in, wielding her umbrella in a very inappropriate way, eliciting several yelps as it connected and a cry of agonised pain from someone, who had stupidly tried resisting her attentions.

What surprised me, was that Bert Rudge had been left in the hall. It had been his comments that had ignited the whole situation in the first place. Perhaps the Colonel didn't fancy the other eye blackened?

After the meeting, Dominic and I went to see where they were. The obvious port of call was the inn.

"Are you alright?"

"T'were unfair, them a-chuckin' us out, Miss Jane," Dick complained bitterly. "Oi hardly said a word and Jack only tried to defend Olga's honour."

"How could I sit and listen to that swine's accusations," Jack snorted. "It was all a pack of lies."

Sheila Tomlinson walked from behind the bar. "You're supposed to obey the chairman, not shout and yell, causing a fight into the bargain."

"That was Bert Rudge," Jack said. "He did all the stirring up and shouting things, it was him who socked the Colonel in his eye, too."

Sheila's eyes softened. "Go on, I'll treat you to that round."

"I've had a word with the Colonel about his attitude, pointing out how very unfair it was to you two, too," Dominic replied. "He said sorry about that, but was concerned anything of Friday's escapade might leak out in the row going on, so wanted you two out of it, you know far too much."

"Thanks, revrund, you're a fair man, if ever oi met one."

"Well, what happened," Sheila asked. "The suspense is killing me."

"Oh, the meeting," Dominic replied, springing to voice. "The WI will replace anything lost in the church, and Smith is coming to deal with the rats. However, you know how superstitious people are around here, several of the WI still insist there's a ghost on the loose so the Colonel set up a sub-committee to look into that, which seemed to satisfy everyone. So that's, that."

"And the incident in the hall?" Jack enquired.

"We all know who was behind that, it'll fade," I added.

"Oi reckons the Colonel will have a nice black eye. He shouldn't have interfered in the scuffle, silly old goat."

"That will take longer to fade," I replied. "Now you know why he did it, perhaps you'll forgive him?"

"Oi guess so. We needs him on Friday, anyways."

Bale of Hay

Dominic still slept, so slipping from beneath the sheets, had a little breakfast, was dressed and went for my morning walk to check on the occupants of Briar Cottage. As usual, the black car stood in the road and the place appeared silent.

"Mornin' Miss Jane."

Dick's greeting startled me a little, my thoughts had been elsewhere. "Good morning, Dick. No Jack?" I asked, searching around.

"Oi s'pect he be at the farm, Miss. He gets up earlier then oi. We're a-getting the bales in today, a-stacking them in the old Dutch barn."

"Do be careful, you aren't used to farm work, are you?"

He grinned back. "Oi used to do a bit when oi were a lad, a-givin' an hand to moi dad on the farm we lived on afore Sharpe bought it. T'were called Swaggs farm then. Oi knows what to do."

"Remember, we need you on Friday, that's only a couple of days away. Don't get injured."

"Where you a-goin', Miss?"

"I'll walk on with you, don't want these crooks to know we're keeping an eye on them, do we?"

The sound of tractor engines wafted out of the shed. Plainly somebody was getting equipment ready.

"Morning Jane," Jack greeted.

A smile and a nod went from me. It had come as a surprise just how willing both the lads had been doing this little job for Josh Rogan, helping him out while his normal staff were off sick. Now it was about the last day, everything had slotted in very well to end before whatever was going to happen, happened. If only we had a better idea what it was, but the Colonel said to lay low, which we had.

"I'll drive, you hop on the trailer, mate," Jack said. "Got the prong?"

"Oi have that too, our Jack," he said, hopping onto the flatbed. "See you later Miss Jane."

Waving an arm and departing the farm, I left them to get on with the job.

"Mornin' Jane," came Margaret's voice. "Seen moi Dick?"

It seems she had forgiven him, yet again. "They're in the field getting bales in."

"Oh ta, oi'll go say hello then. Bye Jane, maybe see you later?"

"Just keep an eye on them, please. Important goings on tomorrow, we don't want to be short of hands."

"Oi'll be sure to do that." Her face broke into a lovely smile. It had to be admitted that both the sisters had a hidden charm about them, I would go as far as say, very pretty with it, in Annabel's case, beautiful. She was a bit of a mystery to me, never having had much to do with her. Then, unfortunately after that heart-breaking experience of being jilted at the altar, refused point blank to join in anything, taking to dressing in a very plain, rather frumpy way. Perhaps she needed a little boost in her confidence?

We were sitting in Dominic's study when the thumping on the vicarage door started. It was so violent Dominic jumped an inch or so. "Who on earth is that?" he cried.

"We had best go to see, before whoever it is knocks it down."

It was opened to find Margaret gasping for air. She had

plainly been running, running hard at that.

Her appearance remined me of the day she had burst into the village hall, having run that day from the church to report the findings in the belfry. To support herself, each hand rested on a side of the doorframe, slightly at a down angle, just as they had previously, her shadow imitating the CND Cross on the passage floor. Talk about Déjà vu!

"What's the matter, Margaret," Dominic asked, somewhat warily.

One never knew with the Drummond crew, anything at all could have occurred, to Dominic's dismay, often did.

"It be moi Dick, oi think he's dead."

"Dead!" Shrieked Dominic.

His outburst made me jump, having rarely if ever, heard such a loud noise emit from him.

"Come in," I said, "sit down, tell us what has happened."

"Oi b'ain't got time for a-sittin', Jane, 'tis urgent. Please come, revrund, he's a-lyin' on the ground not a-movin'." She had hold of his sleeve, pulling for all her worth. "Please," she begged.

"We will, first I'll call an ambulance then Doctor Monday, let's get help on the way. Here's your coat, my love."

At the field we found Jack sitting beside a prostrate Dick, patting a hand. "He won't come round."

Jack never sounded panicky, wild or annoyed at times, but never like this.

"Help is on the way, Jack, let's get him in recovery."

"What's that, Jane?"

"Like this, it's easy, helps the patient breath better."

"What happened?" Dominic asked.

"I told him it was too high, but he said he could do it."

"Do what, Jack, you're not making any sense," I continued.

He kind of gasped out in anguish. "We had a good load on, Jane, right high it was, there were only a few bales left. I said we should take the load in, then come back for the others, but Dick decided to try hoisting them up. You know how he is when he gets cocky about doing something. At first he managed okay, it was a job though, only barely made it. I don't think he had enough strength for the second one, but he tried anyway. It got as far as the edge of the load and I made a grab for it, when it suddenly vanished over the edge, falling on him, straight on his head. Bales are heavy, Jane, from that height you don't want to be clobbered by one. He went down like a sack of potatoes, out like a light, nor hasn't moved since."

Taking a hand, I felt for a pulse. "He has one, so isn't dead, Margaret, just unconscious. Ah, here's the doctor."

Taking Margaret in my arms to comfort her, I whispered, "The doctor will get him round, an ambulance is on the way as well, try not to worry."

"Oi love him, Jane," Margaret wailed. "Look at him now, a-lyin' there in an heap."

"He's a good strong pulse, try not to distress yourself."

"Will you come with oi to the hospital, please?"

"Yes, of course. We'll go together."

"Oh, thank you, you're a good friend, Jane. You've been good to moi Dick, as well. Oi know he's not very popular in the village, but he does try to help out."

"Yes, he does, especially for you, now your sister as well. It's why he took this little job. We'll have to try getting his old one back soon, too."

She cried softly on my shoulder then, the poor love.

"He's a good man at heart, he'll be okay, you'll see." There wasn't such conviction of any such thing in my heart, but kept those concerns to myself.

A wail of a siren sounded as the ambulance swung into the field. Men jumped out; a stretcher was quickly placed on the ground with Dick on it.

Dick suddenly leaped into life as soon as they tried to lift the stretcher up, beginning to fight the men and creating merry hell, but was finally moved onto into the ambulance.

I got in with Margaret, then with a wave to Dominic as the doors closed, we soon found ourselves dashing to the hospital.

Dick remained motionless once firmly secured all through, uttering nothing. On arrival was put onto an A and E bed, which was possible back then, without having to wait hours in a corridor.

Doctors came to run tests, confirming to Margaret, that his bodily functions were working as they should be. They were however, puzzled why he had so quickly relapsed into unconsciousness after being so lively on the stretcher.

Margaret still wept occasionally.

Patting her hand for support. "He's in the best place and they are optimistic, that's good news, Margaret."

"Oi suppose so, Jane," she almost whispered.

Suddenly a leg twitched. It was Dick's, not Margaret's.

Life in the chap yet, I thought. Thank goodness.

He muttered something so low, we couldn't make out what exactly, then lapsed into silence for a while once more. I had to admit, it was very unusual behaviour.

"What did he say, Jane?"

"I've no idea, Margaret, although it sounded like press something or other. Has he been pressing anything?"

"She laughed for the first time since hammering on the vicarage door. "Moi Dick press anythin', ha, you gotta be jokin', Jane. Our Annabel does all that."

"Shss, listen, he's saying something else. Who's Sam? Is he a relative?"

"Oi don't know any Sam, not ever. Are you sure?"

"That's what it sounded like."

To our surprise, Dick sat bolt upright shouting at the top of his voice, **"Aye, aye, sir."** Once what mouthful was out, he collapsed back again.

We stared at each other.

A nurse dashed over, checking his pulse and temperature. She seemed satisfied.

Margaret looked blankly at me. "What's aye, aye, mean?"

"Isn't that what they say in the navy?"

"Oi don't know, moi Dick's never been in the navy, not ever. Nor have oi."

Those statements were truly believable.

He began muttering again. "Rum, oi don't like rum, Sam, oi drinks ale."

That was also gospel truth, I'd seen it disappear with frightening speed down his gullet on many an occasion with my own eyes. Why was he talking about rum? Wasn't that a navy drink?

"He don't drink that, Jane, oi've never known it. Gin and brandy sometimes, never rum though."

"Yaaa!" Dick hooted, leaping up again. "Bloody Frenchie, that shot just missed oi."

"What shot?" Margaret asked.

Two nurses appeared. "Stop shouting, patients are trying to sleep."

"Aye, in their hammocks," Dick whispered back conspiratorially. "Now, over the side my lads." Arms waved about frantically.

"He be swimmin'," Margaret said in amazement.

"Can he?"

"No Jane, he hates the water."

She was accurate about that, too, and remembered how he had to be fished out of the canal once or twice!

Someone arrived with a straightjacket to subdue poor Dick, who was obviously having some kind of traumatic dream.

He quietened after that, just muttered every now and then, but nothing made any sense at all. About dawn his eyes opened.

"You're back with us, moi love!" Margaret exclaimed.

"Where's Sam?"

"Who?

"Young Sam, the lad oi escaped with."

"You talking in riddles, moi love. You've had a bad dream, that's all," Margaret soothed.

"No, no," Dick yelled, "oi left him up in the tower."

"Please try to keep him quiet," a doctor said. "Otherwise, we will have to sedate him."

"Can oi have this set of irons taken off now?"

"Irons?" the doctor asked.

"Those things what's a-holdin' moi arms tight?"

"Only if you promise to stay silent."

"Just say yes, moi Dick. It's a straightjacket, you were makin' a lot of noise and wavin' your arms about, they put it on to keep you from hurtin' yourself."

"Where am oi, not 'tween decks, is it?"

"'Tween decks? What does that mean? You're in the hospital moi love. Don't you remember that bale a-fallin' on your head?"

"Hospital? Bale? No, oi don't. Be careful, you two, they don't allow women on ships."

"Oh dear, that blow may have caused a loss of memory, Margaret. We had better agree, just to keep him calm for now."

Jack's cheery face appeared. "How is he?"

An explanation followed.

"Crikey, Jane, that's not good. We need him with all his marbles later. Can't they sort him out here?"

My head shook. "I don't think they realise what's happened. If they do, they'll want to keep him in for observation, which could take days."

"I see. What can we do, then?"

"Get him home, perhaps that will help. He'll be in a familiar environment there."

"Good idea. We need him later. I'll have to get him discharged," Jack muttered. "Leave that with me."

How he managed that remained a mystery, but he did. A call to Dominic brought the car to collect us, solving a transport problem.

"Is he well enough?" Dominic asked, looking doubtfully at our patient. "He still seems in a daze to me."

"He is, darling. But we need him for the event, later."

"Oh, I had forgotten about that in this excitement."

"Yes, my dear, it has been a bit of a trial. He keeps talking nonsense, about a young Sam, whoever that is. His mind seems locked away somewhere, the bang on the head caused that, most likely."

"He needs a hypnotist then, to get it out of his system," Dominic answered.

"We can't get just anybody in case he says anything people shouldn't hear, like the cove and all that business," Jack pointed out.

Dominic shrugged his shoulders. "I've no idea in that case. Who else is there?"

A stroke of brilliance hit me. "Maureen! She does that sort of thing. Let's go see Danny."

"The top of the morning to you all," Danny welcomed cheerfully. "Tis later we go to the Colonel's, isn't it?"

"Yes, Danny, it is. But we have a problem with Dick," I cut in quickly

"He's not got blind drunk, has he?"

"No, not this time, my friend, he's had a bang on the head so has lost his memory."

"Oh, I see. Bring him in, Jane. I'll get the Colleen."

Dominic told her of events leading up to our present situation.

"By the Sacred Virgin Mary, the poor lad. His mind is all mixed up. He needs to regress, get troo this muddle then back out again as he was before. Tat'll get this mess out of his system. Tis a terrible ting, to be held in the past."

"Well, what then…" Dominic looked at her, puzzled.

"Don't be worrying yourself, vicar. It can be done, for sure right enough. But I want complete silence, no matter what he does or says. He may live out all the parts, so his voice may change, you'll all need to be ready for dat."

"How can it change?" Jack asked. "It's only his voice."

"No, Jack, not in regression. He may take every part, every person he tinks he met, you must be ready to just listen, no touching him. Do you all understand what I'm saying?" Maureen looked meaningfully from one to the other.

"Oi want moi Dick back," Margaret said softly. "He be a stranger right now."

"So you shall," Danny put in. "Maureen's very good at this. She'll find out what the problem is. But do as she says, stay silent all troo her regression."

All heads nodded. No matter what Dick may have been like, I was sure we all wanted him to be his old self again.

"Lay him on the sofa, put this pillow behind his head," Maureen said. "Now, be very quiet." Her eyes closed slowly, lids fluttering a little. "Master Drummond, you must speak to me, where are you?"

Dick didn't respond, just moaned a bit.

"You must answer. Where are you?"

"Oi got knocked out, so oi didn't rightly know straight off, not until the shakin' started."

"What shaking was dat?"

"Moi shoulder, bein' tugged somethin' terrible. Oi thought it t'were a girl, a-corse it were such a squeaky voice, but when moi eyes opened, oi were a-lookin' at a young lad."

"I see," Maureen whispered back. "Then what happened?"

"He were a-callin' out, that's what happened."

"What did the lad say?"

Regression

'*Wake up, Dick, for God's sake wake up. The Captain'll be here any minute and if you're caught still in your hammock, he'll have you flogged, that's no error.*'

"Sounds began to clear. Captain? Flogged? Do you mean sell oi off? Why is there a strange mist about oi and why are the walls a-movin' up and down?

A booming voice came near. '*Has that lazy dog of a sailmaker shown a leg yet? He'll be lashed to a grating and shown the cat if he isn't up and working.*'

Crikey, I thought, where am oi and who's that a-doin' all the shoutin' about a sailmaker? That young voice whispered in moi ear again.

'*Get up Dick, for God's sake, get up.*'

Who are you?

'*Stop skylarking about, just get on your feet, he's coming down the companionway.*'

Companionway? Who's a-comin' down what companionway? However, the urgency from this lad was genuine, so with that something told moi leg muscles to work. Then moi feet touched the floor, but it went sideways, flinging oi down onto wooden boards. Where the hell did they come from?

'*Stand up, come on, get on your feet.*'

The youngster put an arm under moi armpit, to help heave oi up.

Heavy footstep approached.

'Where is the wretch?' a booming voice yelled out.

'He's here Sir, all shipshape and Bristol fashion, ready for work, Sir,' the youngster replied, touching his forehead with a knuckle.

'Ah, so you've recovered from last night's so-called illness, have you, damned scurvy knave? You can thank your lucky star Lieutenant Rudge wasn't sure if you were drunk or not, otherwise it would have meant thirty strokes of the cat for you. Nobody has ever survived thirty strokes of the lash before.'

The ugly brute walked away a short distance.

"Oi don't like cats, oi said to this lad. Do oi have to stroke one thirty times?

The lad shook his head. *'Not a real cat, you idiot, the cat of nine tails, as well you know. It's a very bad punishment.'*

Oi noticed the man had stopped further along to have a go at somebody else.

'Look at me when I'm speaking to you, I won't tolerate insolence. Clap him in irons.'

Men dragged the poor devil away.

Dick lapsed into silence…

Maureen cast us a puzzled look. "Then what happened, who was this man?" she encouraged.

"T'were like this, oi gave him an eye all over, a medium height man but stocky with it, almost as broad as he were tall. He had a neatly trimmed black beard, but what took oi aback most of all, were his clothes, a jacket cut away at the front at the waist, but with tails behind. T'were a dark blue with wide lapels that turned back to show a white facin'. On each shoulder lay a gold epaulette, along with gold lacing on the lapels and collar, too. White trousers covered his thighs to his knees, with white stockings to his feet. At his neck was a black cravat, together with the strange half-moon shaped hat he wore across his head with the edges turned upwards, there sat on the front were clipped a black cockade in the shape of a rosette. T'were a funny set of togs, that's for sure."

'Best get to work, Dick, we've sails to repair. After all, you are our sailmaker.'

Oi looked back blankly. "What are you a-talkin' about?"

'Don't upset him, you can be keel hauled for insubordination, which would kill, or at best kiss the gunner's daughter.'

"Oi'm a married man, but is she a looker?"

'If you like being strapped across a cannon and flogged, yes, she is.'

"Oh," oi thought, a-lookin' at him again, but oi could see what this lad meant about that oaf of a man. Cruel eyes, deep set and black as night, a mouth set inside thick fleshy lips, their redness made brighter by the paleness of the man's skin, as if he was sick or had a weakness of some kind.

'Well, get on with it then,' the aberration snapped.

"Oh ah, oi'll be a-doin' that right away."

'It's aye, aye, Sir, and well you know it.' He stood, legs slightly apart, hands on hips, his body balancing the movement of the floor. *'Learn your seamanship, otherwise you'll feel the bite of the bo'sun's rattan.'*

"Oh, right, aye, aye Sir, that's exactly what oi means, Sir." He gave oi the creeps.

'You were lucky there, Dick,' the youngster said.

Oi looked at him close now. He'd just saved moi bacon.

His young face broke into a grin. *'Don't do that again on board. T'were really stupid.'*

"Do what again, on board what? Who are you?"

'You had too much drink last night, that's what you don't do again.'

"Drink?" oi muttered. "But oi were on the farm."

'No, you're not. I expect you were dreaming about that, old memories of better times, eh?'

"Now look here, oi were helpin' our Jack," oi shouted.

'Shss, don't start hollering again. You were pressed over a year ago, and in all that time, you've never mentioned it before.'

"Just a minute, let's get one or two things straight. Who are you, why is this floor a-goin' up and down?"

'What the hell do you mean, who am oi? You've got a bleeding cheek, us who have been shipmates together all this time. Have you gone soft in the head? For goodness sake don't call it a floor, it's a deck.'

"All what time?" Oi realised oi had to relent a bit, the lad looked so sad about my statement, offended even I apologised. "Oi'm sorry, that fall musta knocked my brains off their gate hinges. Oi can't remember anything."

'Shss, oi told you not to start that yelling. God help us, you must have lost your mind. P'raps oi can jog your memory. Moi names Sam, they call me Young Sam on account of moi surname being Kidd. You're the sailmaker and oi'm your assistant on this ship. Nowwe've gotta make some new sails a bit sharpish after that storm, else we'll be in real trouble. Now, can I get some sail cloth and cord, then we'd better get on with it?'

"Ship! Oi don't understand, how did oi get here?"

'Oi told you, we were a-taken by the press gang.'

"Press gang? Who are they?"

'Officers or trusted seamen from the ship. They go ashore asking for volunteers, or just take people by force if they resist.'

"That's kidnappin', that is. It's illegal and against the law."

'Be that as it may. The navy's a law unto itself when the press is out.'

"Some dream this be," oi moaned. "Why can't oi have a nice one where oi gets lots of ale and money?"

'It's no dream, Dick. If you don't stop skylarking about, you'll be flung in the brig.'

Oi looked at the lad blankly. "Look, Sam, you'd best show oi, to remind oi how to go on, mate," oi added hastily, seeing the lad's look of exasperation. "It'll come flooding back, sure as hens lay eggs."

'It's shipmate, not mate, try to get that into your thick head. This way to the sail loft, follow me.'

"Tell me, young fella moi lad, what's this Captain like, even more to the point, where are we?"

'That was the Captain you crossed with just now.'

"Oh, bit of a tyrant, is he?"

'Captain Hugo Blackwater, a nasty piece of work with a heart blacker than tar. He wangled command of this ship bribing someone at the Admiralty. He took an instant dislike to you the moment he stepped aboard.'

Now I seemed to remember that name, way back in moi

mind...

This is HMS Vanessa of his Majesty's navy, a sixteen gun sloop of war on a spying voyage off the French coast. That storm hit us two days ago, blowing several sails out. Fresh ones have been bent onto the yards, but the Captain wants us to make more to replace them as spares.'

"Why have oi got this headache?"

A grin went from ear to ear. *'You pinched some rum last night, getting blind drunk. T'were oi that got you into your hammock to sleep it off. Oi told Lieutenant Rudge you weren't very well, 'cause if he knew what had really happened, you'd have been keelhauled next morning.'*

"Keelhauled! What's that?"

They ties a rope around you, pass it under the ship, and then chuck you over the side, pulling you back up to the other. It's certain death.'

"This is givin' oi a bigger headache than the ale," oi groaned.

'Not ale, t'were rum, that's what we drink aboard ships. Every mess gets a ration daily.'

"Every day! For nothin'. That's not bad," oi says, the news cheerin' oi up a lot. "One more thing, young Sam, what are we a-doin' spyin' off France?"

Sam laughed. *'We're at war with the Frenchies, of course. Napoleon's up to no good, the Captain said so. He thinks they might be about to invade England, so it's our job to find out.'*

Oi slumped down on a coil of rope. "Stripe oi with a swage of hay, how did oi get here?"

'Don't start that all over again, I told you how,' Sam muttered impatiently.

"Oi don't wanna get caught up in some war, especially on a boat."

'Ship!' Sam snapped. *The Captain hates her being called a boat, if he hears it, he goes raving bleeding mad.'*

"Oi'd not like to see him ravin' mad, oi saw some of that just now."

'He was in a good mood then,' Sam replied. *'He's had men hung from the yardarm for less than you did.'*

"Hung! By the neck, you mean?"

'Yes, that's the truth and no error. But he needs us right now to repair sails, that's why he let you off.'

A staccato drumbeat rent the air.

"What's all that racket a-comin' from above, oi've got an headache."

'Crikey, you have lost your memory, that's no error. They're beating to quarters, looks like a fight in the offing.'

"A fight! What, with fists?"

'No, ship to ship, with our cannons. Come on, let's get on deck to see. Look, a sail off our port bow. Don't worry, the Captain will want to get away and report to the squadron offshore. We're just unlucky getting trapped inshore. On the other hand, if it's a coaster and we take it alone, the prize money will be all ours. We caught one once before, their Captain wouldn't tell what they were up to, but Blackwater has ways of making people talk.'

Oi swallowed hard with a hand to moi throat. Oi could just imagine some of the Captains 'ways'. "What happened?"

'It turned out to be a load of timber for Calais.'

"Timber! What does that mean?"

'It means making landing barges, you nitwit. Look, there she is, rounding that headland, a ship of war and bigger than Vanessa, about twenty-four or more guns, I'd say. It could get messy, them with the wind gage.'

"Oi'd rather be back on the farm, oi could do with somethin' less excitin' than this. What are those racks?"

'For storing ammunition on, see the cannonballs. They are called monkeys on account of the three brass rods sticking out the ends, they look like a monkey's face. In the winter the cannon balls get frozen fast on the brass bars, so have to be heated up to get them off. We call it freezing the balls off a brass monkey.'

"Are there any more lads like you?"

'Yes, lots, called powder monkeys, they bring black powder up from the magazine below decks for the gunners.'

Oi nearly got knocked over by some big fella. Sam said he was a gunner, getting the cannon ready to fire.

"Why are the hammocks bein' hung over the sides."

'To help stop the wood from splintering when a ball hits us.'

"Stripe oi, they b'ain't a-gonna shoot those balls at us, are they?"

Into Action

Dick had gone very quiet. "Is he alright?" I whispered to Maureen.

"'Tis a little shock, it happens at times during dramatic moments. Be patient, please Jane."

I wasn't sure about that. Say he went into deep shock then never came out? How awful that would be.

"Now then, Dick, you're on the deck of a warship going into a battle. What happened then?" Maureen prompted.

Her words seemed to jerk him back to the moment, hopefully not too far back… yet his voice came clear and strong.

"Sam laughed. *'Course they are, we're at war. It won't be long now, up and at them with our guns. But she's farther offshore than us, putting us at a disadvantage with less sea room to play with.'*

"Is that bad, young Sam?"

'Aye, it can be, although the wind's offshore, so that will help.'

"Oi'll waked up in a minute, best give oi a good pinch."

BOOM, BOOM, BOOM… An incessant crashin' roared across the water, numbin' moi senses. Oi had to clap both moi hands over moi ears. "Ahh, moi bleedin' earholes."

They've opened fire,' Sam shouted, givin' oi a dig in moi ribs.

"Flippin' heck, oi can hear that!"

'Wait till ours fire.'

As Sam said that, a row of water spouts shot into the air about twenty feet away.

'They fired on the wrong roll' Sam cried excitedly. *They have to reload*

now, that takes time, it's our turn.'

"Crikey, oi'm too young to die," I wailed. T'were real scary.

'Don't fret, shipmate. Whatever else he might be, the Captain's a good seaman. He can handle this ship as if it was a part of him. We'll probably squeeze out of this scrape. The Frenchie thinks he's got us trapped against the shore, but I'll wager he's in for a shock, that's no error.'

'Lieutenant Rudge' the Captain shouted.

'Aye Sir?'

'We'll hold this course across her bow, but stand by to change tack on my command, and look lively about it.'

'Aye Sir,' Rudge replied, touching his hat as calm as you like, as if he were out on a Sunday stroll.

'I've a mind to let them think we're going for the channel and open sea, but we'll go for the gap between them and the rocks,' the Captain ordered.

'Hell, Dick, it's going to be very close,' Sam uttered.

'Stand by! Ready about…' yelled Blackwater.

'Helm's alee,' returned Rudge, as the ship lurched to one side as Vanessa's bow swung across the enemy vessel, so close oi thought we might collide.

'Fire as your guns bear,' the Captain shouted.

'Fire!' the Lieutenant screamed at his teams. *'Make every shot count, my hearties.'*

The wood beneath moi feet shook and shuddered so much, oi thought the ship might fall apart. But it didn't, it held fast.

BER-BOOM, BER-BOOM, BOOM BOOM, went the crash of our cannons, each leapin' back on its ropes to stop a few feet inboard ready for a reload. Clouds of smoke hid the view for a while until the breeze blew it away.

"*Two, six, heave,*" someone yelled.

"Who's two, six?"

'Twit, it's the gun crew numbers that haul them out through the ports again.'

"Oh, oi see."

Sam was jumpin' up and down with glee. *The Frenchie hadn't expected that, not between him and the shore so close, the Captain took a gamble. Look at the Frenchie, her fores down and half the mainmast has gone as well. That'll slow them up.'*

Huge pieces of wood floated near the enemy ship, great gapin' holes showed in her side, torn in her by Vanessa's cannonade. Painstakingly she turned towards the open sea.

'She's trying to bring her remaining guns to bear, blocking our escape,' Sam said.

The crash of cannon echoed across the gap between us, quickly followed by the howl and whump as shot pierced our sails or slammed into Vanessa's timbers.

Oi jumped with every thud. "Ah, oi've a splinter in moi arm."

'Hold still, let me see.'

"Oi'm wounded, there's blood a-flowin' down to moi wrist and the jagged end's a-showin' through moi shirt. Oi can't stand the sight of blood, especially moi own."

'You'll live,' Sam assured grinning, and with a quick tug, pulled it out. *'It was only a tiny one. It's not as bad as it could have been, a lot of shots missed.'*

"Yeah, a lot didn't though. Come on, it looks like we'll have our work cut out with all this damage."

'Stand by to wear ship,' the Captain shouted. *'Wear!'*

The ship tilted only slightly this time, turning with the wind across our stern helped a lot. Suddenly, the Frenchie seemed to be spinning in front of us, but it was swingin' round that made it look like that, then as quick as a flash, the Vanessa completed her turn, bringing a fresh broadside to bear. To oi, it looked like we were a-dancin' a deadly waltz of death.

The enemy's bowsprit pointed at our side, to be blown apart within moments as our cannons roared again, the shot well aimed.

'We raked her right through the length of her decks with that broadside,' Sam cried in delight. *'Knocked every single gun off its carriage, I'll wager, killing most of their gunners.'*

We stumbled along the deck, dodgin' guns cast askew with great jagged splinters sticking up out of the planks, ready to pierce or cut any unwary naked foot. Men fought to get cannons upright

156

and back on their carriages as powder monkeys replaced shot and black powder in their pouches. Bodies had to be moved, decks cleaned as quickly as possible lest people slip on the blood that flowed about.

'*Their trying to reload,*' Sam cried. '*Come on lads, get our guns back into action.*'

'*Ready to fire, Sir,*' Lieutenant Rudge called to the quarterdeck.

A nod from the Captain as he gave permission.

'*Fire!*'

To be honest, oi couldn't hear them anymore, my ears had gone numb, it was like watchin' a mute pantomime bein' acted out, but oi felt the broadside go. No sooner had each cannon sent its ball at the enemy, the gunners were rakin' and swabbin' them out ready for another round, like well-oiled machines.

'*Hard to port,*' somebody yelled through a lull in the racket. The wheel spun and Vanessa came back on her original course, passing close alongside the French ship.

'*That's it,*' Sam grinned. '*She's finished, it's all over.*'

"Now what?"

'*We'll be out to the squadron to pass any news.*'

"And after that?" oi asked.

'*Who knows? Maybe England,*' Sam said. '*But she hasn't struck her colours yet.*'

"What does that mean?"

'*Not given in, surrendered if you like.*'

'*One last round for England,*' oi heard Rudge call.

As we sailed serenely along, our guns spoke for the last time, shattering what was left of a mast and any wood that had miraculously survived until now. Her masts lay over her side, dragging the ship slowly round, like sea anchors.

'*She'll not be going anywhere,*' Sam remarked, as he gazed at the wreck. '*We'd better get sail cloth and twine from the for'ard store. There'll be plenty to mend and replace. T'were a narrow escape, to get away with just one broadside fired at us was nothing short of a miracle.*'

"Will they follow?"

'*Nah, doubt they'll get her repaired in time, shipmate. Anyway, Vanessa's got a fine turn of speed,*' Sam replied, a-pattin' the ship like oi would a pet dog.

⸎

Dick lapsed again. "Bring some water, please Jane, to dampen his lips and forehead."

If Dick had known what she had said, he'd have had a fit, water was bordering on sacrilege. But the cupful was given so Maureen could trickle a little onto them.

He groaned.

I wondered how much more there was, or even he could actually take? The tale plainly hadn't had an ending as yet. But everybody had complied with Maureen's requests about remaining silent. Margaret must be busting at the seams with worry, but again, and to her credit, she had obeyed Maureen to the letter. A comforting arm slipped around her shoulders.

"Did you find that squadron?" Maureen ventured.

"Oh, aye, we did, eventually. Sam and oi were below decks a-workin' when someone shouted a sail had been sighted. Oi hoped it was a friendly one, oi didn't fancy another battle like the last.

'*It'll be our squadron, shipmate. Come on, let's go and look.*'

"T'were a sight to see, too. Oi let out a low whistle, ships as far as oi could see, their white sails billowing out against the blue sky, like swan's feathers bein' blown along a lake by a light breeze. The Captain went over to the flagship in his gig, coming back with orders that pleased every soul aboard.

'*Tis England, we're bound,*' young Sam shouted for joy. '*I heard Lieutenant Rudge say so.*'

That was good news. "Maybe we'll get off this ship and back to our homes?"

'*Stop gossiping and get on with your work,*' the Lieutenant snapped.

"Bleedin' old crow," oi muttered.

'*What did you say?*' the officer demanded, spinning on oi.

"Sew Sir, oi told him to get on and bleedin' sew, Sir."

You're sailing a dangerous course, scum, running so close to the wind with me,' Rudge snarled. *'I didn't like the set of your jib the moment you came aboard. I've got my eye on you, just one wrong move, that's all it will take.'*

Oi watched him go, then once sure he was out of earshot, said to Sam, "Only one eye, where's he a-lookin' with t'other?"

A weak smile flitted across the lad's face, but was gone in an instant. *'Be careful, shipmate. He's a mean, cruel man who'll stop at nothing to keep in the Captain's good books with a weather eye for promotion. Dick, I haven't got a home,'* Sam went on, a sadness in his voice. *'You're lucky if you have.'*

"Come and live with oi, then. How does that set your jib?"

'Thanks, shipmate. You really are a good friend. But it's very risky deserting, it's the drop if caught.'

"Can't be much worse than a life on here, our Sam. Hardtack and rum, b'ain't be the best of diets. Mind you, we get meat from the weevils in the ship's biscuits."

'At least the men don't call you the drunken sailor any more, on account of you getting your sea legs. Now you're not wobbling all over the place,' he said with a laugh.

"Yeah, but moi hands get so sore with the sailcloth and yarn."

'It's because you have soft skin. Didn't you do any rough worked before getting pressed?'

'Land Ho!'

"Be that another Frenchie, Sam?" Didn't fancy another battle with bleedin' great cannon balls a-flyin' by moi ears.

'Let's go see,' Sam said excitedly. *'It's land, England at that, I'll wager.'*

'Where away?' Rudge called up.

'Fine off the starboard bow,' the lookout yelled back.

Some hands stopped what they were a-doin' to see where.

'Get back to your work, scurvy dogs,' Lieutenant Rudge scolded, *'else you'll be flogged.'*

"He's right handy at dishin' out the floggings," I muttered to

Sam.

'Shhs, he'll hear you.'

"Oi needs to go."

'Go where, below?'

"No, you daft banana. Oi means oi can't stay on this here ship any longer, oi've gotta get off."

'That's crazy talk, shipmate. Nobody ever gets off a ship of war, that's desertion and means death if caught.' He paused, casting his eyes aloft at the huge yards the held the sails. 'Hanging from one of those as a warning to everybody who thinks about escape.'

"Maybe that's a better way to go than rottin' in a hell hole like this," oi replied.

'Perhaps you're right. Can I come with you,' Sam pleaded? 'I don't want to be left here to my fate.'

"S'pose so, Sam. You've stood by me, so one good turn deserves another."

'Dick, can I ask a question?'

"Yes, young Sam, what be it?"

'What's a banana?'

"Well, stick oi with a prong. B'ain't you ever seen one of those? They called these the good old days, too."

'Who does? I don't understand what you mean?'

"No, moi young whipper snapper, oi don't expect you do, not at all."

Escape

$\mathcal{A}$ touch on Maureen's arm brought her attention. "How long can he go on for, is it dangerous?"

"No more than having him stuck in another time. Don't worry your head, I've done several regressions, they've all lived to tell the tale." She bent moistening his lips again. "Let's see if we can't finish this."

"Now tell me, Dick, did you escape? Maureen asked.

He lay silent for a few seconds, then stirred. "No, not right then, we had to plan a bit, see. We went on the upper deck to look at England as it hove into view, what a beautiful sight it were, oi can tell you. Oi knows oi moaned about work in the past, but those lovely green hills with the sun lightin' them up, was a sight for sore eyes."

'Tis lovely, shipmate,' Sam mused. *'I've not set a foot on my country for several years.'*

"Where are we?"

'We got pushed farther west than the Captain wanted, so I'm not sure. He had wanted to make landfall off Portsmouth, so maybe nearer Exeter.'

"That's handy, oi lived inland of there. But how are you so sure of that?"

'One of my duties is to clean his cabin. They don't know I can read and I've never let on.'

"Bet'cher can, young Sam. You're a bright'un, that's for sure."

'Drop anchor,' a command came, its splash rippling the calm waters of a bay.

"We're very close to the beach," Oi pointed out. "B'ain't that dangerous?"

The Vanessa was a Frenchie before she was captured and put into His Majesties service, so French built with shallow draught. It's why she's sent inshore off the French coast a lot, spying.'

"That's interestin'. Oi expect most were a-taken by the press and would love to go."

The deep voice from behind us surprised oi.

'Aye, taken away from their loved ones, families or work.'

We turned to see a wizened old sea salt smiling at us.

Just thinkin' aloud, shipmate.' The oldish chap said. *We all have the same thoughts when anchored close in like this, sailmaker. Most sailors have broad and strong shoulders, made that way from years slaving on one of His Majesties ships. But most can't swim, so can't make it.'*

"Ever tried?"

He gave oi a long, hard look. *It would be more than your life's worth, just as your young friend said.'*

"There must be a way," oi parried.

His voice dropped conspiratorially. *Yes, shipmate, there is, but it is very risky.'*

"Okay, how many to go?"

Two or three, but no more, that would draw attention. First, an escape route?'

"We drop over the side quietly then swim for it."

He shook his head. *No good, a sentry would hear the splash. Gunner Crocker got himself shot last year doing that, and I don't fancy a ball in my back."*

"Then hand-over-hand down a rope?"

That would take ages and we'd be spotted. It's obvious you don't know the way of doing things on a ship,' the sailor replied.

"Oi can't see any other way, then."

You're a sailmaker, you have access to leather. We make straps to put over an anchor cable, grease them then slide down. Nice and quick and quiet, see, and it's possible to control your descent by tightening the straps. You get the leather, it should be simple.'

"Oi'm on, that's what we'll do. When?"

'As soon as possible, tonight if we can. Can you manage that? It's in case we up anchor and sail out of this bay.'

"Leave it with oi. As soon as it gets dark."

'It'll be dark soon enough, another hour maybe. Best time is on the change of the watch, people will be going in all directions then, they won't notice us,' the man said.

'It's at times like that they double the sentries to stop anyone going over the side. If you dive, it makes a splash and the Marines open fire. It's often just too far to swim, especially around these coasts with fast currents. It isn't as simple as you think, shipmate.'

"Oh, that be a bugger then, young Sam. How about a boat?"

'Don't be daft, they have to be swung out, so need a capstan to lower them,' Sam explained.

"We needs a sensible plan," says oi.

'Meet me here when the watches change, like oi said. Just one more point, we must be aware where we're off to. No good getting ashore then not knowing where we are.'

"Leave that with oi. What's your name, by the way?"

'Crowthorn the Carpenter, call me Jake, shipmate.'

Oi looked Jake square in his eyes, held a hand out for us to shake, at the same time pulling young Sam to moi side. "Here's one other. This is our chance, it's now or never."

The ship's bell rang out for the watch change, when pandemonium cut loose with people a-goin' all way. We made our way along the main deck. Oi kept young Sam close by me, after all, we had a right to access the store room for'ard.

Jake stood waiting in the shadows.

'Where are you two going?' Lieutenant Rudge's voice cracked out of the dark.

"For twine, Sir, the front store."

'It's for'ard. You've been at sea long enough to know that. Be quick about it.'

"Yes Sir, a-corse it be, for'ard."

Tomorrow, I'll have you lashed to a grating, mistakes or not. Your time is up, you useless dog.'

The Captain bellowed. *'Rudge!'*

The man vanished.

"Phew, that were close, Sam. He has a charmin' way of addressin' a person, too, really makes you feel good. Oi've been here too bloody long as well, high time oi were back on dry land."

'You've upset him now. He means it, he's done it before, made some false claim of insubordination and had punishment given by the cat.'

"All the more reason to go through with this plan. Oi don't want no cats."

'It's not an animal, it's a whip with nine ends, you nitwit.'

"Crikey! That's worse."

'Here, take one of these as well.'

"What is it?"

'A marlin spike, might come in handy for persuading someone to see things our way,' Sam said with a grin.

Oi patted moi palm with the thing. "Fair give you an headache, this would, it's a lumpy bit of kit."

'I'll take a sailmaker's palm, too.'

Oi gave the lad an enquiring look.

'Old habits die hard. Anyway, I'd be lost without one.'

"Come on, for'ard, as clever clogs calls it, there's Jake, by the anchor cable."

'All set?'

"Here's your leather thong, double sewn for strength," oi says. "Have you the grease?"

'Aye. Put some on your sling, now let's go.'

Moi heart were in moi mouth, oi tells you. After a few paces oi held an hand up. "A marine, just there," oi hissed through moi teeth. "We'll not be able to slip off here. What now?"

Jake indicated to go down a deck.

"Got any more ideas," oi says, as we got to the bottom.

'What about the bow cable locker?' Sam suggested.

'The eyes of the ship, aye, good thinking young'un. There's a small port we could squeeze through,' Jake explained.

Men slept in their hammocks, rocking gently as the ship swayed at her anchors.

'Here it is,' Sam said. *'Damn its eyes, it's locked.'*

'Give oi that belaying pin, I'll shift it,' Jake whispered.

A light clunk told oi he'd done it. "Be careful, that door might creak," oi warned.

Creak…

"There, oi told you so, you great muffin, you could have woken half the ship up."

Jake looked around. *'S'okay, shipmate. Mind how you tread in here, I knows .this locker.'*

"It's bleedin' pitch black."

'Keep close and follow on,' Jake's voice came back.

'Have you got that belaying pin, Dick?' Sam asked.

"Yeah, oi have, tucked in moi waistband. Pause a minute, listen, see if all's quiet."

'Come on, we've not time for listening,' Jake snapped. *'Let's make headway.'*

Oi felt Sam move to push the port open. A glimmer of light came in, showing a cable stretching to the water in a gentle arc.

'Off you go lad, you're the smallest, Dick'll follow, and I'll be last.'

Pokin' moi head through, oi could see Sam, standing on the side of the Vanessa, a-waiting for the ship to swing and slacken the hawser. Then, flippin' his strap over the rope, began the slide down.

Oi followed through the port, but it'were small and moi shoulders got stuck. "Oi ain't gonna make it," oi cried.

An hefty shove got oi a-movin'.

'See you soon, good luck,' Jake called.

Oi were out, but wobbled, so grabbed the hawser, flung moi sling around it and givin' a last glance along the ship's side, closed moi eyes to launch moiself into space.

Whirrrr…

The sound of the strop echoed off the ship's timbers and seemed so noisy, oi thought every livin' soul for miles around must be able to hear it, expectin' an hail of shot a-comin' after oi any moment. Oi knew oi needed to slow moi fall, so tightened the sling and just in time, hittin' the water a second later. The shock almost made oi cry out, it'were freezin'. Suddenly oi was under water and a-strugglin' up with moi lungs almost a-burstin'.

On a-breakin' surface, oi found Sam a-grinnin' at me, his eyes and teeth white with moonlight reflectin' off them.

'Bit of a shock, was it, shipmate?'

"Shss, someone might hear."

'I doubt it, matey, not after the racket you made coming down.'

"Are you alright, young Sam?"

He grinned again. *'As sure as hen's lay eggs.'*

"Cheeky young beggar, that's what oi says."

'Look out, here comes Jake. Swim close in to the hull, give him room.'

We saw him leave the ship, then gasp out loudly. *'Ah. My ruddy hand.'*

'Man overboard,' a sentry yelled at the top of his voice.

'We're rumbled,' Sam said. *'Dive!'*

Even under water we felt Jake hit hard, it must have made a hell of a noise and a huge splash. By now, moi lungs were a-burstin' again, so oi had to surface, comin' up right close under the ship. Sam popped up beside me.

Jake was thrashing about as he began swimmin' towards the shore.

"He'll be shot for sure makin' that much noise, splashin' all over," oi whispered to Sam.

'It's to give us a chance, Dick, they'll think he's the only one, for a while anyway.'

Bang, bang, bang. Balls thudded into the sea all around Jake as he swam noisily. More marines came on deck to open fire, the sea began to boil around him.

'Ah' he gasped, as a ball found its mark. Slowly the thrashin' eased, to finally stop.

'Hold your fire. Well done men, another stinking deserter shot.'

"He's a-done for, poor beggar," oi muttered. "Let's get around t'other side, it be quieter there."

After a-waitin' a while, we shoved off, slowly swimmin' the last few yards to keep water disturbance down.

Soon, we were a-scramblin' up the beach, collapsin' on a band of grass at high water mark.

We should get off this beach and inland as quick as we can. You said you know this area, so lead on,' Sam said.

"Were there any marks on that chart?"

'Yes, a place called Eastwich. Do you know it?'

"You're a good lad, young Sam. Yeah, oi knows it well."

'Seems funny to be on land again, it's still going up and down like the ship's deck. Look, there's a lane, which way now?'

Oi shook moi head. In truth oi hadn't a clue. "Go left Sam, let's find a signpost or directions of some sorts. We must put distance a-tween us and the ship afore dawn."

Sam pointed. *'A track over there, it's grassed over so not used much.'*

"Right, let's get off this road, it's not safe."

We walked for goodness knows how long, until it began getting' light. "Let's have a break, oi'm pooped. Just five minutes or so."

'There's stone walls ahead, see, set against the sky. Looks like a building,' Sam uttered.

"Maybe a barn, that'll be somewhere to rest. There might be someone about, so best be careful."

'Looks old to me, Dick. These gateposts haven't seen attention for years, this one's falling over.'

"You're right there, young Sam. There's somethin' queer about this place, seems deserted to oi."

Sam ventured further in, pokin' his head into a room. *'It's empty, nobody's been here for some time.'*

"Musta been a church or abbey a while back. Oi'm gonna rest moi feet, get them up on some hay, they're barkin' their heads off."

'Barking?'

"Just a sayin' oi heard a long time ago."

'Dick! Come here, quick.'

Oi were on my feet in a flash. "What is it, a search party?"

'No, a light flickering over there,' Sam said, pointing an arm *'Might be a farm.'*

"Okay, let's go see. Oi'm starving', and farms mean food, don't they?"

Moving across a field we found it were a lamp hung outside a door.

'It's a farmhouse right enough, that's no error,' Sam muttered. *'There's a barn beside it too, looks inviting and cosy, I'm about all in. Can we rest up a while?'*

"Yeah, I suppose so, just for an hour."

T'were warm once out of the wind, hay was strewn about from a broken bale, makin' it soft under our feet. Layin' down, oi stretched out and relaxed, the first time since a-slidin' down the ship's hawser hours ago.

The Church

*G*lancing at Maureen, who had an equally puzzled expression. "Is this normal. It seems very detailed."

"To be sure, I've never known one like it, seems uncanny to me, how he knows so much about his surroundings and people."

"He's not gone off his rocker, has he?" Jack wanted to know, worry in his voice.

"No, I don't tink so, oterwise it would be a rambling jumble, and this isn't. He's very sure what's happening."

"Shouldn't we wake him up?" Danny asked, a concerned look on his face.

Maureen shook her head. "No, not at all, Danny. His mind might be at a critical point, awaking him would destroy it."

"From what he's babbling about, it sounds as if it has already," Jack snorted.

"Shss, keep your voice down. I'll ask him a question now he's gone quiet again."

"That's peculiar for a start," Jack snapped. "We can't shut him up usually."

"Dick, Dick, can you hear me? What happened in that barn?"

"Oh ah, in the barn, so we were."

Dick's voice was softer, as if miles away, which he probably was.

There were a bang, clatter, clatter.

Oi leaped up. "Action Stations, Sam," Oi said, shakin' his shoulder. Thud, moi head hit a beam.

'*No, it isn't, we're not on the ship, keep the noise down, let's find out what's going on.*'

"Oh ah, that be right, young Sam, oi forgot."

'*Shss, be silent, there's somebody in here,*' Sam whispered.

"Great lumps of grapeshot, it'll be the press."

'*Or a party from Vanessa.*' Sam's voice wavered with fear through his words.

Oi sneaked to a wall to peer over. "It's okay, it's a woman getting ready to milk her cows."

'*Thank the good Lord for that. I'll see if I can pinch a loaf from the kitchen while she's out here.*'

"But…"

A cheeky grin came from Sam, then he was gone.

As Sam vanished, a call came from the house. '*Aggie, where's the milk for moi breakfast?*'

'*Comin' moi dear,*' she called back as she left the barn.

"Milk, now there's a thought," oi muttered to moiself. "That be as good as food."

A quick dash put oi beside the pail that stood half full. Grabbing a jug, oi dipped it in the bucket, nearly fillin' it to the top.

Mooooo…

'*Alright Daisy, don't fret yourself, oi'm a-coming.*'

The cow struck out with a hind leg, kicking the bucket over, propelling it into moi rib cage.

"Ahhh. Oi'd best get out of here."

'*Shame on you, Daisy,*' Aggie scolded. '*You lost all the milk now. Why did you do that?*'

Just as well cows can't talk, oi thought, else the game would be up.

Sam slipped back in, a grin of success on his face.

"What's made you grin like a Cheshire cat?"

'*I freed some meat from captivity, found it in the larder. It looked lonely hanging there, so I brought it back for some company.*'

"Oi tells you, Sam, oi'm right famished, well done. We'll eat this, then get a-movin. Here, have a slug of this milk, lad."

'Listen,' Sam said. 'Sounds of a horse thundering into the yard.'

That put us on alert again.

"Was it the soldiers?"

'Father, father,' a chap called, provin' t'weren't the military.

Someone dashed out the house. 'What's the matter, Josh? A-comin' in the yard like Old Nick Himself, were after you?'

'A ship... the sailors...'

'Calm yourself lad. Afore you go any further, Josh Sandcastle, where have you been all night?'

'Never mind that,' Josh babbled, 'they're here, in the bay.'

'Josh!' the man snapped. 'You answer your father properly.'

'Sorry, father. I stayed at the Maybrook's farm. Had oi not, oi would never have known the news, would oi?'

'Mmm, that's alright, then. Well, out with it, oi ain't got all day to stand a-gossipin' like the women do.'

'It's the press, father. They landed early this morning hopin' to catch folks in their beds. All the men have fled into the countryside, should oi do the same?'

'The press, you say. Are you sure?'

'There's a warship anchored in the bay, real close in. It's said some escaped ashore in the night. That means they'll be a-lookin' for them, or wantin' more to replace any missin'.'

"Well, swipe oi with a swage of hay, they didn't waste much time, did they, young Sam?"

'We've had it, Dick, not many escape the rope,' he uttered mournfully.

"Here, here, matey, don't let's be havin' that kind of talk. They b'ain't caught us yet, that's for sure, so cheer up."

'Get some things packed,' the farmer shouted. 'Then get you and that horse far away. The press will take you whether they need you or not. Those deserters aren't here, a-corse your mother and oi, have been about all mornin. Put your horse, Captain, in the barn out of sight for a while, just in case.'

'God help us, Dick,' Sam wailed with fear. 'We'd best up anchor and sail out of here as quick as we can. We need to get some sea room between us *and the search party.'*

"You ain't wrong there, young Sam, that's no error. Hark at me, you've got oi a-sayin' it now. Can you ride an horse?"

'Ride a horse! Of 'cause I can't, I've been at sea for years. Can you?'

"Yeah, tis easy." Oi had to make oi sound confident, a-corse oi'd never been on one moiself. So, a-takin' the reins, slipped moi foot in a stirrup as oi'd seen it done so often enough, grabbed the saddle and heaved moiself up. "Give oi your arm, oi'll pull, you swing up behind oi. Hang on tight around moi waist, else you'll be off afore you can say Vanessa."

We sat, nothin' happened.

'Aren't you supposed to say giddyap or something?' Sam asked.

Oi pushed moi heels into its sides, it still didn't budge. "Bloomin' heck, what a time to get on a temperamental nag like this'un. Young Sam, give it a smack on its rear end."

Whack!!!

Neigh… The blinkin' thing shot out the barn like a ball from a cannon with a weather eye on the shut farmyard gate, began a-pacin' itself.

"You blinkin' great hayrick, why did you hit it that hard?"

People appeared at the farm door.

'Hey you, bring that horse back here. Thieves, rogues and bloody gypsies, you'll be hung for this.'

Oi noticed the gate passin' under us, then the jolt as the animal landed, once more we were off on a frantic dash along lanes and fields.

'Ohhh…' Sam wailed. *'I think I'd rather be on the ship, I feel land sick. How far have we gone?'*

"Oi don't know, all oi hope is it doesn't start a-jumpin' any hedges or walls again."

'I can't take much more.'

"We're headin' for a bunch of houses, best we don't go in there at this speed, or else the game'll be up." Oi gave an hard tug on the reins, then the horse slowed just in time. "As soon as it stops, slip off, Sam."

Oi think he fell more'un slipped, oi heard him cry out.

'I feel like I've had a taste of the gunner's daughter,' he moaned, rubbing his backside.

"Turn it round, quick." Oi gave the horse another slap across its rump, and off it went. "Let's hope that'll throw them off course."

'What'll we do now?' Sam asked.

"We can't stick around this neck of the woods, that's as sure as hens lay eggs. The search parties will find us. Trouble is, we've no money and without that, we won't get far."

'Can't we steal what we want?'

"Commit a robbery! Where's your Christian soul, young Sam? To start nicking things wholesale will arouse the local law, then we'd have two lots hunting us."

'What about food? My tummy's fair grumbling, thinks my throats been cut by Rudge's cutlass.'

"It's best we buy food. What we need is some small change," oi said, grinning.

'You mean pinch somebody's money,' Sam gasped. *'That's dishonest.'*

"You were all for it a minute ago. Now you've gone holy on me," oi replied. "Oi'm open to suggestions, young Sam, but oi've a notion there b'ain't be many."

Sam shrugged his shoulders. *'I don't know.'*

We sat silent for a while.

'Okay, I agree. There's little else left, is there?'

"Cheer up, young Sam, it b'ain't the end of the world. We've only got to do it the once, then maybe we can find some work."

'Let's move on, we can't stay in one place too long.'

"That's better. We'll go into the village for a look around, see what's about."

'Just a cluster of houses,' Sam viewed.

"There's a farm to our left and a church over there. Oi'll take the farm, you see what's in the church."

Sam backed away. *'N… no thanks, I'm superstitious about churches. Anyway, I proved I can pinch things at the barn, you do the church, I'll see to that house.'*

Oi had to smile as he went off, a proper scamp if ever oi saw one, a chip of moi own block when oi were his age. Right, the church. Best take it steady in case anybody's about. What with scalin' a wall and a-goin' through a wood, it took oi a while to get to the old wooden door. Turned the handle, but nothin' happened, it needed a bit more of a shove. Settin' moi shoulder to it, oi pushed.

Creak…

T'were a loud noise, oi were surprised the whole village hadn't heard it. A quick cast around, but not a soul stirred and nobody came or called out. Breathin' a sigh of relief, I gave the door a push open. Havin' stepped in, found t'were like midnight with no moon in there, so in case oi stumbled, waited a minute or two for moi eyes to get used to it. The door had put me halfway along the nave. On moi left was the bottom of a tower, to the right lay an altar, so oi went there. Across the front they'd erected a fence thing with a small gate in the middle. T'were open, so movin' with a reverential step, as you do in churches, oi walked to the altar.

"Why am oi being's so quiet? Yet oi couldn't help feelin' it were wrong bein' here," So oi crossed moiself, it seemed the right thing to do. As oi turned to leave something glinted on the altar. A-lookin' closer, found it were two gold candlesticks. "Crikey, these must be worth a King's ransom." They mesmerised oi, so lovely and well, all made of gold. Oi reaches out, moi fingers were about an inch away, when… An hand fell on moi shoulder…

"Ahhh…" oi yelled out loud.

'Cripes, be quiet you ninny,' Sam said. *What are you making all that row for, it echoes around the church and half the village'll be here in a minute.'*

"What the hell are you doin' a-creepin' up on oi, you great hayrick? Nearly gave oi an heart attack."

'Sorry, shipmate,' Sam said reproachfully.

"Did you find anythin'?"

Sam shook his head. 'Just a couple of houses, could see any food lying around."

"Well, we had better find somethin' soon, Oi'm starving'?"

There's a big house along the lane away, though. Might find something there.'

"Too risky, young Sam. Bound to be loads of servants about. What'cher reckon on this place? Oi says it'll be safe enough for now. Let's nip out and see what's along the lane."

'I came along there. It's as empty as Lieutenant Rudge's head.'

"That's more like it, young Sam. There's an inn over there and oi could sure do with an ale, right about now."

'Come on then,' Sam cried excitedly. *'So could I. What's ale like?'*

"Real refreshin'. Let's go, but not front on, round by the stern, through those bushes."

'There's a window,' Sam whispered, lookin' in. *'Nothing, just living quarters.'*

"We can't walk straight in, not a-bein' known around here. People will be suspicious."

'I wonder if they found that horse, Captain, its name was?'

"Talking of Captains, we'd best get back to that church, young Sam, it's safer there."

'Well, what's our next move,' Sam uttered as he sat on a pew.

"Shss, there's someone a-comin'."

'Quick, in here,' Sam cried, grabbin' moi sleeve to tug oi through a door behind the pulpit.

"It's a little room. Must be where the vicar gets his togs on. Try not to worry, Sam, oi can see you're scared. We're in this together, so together us stay."

'Cripes, they're coming in here,' Sam stuttered, panic stricken.

'Who's there, who's in my vestry? Come out, I'm the vicar of this church.'

"Oi reckon he's safe enough. Let's show ourselves."

We stepped into the church. "Hello revrund," oi says, grinnin' sheepishly. "Nice day."

'What are you doing? Stealing?'

'We'd best tell,' Sam said. *'He's a vicar, so we can't lie.'*

Oi took a deep breath. "It's like this, revrund, we're deserters off that ship in the bay."

176

'I see. Tell me one thing, did you volunteer for the King's service?'

'No, vicar, I was taken,' Sam cried out.

'The press?'

'Aye,' Sam answered.

'And you too?' the vicar asked oi. Well, oi weren't sure how oi'd ended up here at all, so couldn't explain that. "Aye, that be right, revrund, oi as well."

'I see. I don't agree with snatching men away from their families, it's neither Christian nor right.'

"Well done, revrund."

'But I don't approve of stealing either,' he snapped. 'Have you stolen?'

'Of course not,' Sam put in with a cheery grin.

'Very well, that's good enough. Have you eaten?'

"No revrund, we're starving', but oi never stole."

'Stay here, I'll bring you something. People will spot you dressed in rags.'

Oi saw Sam's head turn moi way to look oi up and down.

"The vicar's right, we look right ragamuffins.'

'Stay put,' the vicar added, vanishing out a door.

It was ages afore that door creaked again. I got the belayin' pin out ready to donk a searcher.

'It's alright, just me,' the vicar called. 'Here, food and drink.'

"Thank you kindly, revrund, but we can't pay you."

'That's alright, this is God's house, so there's no charge for those in need,' he said with a smile.

Oi had to admit, oi took a likin' to this man.

'Enjoy your food. I have to go now to an appointment at the Manor with Lord Wymondham. Not a nice man, but perhaps his soul can be saved. Don't go anywhere near there. Goodbye.'

"Same to you revrund." We waved as he left.

"Phew! Oi feel shattered after that food, young Sam."

'Have forty winks, I'll keep a watch.'

Search Parties

"*H*as he dozed off?" Jack asked.

"Shss, no, but he thinks he has. It's all part of this drama he's acting out in his mind."

"Maureen, my dear Colleen, are you certain he's alright," Danny muttered, plainly worried. "To be sure it is, that you've done a few of these, but never like this one."

"We can't stop now. Someting else will happen soon, let him rest a few moments. Why not make some tea?"

Dick stirred, stretching an arm as though yawning.

"'Tis starting again," Maureen warned. "Right, my darlin', what's goin' on now?" she uttered, just before Dick spoke.

"Oi woke with a start at a noise. Sam was asleep beside oi, so it t'weren't him, voices came from outside.

'Look here, Blackwater,' the voice said with authority, *I'm in command of this search party, it will be done the way I blasted well want it, so both you and your scruffy band of sailors, do what I say.'*

Oi woke Sam, clampin' an hand over his mouth in case he yelled out. "Shss, we've got company."

'W… what's the matter?'

"There's somebody in the lane. Have a quick look, lad."

'Sorry Dick, I dozed off.'

"You were as tired as oi was, oi'm not surprised."

'There's a party of soldiers out there, formed up and awaiting orders. They'll find us for sure, Dick.'

Another voice barked out commands. *'Corporal, detail a search of the village.'*

'Right away, Colonel.'

"Let oi see, young Sam. Moi God, Captain Blackwater is with them along with some marines."

'My men should be doing this, its navy business, not the damned army's. How dare you speak to me like that in front of other ranks, Colonel or not, show respect to a King's Commission.'

A soldier ran up. *'S'cuse me Sir, sorry to but in, I've something to report.'*

'What is it, sergeant?'

'The horse has been found, only a few fields away.'

'Capital, capital, the pair of blackguards must be here somewhere. Did you hear that, Captain? They're almost in the bag. It's just a pity you didn't take more care in the first place, allowing them to just swim away.'

'That swine Drummond should have hung in the first place, never did like him, a scurvy trouble maker. He said he was a sailmaker, but I have my doubts about that as well. I'll take my men and search the inn area.'

Oi gave a gulp in an attempt at a-shiftin' the lump in moi throat. "Hang oi!"

'Do something, Dick.' Young Sam's voice shook with fear.

"We'll separate and hide somewhere, till the excitement dies down." Glancin' around, oi realised there weren't many a place to hide. "Through that door in the corner, lad, quick, up those stairs."

'It's a dead end,' Sam wailed. *'We're trapped like rats on a sinking ship.'*

"There's a trapdoor in the ceilin'."

'That's the deckhead, but it won't go anywhere,' Sam said. *'Just into the belfry.'*

"Wait here, I'll bring something for a rainy day." At the altar, oi grabbed the candlesticks.

'What are you going to do with them?' Sam asked, horrified. *'You can't steal from a church, not after that vicar was so kind. It'll bring a curse down on us.'*

"For a ruse. Tell them you were stowin' them away up here.

Now, get up in there," oi says, pullin' a trapdoor down."

'Crikey, Dick, it's blooming cold up here, and that's no error.'

"You ain't half bleedin' fussy. I'll get some of those monk's cloths from the vestry, put them on. Keep your belaying pin handy, just in case."

'You take it, I don't need it, not up here.'

"Get your anchor up in there. Sit on that chest and be quiet. Oi'll be back as soon as oi can to get you out again." Oi waved as oi slammed the trapdoor up, turning the ring, which seemed to lock it in place.

Shootin' out of the side door oi first came in, oi paused to look at the road.

'You two, come with me,' the sergeant snapped. 'Brown, take the vestry, Clayburn, with me, we'll search the church itself.'

"Crikey, if oi don't get away from here, oi'll be taken." Bending low, oi runs between gravestones, jumpin' the perimeter wall, a-landin' in a track. Followin' that along, took oi to the road, which oi were about to run across when the Colonel stopped a wagon.

'Where are you going?'

'To my farm along the way, that's all.'

'What's your cargo?'

'Pig feed.'

'Oh, right, you're free to go.'

'What'cher say?'

'On your way, man. Are you deaf?'

'Oi am that, too,' the driver nodded.

T'were moi chance. If they searched it and found nothin', oi could nip out, jump on the back and hide. Sam should be okay, that door only opened from the vestry side, so nobody could get in and close it, a-corse there weren't a ring on the inside.

Gently slapping the reins across the horse's rump, the man got it a-walkin' on.

That stupid Colonel turned away, so out oi goes, a-leapin' in. Trouble was oi misjudged it, landing with a thud.

180

'What's up, lad?'
"Don't give oi away, please, shipmate."
'Oi see, away off that ship in the bay, are you. Lay still.'
'Hey, you!' the Captain yelled. 'Stop that cart immediately.'
'Who, oi sir?'
'Yes, you blithering idiot. Stop I say and be searched.'
'Oi've just been searched, Admiral.'
'When?'
'Who's Ben?' my driver said, cupping an ear.
'Not Ben, you imbecile. When were you searched,' the Captain bellowed?
'No need to yell at oi like that, oi b'ain't deaf. T'were just there, by those soldiers.'
'I see, okay. I'm a Captain, not an Admiral.'
'You looks like an Admiral to oi, Sir, all that gold braid, real important.'
'Go on, move your cart. Keep a weather eye out, there are a couple of cutthroats on the loose, deserters from my ship.'
'Righto Sir, oi'll be sure and do that. Don't want moi throat cut.'
'Good man. There's a sovereign in it for any information you bring me.'
'Sorry, Cap'n Sir, but oi b'ain't seen nothin' hereabouts.'
The movement of the wagon gave oi a sigh of relief. Oi knew the man had given up a lot of money just then, and wondered why. A golden sovereign were a fair lump for a farmer to turn down.

Eventually the motion stopped.
'It's okay, you can come out now, young'un.'
"Thanks, old timer. You gave up that reward, why?"
The old man smiled, crinklin' his creased, weather worn face even more. *'You might well ask that, moi lad. S'pect you were pressed into service?'*
"Aye, old timer, something like that."
'Oi guessed that,' he replied, turning to look out across the fields, his mind flittin' back to some past event. *'One day a few years ago, the press came here as we're near the sea. Took a lot of men, dragged them away, some screamin' and a-yellin' to be left with their wives and children. T'were a*

black day for oi, too, moi only son were taken, got him at the inn, they did. So oi've nothin' to say to the likes of they.'

"You just saved moi bacon, old man, just thanks don't seem enough, but oi'm right broke."

'Get yourself away from this coast, make a decent livin' for yourself. Here, take this bag of coins, t'ain't much, but it'll get you started. Take moi scarf to Swaggs Farm, give it to Jethro, he's moi brother and when he sees this, he'll know oi've sent you.'

"Who do oi say?"

'Tell him, Jasper Crowthorne.'

"Oi think oi knew your son, Jake, was it?'

'That be right. How is he?'

Oi never had the heart to say oi had been a witness to his death yesterday, a-givin' his life to save Sam and oi. "He's fine, big strong fella, knows how to look after himself."

The man's chest swelled with pride. *'He's a boy to be proud of, one day he'll come home with a stack of prize money worth a King's fortune to see us all well.'*

"Maybe, old timer. Look after yourself."

'Goodbye, young'un, look after yourself, too.'

Oi watched his cart go bumping along the small lane. "God rest his son. Good Lord, and thinking of sons, Sam's still shut up in that tower. Oi'll have to go back to let him out."

When oi got there, it was a mass of activity around the church, the search parties must have billeted themselves here, which meant waitin' until it was dark. "Oi'll try moi luck then, there were no lights in that building so oi won't be seen," oi said to moiself.

It took ages afore night fell. Oi gave the front a wide birth, slippin' over the wall, a-creepin' across the graves to the side door. "It's now or never," Oi mutters, a-pushin' the door open with that creakin' noise. Oi waited a few moments in case anybody had heard it, but nothin' happened. Turnin' left and moving along the aisle to where oi knew the base of the tower lay, found the door in the gloom of a candle alight on the altar. Takin' the last couple of steps to let Sam out of the belfry, bumped smack bang into the open arms of Captain Blackwater.

'*Got you, my beauty,*' he cried triumphantly. '*To me, the marines, I have the blackguard, lads.*'

The twine cut into moi wrists as they were lashed tightly together behind moi back.

'*Right, Drummond, where's your accomplice. Speak up man,*' he shouted in moi face. His hands came around moi neck, a-grabbin' it in his fingers and a-squeezin' until oi almost choked. '*Your silence won't help him, he'll be found.*'

Oi bloody hope not by you, oi thought, maybe the vicar, oi hopes. His finger's pressure increased until oi were a-losin' consciousness.

It eased enough for oi to gasp. "He's well away, gone off on his own as we thought it best to split up."

'*You'll swing for this, make no mistake.*'

Oi remembered they got a cart from somewhere and oi were thrown' in the back.

'*Bo'sun, keep a close eye on him. Never let up once, if he escapes, you'll be swinging in his stead.*'

T'were a rotten journey back, bein' bashed constantly and hit with the bo's'ns' rattan until oi were nearly black and blue. They had poured water on moi wrist bindings, making them tighten even more. Somehow oi had to escape, get back to let poor Sam out of the belfry, but oi didn't stand much of a chance of that yet. He was safe as long as oi kept my mouth shut about him, then maybe someone aboard would get a message to that vicar, he seemed a decent sort.

'*Clap him in irons and lock him in the brig,*' Blackwater ordered. '*Let nobody near him, he must be totally confined without a chance of passing messages to any sympathisers. You marines must stand a permanent guard.*'

So that was the strength of it, was it? Oi thought. The chance of a-getting' a message off this ship had just gone right out of a gun port about as fast as a six-pound ball.

'*Come on you,*' a voice broke into moi thoughts. '*It's time for your appointment on deck.*' The Master at Arms stood grinning down at oi.

"Is it morning already?"

'Your last, sailmaker,' he gloated.

Havin' been dragged from the bowels of the ship, oi was blinded by the brightness of the day. Oi staggered.

'Move, damn your eyes. An hand shoved oi in the back.

I'm making an example of you, scum, nobody deserts from my ship,' Blackwater boasted.

A noose came around moi neck, somebody shouted 'Haul away', and then oi felt moiself floating up in the air, a-soarin' skywards, chokin' all the time.

"Sam be in the tower," oi tried to shout, but couldn't, so kicked out in a desperate attempt to get air… if only oi could free moi hands from behind moi back…

A white mist drifted in front of moi eyes, a-getting' lighter all the time…

Why were Jack and Maggy's faces a-lookin' at oi halfway up to the yard with that shssin' noise?

"I've got his hands behind his back," Jack was saying. "For goodness sake, get Maureen's scarf off his neck and face, it's got tightened in that struggle."

"Oi'll do moi best," Margaret cried loudly, "but he's a-strugglin' like a thin' possessed. Shss, moi dear, it's alright, it's me. Shss, be calm now."

"Gordon Bennett, what a lunatic, even I'm having a job holding him still," Jack shouted.

"Watch you don't get a smack in an eye, and look out for his legs, he's thrashin' about like one of Farmer Rogan's cows at slaughter, he is," Margaret warned.

"I think he's coming out of it. Danny, get a drop of brandy, please," I called.

"What are you a-doin' up here, our Jack, and where's the Captain," Dick shrieked. "Get this rope off oi."

"Calm down Dick, this is Jane, the vicar's wife, you remember me?"

"You idiot, Maureen," Danny snapped. "Fancy letting it go as far as that."

"It had to come out. Now he's free, he'll soon recover."

"Free, to be true, we nearly had a casualty on our hands, woman," Danny retorted.

"Take it easy, my old china, there ain't no Captains around here. You're in Danny's caravan. We got you out of hospital."

"Caravan? How did oi get here, and where's the ship?"

"You had a bad dream, matey, Maureen took you back in time, but you're back with us now. Just lie still, here, sip this brandy."

"Brandy! Not rum?"

"No, where did you get rum from?"

"Why were oi in hospital?"

"Don't you remember? That bang on your head when the bale fell off the trailer."

"Trailer? Why were oi on a trailer, it were a cart," our Jack.

"We were picking up bales to put in the Dutch barn. One fell off, knocking you out. Then you went all weird on us, babbling about being at sea, ships and escaping."

"Can oi have another of those brandies, matey. Oi'm starting to feel better now."

"Thank goodness for that," I exclaimed. "Lay still, just get your bearings, Dick. I got an ambulance, they put you on a stretcher but you went mad and fell off, banging your head on a lump of flint, shouting rubbish about a hammock."

"Oi arrived then," Margaret cut in. "They finally got you into the ambulance, banging doors about making an hell of a row, oi was surprised it didn't wake you up. Jane'n oi, came with you, siren a-wailin' and bouncin' all over the place. Bloomin' thing rocked so bad you had to be strapped down. Then you started hollerin' about a French ship, a right load of gibberish, it were."

Dick looked bemused.

"They gave you an injection to calm you down and what a fuss you made about that, screaming your head off about wood splinter sticking in your arm. After a while you settled down, a good job too, it was very embarrassing," I finished.

"Embarrassin' ain't the word," Margaret snorted. "Who's this young Sam? You went on something terrible about him. You don't know any Sams, as far as oi know."

"He were…" Dick began, but lapsed into silence.

"He was what?" Jack asked.

Oh, nothin', must have been in the dream."

"When they took you for an x-ray, they said you went potty again, screaming about escaping and the water was freezing cold. They didn't believe me when we said nobody had a clue what you were on about," I said.

"Yes," Margaret snapped, "you came back on that trolley hootin' about bein' on a cart and tied up by soldiers." Margaret shook her head. "Oi reckon it was that first jab that sent you off your head."

"You kicked up such a rumpus, they were glad when I said we'd bring you home," Jack put in. "Maureen said she could get to the bottom of it, so put you in some kind of trance. That was fine until you got hold of her scarf and had it tangled around your neck. I had to hold you down while Maggy unwrapped you."

"You came around then," Margaret went on. "Not afore time. Still, that brandy seems to have worked a treat, you're back with us now, moi love." She gave him a peck on a cheek.

"You shouldn't do that, 'specially in moi state of health," Dick cried out.

"Oi don't know about health, state of mind would be more like it," Margaret snapped, sarcastically.

"You seem okay now, mate. My nephew has come to stay for a couple of weeks, he's over from London. Want a visitor?"

Dick nodded. "Oh ah, our Jack. Be he a nice lad?"

"One of the best." Jack opened the van door. "Come in, Simon."

"Crikey, that be young Sam!" Dick exclaimed, shooting bolt upright.

"You silly idiot," Margaret cried, "a-jumpin' up like that, made oi start, too."

"Don't start all that again. I said Simon, not Sam. Otherwise we'll have to take you back to the hospital for another injection, then you'll get the point."

"Corse it be, oi just got muddled up, probably that bump on moi head," Dick replied, slowly laying back on Maureen's sofa. "Good to see you made it," he ended with a sigh.

"Rest a while, there's only a day left before Celia's ball and we need you well again," I said as sympathetically as was practical. Yet the story had interesting connotations. There had been bones up in that belfry and gold candlesticks. The robes were like monks of old and Dominic did find a sailmaker's palm in among the bones. However, Dick also knew about those, so perhaps his muddled mind just tied all those things into his story?

The Other GPO

"Celia's Ball is tomorrow evening and we have a meeting tonight about the so-called ghost," I pointed out. "Let's hope it goes better than the last fiasco. That Bert Rudge stirs trouble up. Has the Colonel any more ideas as to who this Mister Big is?"

Dominic shook his head. "No, and we can't think of a way of flushing him out, either."

"It would be nice to catch them all, they don't deserve any leniency."

"Absolutely, Jane. If he gets away the gang will reform and go on being a danger to everybody. But nobody seems to have a clue as to his identity. If CHS knows, she's not said a word. I don't think it's those on the yacht, in fact I'm almost certain it isn't."

"Almost certain? That leaves room for doubt."

"No, I'm not completely sure, my love," Dominic replied. "I don't think its Sandcastle either, I've serious doubts he would be that high up in a foreign organisation. Perhaps the cigar man at Briar Cottage, he seems to have a lot of authority?"

"Mmm, in other words it could be anybody," I mused.

"I'm afraid so, my love."

The phone rang.

"Hello Colonel," Dominic said, lapsing into silence, only adding a few grunts every few seconds. "You had better come up. No, it's no trouble. See you soon."

"Developments?"

"CHS and Olga have had a blazing row. Olga's walked out."

"Good heavens. Where on earth to?"

"The Colonel refused to say over the phone, said he'd tell us personally as it could be touchy."

The door knocked.

"Good day, Colonel. Please come in Dominic is in his study."

"Morning, m'dear. Bad business this."

They shook hands. "What happened," Dominic prompted.

"It was over nothing, so Olga told me. It's Celia, she's starting to crack up, it's hardly surprising really, lots of pressure, don'tcher know."

"Where has Olga gone?"

"She's safe, gone to stay with the count, vicar."

"What!" My exclaimed burst out. "My God, if Jack finds out, there'll be fireworks along with a fight, you know how volatile he is about that situation."

"Not another one," Dominic groaned, sinking his head into his hands.

"We've got to move, Chantril, now."

A tap on the Colonel's arm brought his attention my way. "I'll have a word with Dick, his pal Fred should have that phone-tapping job in hand by now. We need more information before we do anything else."

"Thank you, m'dear. All a bit tricky, what! Bracknell only has to get a whiff of this, then he'll inform Exeter and the balloon could really go up."

"No, please not another balloon, Colonel," Dominic uttered.

"A calculated risk," Colonel Masterson replied. "Steady man, steady."

"One thing's certain," I added. "Celia can't be left in limbo much longer. The poor woman must nearly be driven to distraction. Surely Olga should realise that and allow a little leeway?"

"The Count has been coming on very strong with her. Maybe she's taken advantage of a simple argument?" Dominic viewed.

"If you're going to see Drummond, I'll come as well, I could use a stiff drink."

"Please keep Olga's row under your hat for now, especially with Jack, Colonel," I asked.

Dick seemed okay to us. "Yes, revrund, Fred's ready. We were just a-waitin' the word from you."

"Very well, as soon as possible," the Colonel said with a nod. "All this is against my better judgement, but I can't see any other way."

"Who's house?" Jack asked.

"The gang are in Briar Cottage, that's the best place to start." I viewed Dick thoughtfully. "No messing about, a lot is riding on you doing a good job."

"Most importantly, don't get caught or break the phone lines," the Colonel added, authoritatively.

"Oi'd best not take a breath then," Dick muttered sarcastically.

"What?"

"Oi said, to go and rest, Colonel," Dick retorted, quick as a flash with a suitable reply as ever.

A glare back came from the Colonel. "I must be mad entrusting you, of all people, with a risky mission like this. Remember, what our watchword must be, Care, Drummond, care!"

"Care, rightyo, piece of cake, Colonel," Dick grinned, making an O out of a thumb and first finger. "Come on Jack, let's get Fred."

"You'll want ladders," I put in. "Take those from the vicarage and some rope to make loops out of, and you'll find that in our outhouse. I'll show you."

"Thanks Miss, you're a good organiser. Fred'll bring the other stuff, we'll meet him at the pole opposite the cottage."

It was dark when we arrived.

"Shss," Dick snapped at the gathering. "Best you and all the others get behind the hedge, we don't want a group of people pokin' about by this pole, could raise suspicions across the way."

"It's tall, Dick. Best extend them, to reach the wires," I

suggested.

"Good idea, Miss Jane. Lie them along the ground, all we'll need to do is lift them up then."

That was carried out remarkably quietly, considering who was doing it.

Righto, our Fred, tis done, up you go."

"Oi needs to stay here to tap in. You'll have to go up, our Dick."

"Oi! Why oi?"

"A-corse you used to do window cleanin' so are good at a-goin' up ladders," Fred pointed out. "If you slip, tearing your clothes it won't matter, they already are."

"Oi'll have you know, moi togs are well cared for. Good job moi Missus b'ain't here, she'd bop you one a-sayin' things like that about her abilities at a-lookin' after oi."

"For goodness sake, stop arguing, it'll only attract attention from you know where, then the plan will be finished," I snapped at them.

"You know what to do," Fred said. "Put the clips on each wire, then come down. We'll hide this gear behind the hedge and come back later."

Dick reached the top.

"Secure the rope, just in case," Fred whispered up.

"Oi'll only be a few moments, no need for that, oi'll just hook it on this peg."

Ping, ping, went the wires as each was clipped.

"Make a funny noise, don't they," he said with a giggle, leaning backwards to look down. "Yikes! Oi feel all giddy!"

"Hold on," Jack said urgently as loudly as he dared

"Yah…!"

Crash… the ladders hit the ground with a clatter.

"Gordon Bennet, he's dangling by the rope on that peg."

"Forget him, tuck the ladders under the hedge quickly. Not only did that make a noise that could be heard across the road," I warned, "here comes Constable Bracknell."

"Evening, Jane, what are you all up to? Where's Drummond?" He cast around.

"He's hanging about somewhere around here," Jack replied. "The vicar's dog got free so we're out searching for it."

"Okay, let me know how you get on, then. Whose ladders are those?"

"They were up the pole earlier, most likely the telephone companies. Maybe they'll come back for them tomorrow." Jack tried to sound convincing.

"Mmm, try not to disturb anybody," he ended, glancing around.

"Will do, officer. Good evening," I smiled as innocently as possible.

Bracknell nodded, leaving us with a "Good evening."

"Phew, that was close" I viewed.

"Yes," Fred agreed. "Good job he didn't look up."

"We'd better hop it a bit quick. Let's get him down then off out of it." Come on Jack," I encouraged.

"What's the rush? He's gone now," Fred queried.

"Because we haven't got a dog," I replied. "Bracknell will realise that at any moment thinking it's fishy."

Getting the ladder back up and Dick down took only moments.

"Moi bleedin' back," he complained. "Be fair a-stretched out, hangin' about up there."

"Well done Dick," I encouraged. "We'd better let the Colonel know its set up."

A loud voice spoke, making us all jump.

"By the suffering Jesus, tis the otter GPO," Danny quipped with a broad grin.

"Christ, you frightened the life out of us, you idiot," Dick muttered.

Danny grinned even more. "When do we go? My lads are fair spoiling for a scrap, so they are."

"Tomorrow night, Danny," I explained. "We may have more

information by then, now this is set."

"You're an unusual vicar's wife, to be sure," Danny said with a laugh.

"Come back to the vicarage, better tell Dominic."

"Are you okay, my love?" he greeted, looking me over to be sure all my appendages were intact.

"Yes, fine, thank you, darling."

"All done, reverend," Jack explained.

"I shouldn't be condoning this type of thing at all. It goes against my principles. I've enough problems with the harvest festival and the ghostbusters business, now more goods have been sent."

"We won't let on, if you don't," Dick grinned. His face dropped. "Mmm, I wonder if they've put any ale over there," he muttered.

"Never mind ale, seen anything of Olga, reverend?" Jack asked.

"Olga… um… well…" Dominic stammered.

"Nothing's happened to her, has it?" Jack's voice was terse.

"No, um… not exactly," Dominic fumbled for words.

"Something's wrong, I can sense it," Jack rasped. "Better tell, reverend."

"There was a row between her and Celia, that's all," I put in quickly, hoping to ward off a scene.

"She's moved out," Dick put in.

"Moved out? Where to?"

"Um… in with the Count," Dominic muttered guiltily.

A censorious glare with a hard shake of my head went his way. He had put his foot right in it. That was the last thing he should have said.

"Oh, err… temporarily of course," Dominic tried to calm the situation, but the damage was already done.

"WHAT! I knew he was a no-good son of a bitch, right from the start, now he's seducing my Olga," he ranted.

"Hardly seducing, Jack," I hastily added. "At least she's safe and not roaming the streets."

"Look here, Jack, it's no good calling her your Olga, you're not her favourite person after the bust up at the fete," Dominic snapped. "He has been very polite all through, they speak the same language, so it's natural she should go there for protection."

"There's nothing natural about it," fumed Jack. "I've lost her to that swine."

"Please try to stay calm, Jack. With the other business about to kick off, don't do anything rash," I warned. "Remember, we need all the help we can get with Master William. If he's rescued and taken home, perhaps Olga will return to the Manor to look after him. Then you'll have another chance," It was an attempt at sounding convincingly logical. "See you at this meeting in a short while, please remember, no fireworks."

"Alright, Jane, but if he starts…"

"If he starts you will do nothing, Jack," I cut in sternly. "Everything depends on keeping the peace, no upsets, young William's life could be at stake." That statement went with a waggle of a finger in his direction. "Otherwise, vicar's wife or not, I'll come to brain you myself with the heaviest object I can find, is that clear?"

The startled look on Jack's face was a wonder to see. "Yes, well… um, in that case, I'll be quiet then."

Trapping A Ghost

A small group comprising Colonel Masterson, Major Bragshawe, Miss Wrackham all accompanied by Mister Leggett, sat huddled around a bench outside the inn. They cast our group a glare as we entered.

"Oi wonder what that lot are up to?" Dick mused.

"It's the Colonel's ghost hunting committee, he's gathered some cronies trying to solve that puzzle," Dominic replied. "Leggett said he has some sort of trap rigged up to catch it in the act, put it in place last night."

"What sort of trap?" Dick asked tentatively.

"Beats me, they've all been very secretive about it. Even Jane doesn't know, I asked her."

"Afraid not, Dick," I said in confirmation. "It's very mysterious."

"Oi can't see how anyone can trap a ghost, there b'ain't nothing of them. It's not as if you can get hold of a leg or something and hang on tight, is it? But they all look pretty smug about it." Dick burst out laughing.

"What's so bloody comical?"

"Oi reckons they be a-wastin' their toime. Oi'd have given you credit for more sense, our Jack. If you only half believes, then you're a bigger fool that old Jonas Frogmore, and he was the village idiot."

"Don't mock the dead," Jack snapped. "He couldn't help it."

"You'll have to go ask the Colonel, Dick. I doubt he'll tell you, though." Charlie pointed out.

"A mite underhand, if you asks oi."

"What does it matter," Jack added. "Unless you know more about it than you let on," he ended with a stern look.

"Oi knows nothin', my lad," Dick snorted back. "Oi'll be off home for forty winks before this daft meetin' starts. See you in an hour."

⌘

"Wake up," I whispered in Dick's ear. "Time for the meeting."

"Waaa! Oi never did it," he hollered, sitting bolt upright.

"Be quiet, it be Jane," Margaret said. "She's a-comin' to the hall with us. What b'ain't you supposed to have done?"

"Nothin', oi never did nothin'. Must of been a dream."

"Come on Dick, we're waiting."

"It be excitin', Jane, the Colonel's getting' a picture of it a-stealin' food." Margaret seemed full of it.

"How did the old devil get that? Did he have a portrait done," Dick replied with a nervous laugh.

"Don't be sarky," Margaret snapped back. "The old fox rigged up a camera with a flash. It went off when a light beam got broken somehow, then the flash went poof, just like that. Clever, ain't it?"

"A photograph, cripes!" Dick gulped.

"Yeah, it's away bein' developed, excitin', ain't it?"

A knock came. "Good day revrund," Dick greeted, as Annabel let him in. You come for your missus?"

"Don't be rude. We're all going to the hall, come on. The Colonel said there's an image on the photo, so our ghost may be identified. Can't wait to find out the truth. The odd thing is, I found an apple with teeth marks in it on the floor. Didn't think ghosts lifted things or had teeth. Who knows, perhaps it's a poltergeist? That shop in town has developed it."

"Must Jack and oi come?"

"Really Dick," I scolded. "I would have thought you would be very interested as you have always supported the ghost theory. This time, behave yourself keeping Jack under control. Remember what I said. The Count will be there, none of us want a repeat performance of the last time."

"Wouldn't miss this for the world. The Colonel will make a complete arse of himself and maybe that will cut him down a peg or two, the pompous old fart. Whoever heard of anybody photographing a ghost?" Jack commented.

"He claims it's an animal, he could well be right about that," Dominic added.

"B'ain't it possible to photograph a ghost then?" Dick asked.

"Nah, of course not, how can you take a photo of nothing? There has to be a solid object to reflect the light. Quick, let's get a good seat."

"Crikey, our Jack, the hall's packed tonight."

"Get in," I encouraged. "You're usually in the front row when it comes to the Colonel making a fool of himself, Dick. So, now's your great moment."

Our group sat next to Charlie. "The Colonel's been here ages laying down the law, he's full of it. Goodness knows what he'll do if the negative comes out blank, reckons the flashlight will have lit it up like a Christmas tree."

Colonel Masterson caught sight of Dominic. "There, Chantril," he spouted, "let a military mind come to grips with the problem, then it's soon sorted. Should have let me at it ages ago, could have eased your burden, what?"

Dominic glared back. "It's never been much of a burden, even if it does turn out to be a ghost, which I seriously doubt, it's most likely a disturbed soul that needs help."

"Stuff and nonsense, all this ghost talk. Most likely a rabbit, rat or some tramp getting a night's sleep and stealing half your offerings into the bargain. The picture will show us for sure."

"Well, we'll find out soon enough, won't we," Dominic snorted irritably. "All I hope is the matter will get resolved one way or the other, then we can all get on with our lives. There are more serious matters, Colonel. What time is this chap supposed to arrive?"

"Any moment now, I damn well hope he's prompt. You know what these young whipper snappers are like, no sense of responsibility."

"Dick's curiously quiet tonight," I whispered to Dominic. "Sober, too, what's the event?"

"I've no idea, Jane," Jack put in. "He's been like it all day. Wonder if he's sickening for something?"

"Are you feeling alright, Dick?"

"Yes, Miss Jane. Got one or two things on moi mind, that be all."

"Not another argument with Margaret, I hope?"

"No, revrund. Well, yes, we did have a few words, but it's okay now."

"Thank heaven for that," Dominic whispered in my ear. "Yet I've never seen him so reluctant to talk."

A car door slammed shut outside.

"You had better get up on the stage, darling," I said. "Sounds like he's here."

Dominic nodded, leaving us.

A young man walked into the hall clasping a large brown envelope. He muttered something to Miss Wrackham, who had been guarding the door. He nodded a thank you, making his way to the stage side steps with every eye glued on him. As his foot took the first in the flight, it slipped, obviously nervous at being the full focus of attention.

The Colonel could contain himself no longer. "Come on man, come on. Don't be all day about it."

Dominic gave him a hand. "Hello, thanks for coming and all your efforts on our behalves. I'm the vicar here."

"Look here rector, erm sir, I mean vicar," he stammered. "The results aren't as good as we would have liked, especially as the Colonel insisted on such a big enlargement, it's to do with the grain you see…" he trailed off.

"Yes, alright, although I don't really understand the technical jargon. We are sure you have done your best. Let the Colonel have the prints, please."

The Colonel snatched the envelop, tearing it in his haste.

"Steady on the Blues," Dominic uttered.

"It's Steady the Blues, there's nothing wrong with me, Chantril", the Colonel snapped back, giving Dominic an icy glare. He finally pulled the prints out with a flourish. "Now we'll have him," he went on triumphantly, "mark my words."

Oh, we're back to word marking, I thought that had stopped with Miss Sharpe's demise.

"Remember, the camera never lies." He stood looking at the image for some time.

An expectant hush fell over the hall, every person awaiting the man's shout of victory, some stared dead ahead while others licked lips nervously or tapped a foot.

"Well?" Dominic said impatiently, as seconds ticked by.

"I don't believe it, I just don't believe it," he muttered, sitting down with a plop, defeated bemusement riddled across his face, his fingers opened, dropping the photo to the floor.

Obviously, his plan had gone completely awry. I felt a pang of sympathy, although on the other hand, he didn't deserve any, due to his general rudeness about it all through.

Dominic bent, retrieving the print. "Jane, would you come here, please?"

"Is it of the altar?"

He nodded. "Yes, there's the cloth. But there's something odd about it. What do you think?"

"It seems disjointed, as if in parts."

"There is a ghost, there, in the centre, see?"

"It's certainly something, just an indistinct grey shape, perhaps that's how ghosts look? I've never taken a picture of one before, so have no idea how one might appear."

"The face is blurred, only half turned towards the camera, maybe when the flash went off? That's if there's a face at all. Even so, the figure has a solidarity about it, it's kind of familiar in a way, as if I should know it, if it wasn't so vague and intangible," Dominic muttered. "It might be the ghost."

A loud murmur went around the hall like wildfire, heads nodding in agreement as the hubbub reached deafening proportions.

"It be the ghost, the vicar said so," came Jake Crowe's familiar voice. "I've always a-said there be one. Now all oi hopes is, we haven't upset it with us a-tryin' to take its picture. Who knows what could happen now," he went on? "The wrath of the dead."

Dick suddenly sprang to life after being so subdued all day. "Oi says the revrund should put a stop to all these capers, a-leavin' the spirits of the past well alone. Who agrees with oi?"

This outburst brought shouts of agreement from all and sundry.

Dominic held his arms up for silence. "If that's what you all want, there will be no more attempts at trying to uncover the identity of our lost soul. Colonel, you will agree with this majority vote."

Never before had Dominic been so forceful, he made me proud.

"I agree, Chantril," the Colonel muttered.

"Hooray for the revrund," Dick shouted.

Dick was acting very suspiciously. Was there more to his sudden rejuvenation that met the eyes?

"I second that," Jack said.

"Come on our Jack, oi feels really thirsty now, let's go to the inn."

The hall began clearing. The Colonel departed looking downhearted for a change.

On picking up the discarded print, my eyes cast over the image, studying it carefully. "Look here, my love, I don't want to worry you or upset any apple carts," giving Dominic's sleeve a tug. "But there's another figure on the edge of the light beside the pulpit. It looks like a young man in rags who seems to be watching the other figure, almost as if he knew them."

"I'll be jiggered, you're right, Jane. Well done, there are two figures. Good Lord, that means there must be two ghosts, not one!"

"Mmm, don't know about two. Did you notice how quickly Dick cheered up when nobody could identify the figure? I can't help wondering if he knows more than he lets on?"

"Well, he's always maintained there is a church ghost, maybe this vindicates his view, now he's gone to celebrate," Dominic replied with a laugh. "I hope he doesn't start drinking heavily again, his marriage is already under stress with rows."

The Colonel's voice broke into our thoughts on that point. "We need to talk, Chantril, the other matter, you know…"

"Very well. Let's go to the vicarage, don't want anybody overhearing."

He nodded. "Lead on then."

I thought about that other figure. It was clearer than the main one and as we saw, a young lad who looked hopefully at the wobbly image in the middle. There was a half-smile of familiarity in that gaze. Who could it be? Perhaps the soul of the bones we found in the belfry. They were a puzzle, because that trapdoor could only be opened from below. When Dick had related his shipmate had been put up there during the regression. It almost tied in with everything he had said under Moreen's influence.

Mister Big?

"*H*ere's the tape," Fred said, handing it to the Colonel. "Have you got the player?"

"Of course, it's in my pocket." He pulled it out, opened the lid to click the cassette into it.

Every soul leant forward to see what was on it.

We waited a while, nothing happened.

"Push the play button," Fred said.

That done, the machine whirred a while, then came a ting, then a tinny voice said…

"*Is everything okay?*"

"That's Sid," Dick whispered.

"Why are you whispering?"

"In case he might hear oi, Miss. Sid can be a spiteful man if he thinks he's been a-stabbed in the back."

"It's just a recording, we can only hear him, stop worrying."

"Oh ah, rightyo, Miss."

The squawky voice of Sid went on. "*The Merchandise okay then?*"

"*Sure guvnor, no problem.*"

"*Good, that should please the boss. The party's been arranged, so she's playing along. The move's tonight as soon as it gets dark, do nothing until ten o'clock, understand?*"

"*Okay, we've got it,*" the gruff voice replied.

Click, the machine went dead.

"That means Mister Big isn't in Briar Cottage," Dominic stated.

"Nor neither of those two on the yacht, by Jove," the Colonel added.

"It's somebody else then," Dick muttered.

"Obviously it is, you great banana," Jack snapped. "But who?"

"Plainly he's going through Sandcastle," Dominic pointed out. "That counts him out as well."

"Humph," went the Colonel. "We may have to forget the top man. Our main objective is to rescue young Master William. First priority is to get him out of their clutches, capture the two on the boat and Slimeb… I mean Sandcastle, then we may be able to flush this boss chap out into the open, what!"

"Crikey, that's a tall order," Dick gasped.

"Very risky, too," Jack pointed out. "We should try to avoid anybody getting injured, you know these people are violent."

"What we need is the element of surprise," the Colonel went on. "That should do the trick."

"What's this liniment we have to take? Do we rub it on?" Dick groaned. "Never have been keen on rubbing stuff in, oi b'ain't."

"What are you talking about?" Jack asked impatiently. "Nobody said anything about liniment."

"He said surprise them with this liniment stuff," Dick retorted. "If we don't have to rub it in, do we throw it in their eyes like bank robbers do ammonia? Oi'd enjoy that," he ended with a wicked grin.

"Has he gone completely blasted mad?" Colonel Masterson bellowed.

"Nah, a-corse not. Oi read it in a magazine once. S'pect it's so they can get away nice and easy, after all, who's going to put up a struggle with liniment in their eyes?"

"Humph," went the Colonel. "Element," he snapped. "Element of surprise. God give me strength."

"Oh, oi see, like in an electric kettle. Do we bash them over the head with it? Oi still thinks we'd be better off with the ammonia."

"The man's a damned fool," muttered the Colonel,

unconsciously jabbing Dominic with his cane. "Must we take him along? He'll probably ruin everything. How can I be expected to run this as a military operation with an imbecile like Drummond, beside me?"

"Don't poke me with your stick, Colonel."

"Oh, sorry Chantril, wasn't intentional, I assure you."

"Shouldn't we synchronise watches?" asked the Major.

"Damned good idea, Brageshaw. Ready, let's do that, its twenty-two hundred… now!"

"What's this military plan?" Dominic asked.

"Well, we need to work one out, I hadn't actually thought about it yet."

"There's a way, to be sure," Danny cut in, a finger to his lips as he pondered.

"Well, what is it?" Dominic asked. "It's high time somebody came up with something concrete."

"For a start, we should split this into tree sections, gives us more options."

"Trees" Dick hooted. "Why are we talking about trees? Oi had enough of the liniment."

"Not trees," Danny retorted irritably." Tree I said. One, two tree. One, get them off the boat, two, grab the kid then tree, capture the swines."

The Colonel nodded. "That's not bad, not bad at all. However, I would advise sections four and five. Get Sandcastle in our clutches to flush out Mister Big, whoever he is."

"Or get Sandcastle to flush out this big boss into the open," Dominic added.

"That's it! Well done Chantril," the Colonel exclaimed. "Never thought you had it in you."

"I did, I've known it all along," I said, my eyes full of admiration.

"Tell you what," Dick put in, suddenly coming back to life. "What about getting Maureen to look into her crystal ball, maybe she can see who this Mister Big is?"

"For the suffering Jesus, it's all a lot of nonsense, so it is," Danny snorted. "Don't be after encouraging her, it always ends in death, graves or someting like that."

Dick gave him a knowing look. "Oi've got a feelin' she might see something, that's all. She was right about several things."

"It's worth a try," Jack agreed. "We've got nothing to lose by it anyway."

"Only our sanity," Dominic snapped sarcastically. "I really cannot be associated with this."

"Come on reverend, it's only a bit of fun," Jack went on.

"Don't meddle with things you don't understand, it will come to no good," Dominic warned.

"It's okay, then," Jack said. "Stay here having a cup of tea. Jane will come, she helped with the regression, won't you?"

"Well, I don't know…"

"To be sure, you really helped last time. Come on, please," Danny pleaded.

"Okay then, I agree." Then, giving Dominic a wave, we all departed.

At the caravan, Maureen looked from one to the other. "Foretell the future, is that what you're after me doing? The other day it was silly rubbish, according to Danny, so it was. Now you're all deadly serious."

"Come on, Colleen," Danny said, "we need some help."

"Alright, I'll be after helping, to be sure. Sit yourselves round in a circle touching the person's hand of those next to you forming a complete ring. Jane and Margaret, would you sit opposite me, we spread the feminine source out better that way."

She sat, taking deep breaths as her head slowly tilted back to look with unseeing eyes at the roof. "Ooooh spirits, are you der? Answer me spirits, knock once if you hear me."

A loud rap emanated from the table.

Dick shot up in the air like a scalded cat, being pulled hastily back down again by Jack.

"We seek a name, spirits" Maureen went on. "Give me a

vision… Ah, something is forming, mouths talking silently… people running across fields… a phone box by a junction… an old graveyard, now a tomb… a coffin, a grave… shots, revealing much wealth and riches…"

Danny stood abruptly. "That's enough Colleen. It always ends up with graves or somebody dying."

The woman slumped forward onto the table.

"Crikey, our Danny, you shouldn't have done that. It's not good to stop in the middle of a séance. Where's that brandy?"

"Here," Margaret said. "Don't you go gollopin' it down, neither."

"She's coming round," Jack muttered. "Give a hand sit her up."

"Well, did you get the message?" Maureen asked.

"Do you mean you don't remember saying those things," Jack asked, somewhat shocked.

"Yes, we did," Dick said with a grin. "A good'un, too. Thanks Maureen."

"But it wasn't a name, was it?" Danny challenged. "All she came out with was a lot of gibberish."

"These here mediums never come straight out with an answer," Dick retorted. "You have to interpritate what they say."

"Pah," scoffed Danny. "By the love of Mary, it's a load of blarney, there's noting there in the first place."

A knock came, it was Dominic. "Well?"

"Nothing definite, reverend," Jack informed him. "No name."

Everybody sat while Maureen made tea. We had a while to wait. Dominic seemed edgy, looking at his watch nearly every few minutes.

"Why don't you get the gang together at the vicarage, darling," I suggested. "You can call the Colonel and Major."

"Do I look that restless?" he said with a short laugh. "You're right, we'll all keep each other company, even maybe come up with ideas."

"Yes, you do, sweetheart. I'll put some lagers in the fridge, can't see anyone wanting more tea."

Dominic walked to me. "What would I do without you? You think of so many little details. One thing's certain, I'll never regret the day I proposed. Come here, Missus Reverend, I want to thank you."

We kissed. His warm arms gave me comfort and strength as I rested my head on his shoulder. "I'm glad, too. Glad I left London moving here to meet you, my love. No, I've no regrets either. Except perhaps being called Missus Reverend," I said teasingly with a whimsical smile.

The door knocked.

Shots

"*H*ere are all the others, I'll let them in. Then it will soon be time to go play detectives." As I opened the door, Olga and the Count walked past the gate.

"Crikey," Dick gasped, "look at her!"

I had to admit the vision that met my eyes was a shock.

Olga flounced along hanging onto the Count's arm, dressed as she never had been before, draped in expensive jewellery, a fur coat across her shoulders and sporting a lavish hair do. She looked radiant.

They halted, the Count standing beside her like a proud peacock. "*See 'ow she is now, 'aving been rescue'd from that terrible Manor,*" he puffed proudly.

"She didn't need rescuing," Jack grated. "She was doing just fine until you stuck your oar in."

"*Moi Cherie was under stresses.*"

"It's Lady Celia that's under bloody stress," Jack snapped back, regretting his outburst immediately.

"Jack!" I warned.

"*Why is she, pleases?*" Olga asked.

"Oh, um… I can't say right now. She's just got things on her mind. You should have helped her, not run off with him," Jack ended angrily.

"*You will not threaten my Olga these ways,*" the Count shouted in return, heckles rising.

"You just keep your froggy nose out of it," snarled Jack.

"Jack," I cried again, "don't do anything rash. Remember our other business."

"*Phoo*," the Count sneered. "*'Ee is nothing.*"

Jack moved so fast he became a blur. "I'll give you nothing, take that." His right hook came from way back, landing squarely on the Count's chin.

The Count reeled back several paces, but somehow stayed upright.

Jack had already moved forward to deliver a follow-up blow, catching the man to the side of his head.

This time the Count went down, hitting the ground with a resounding thud.

"Get back to your own sodding country, you big-headed frog," Jack screamed.

Dominic appeared, having heard the scuffle. "What's going on here?"

"*Thees Engleesh pig 'as just struck moi,*" the Count snapped. "*You will live to regret this day, messieur.*"

"Knock it off, our Jack," Dick said. "There's other work to do, or have you forgotten?"

"*You is de 'orrible beasting,*" Olga screamed at Jack. "*You vill be leavinks 'im alones. 'Ee is a gentlesman, a lot more than you is beinks. I vill never be for you, never, never!*"

The pair left.

"Crikey, Jack, that were a real stupid thing to do."

"I agree," Dominic cut in. "All you have succeeded in doing is alienating Olga, driving her further away as well as losing any goodwill we may have had from the Count."

"Sorry reverend, lost my head a bit."

"More than a bit. You very nearly upset the whole applecart for tonight. You can consider yourself lucky there isn't a very heavy object within my grasp," I snorted at him.

"Let's go indoors before anything else happens," Dominic suggested.

Soon the room was humming with activity, the near disaster

forgotten. Dominic had cheered up, the Colonel and Major were in earnest conversation with Danny along with several of his associates.

Jack sat sulking.

Yet it surprised me how easily so many people with such differing backgrounds had welded themselves into a close-knit group with a single purpose. Well, almost knit, I mused, there was no telling what Dick might do when let loose on the crooks, a thought that caused me to laugh. Jack needed cheering up.

"Here, have a larger," I said, holding one out. "I wouldn't really have hit you with a heavy object, you're let off."

That piratical grin came. "Thanks, Jane."

"We've gone hard on a plan, Jane," the Colonel said. "It seems remarkably simple now we have worked through it, but then, simple is always best. Drummond has volunteered to be the first decoy, that will give Jack a chance to snatch young William, then Danny's lads move in to capture the crooks."

"Do you think that will work? Can you manage to get to the yacht, Jack?"

He rose. "No problem, Missus Reverent, no problem at all."

"Well done, Jack. The hardest part will be tempting Sandcastle out to the cove," Dominic mused. "How do we manage that?"

"We'll have to play that by ear," the Colonel mused. "All hell might break loose once things start happening. Brings to mind an action in Malaya, against the Japs, don't you know, Jane. We had planned a raid on a…"

"It's time to go, Colonel," Danny's voice stopped him in his tracks. "Come on, to the cars."

"Phew, rescued in the nick of time," I whispered to Dominic. "Be careful, won't you, my love? I don't want to lose you now I've found you."

"I will, you have my promise," he replied, giving me a kiss. "See you soon."

We paused at the gate.

"You all know your positions?" the Colonel asked.

Crack… wheee… thuck.

"What was that?" Dominic muttered.

"I'll tell you, Chantril, it was a shot, the bullet hit the gatepost beside Sweeny."

"My word, oh, good heavens," Dominic stuttered. "It must have been aimed at one of us."

"Sweeny, I'd say," the Colonel shouted. "Look, over there, by the village hall, there's somebody running away. After him. Tallyho!"

A blur left the spot beside me as Jack took off like a greyhound following a hare. He cleared the fence in a single bound, speeding across the grass in hot pursuit of the distant, fleeing figure.

The assailant swung, crouched, brought the gun to his shoulder, firing again.

Bang!

Jack dived to the ground, our trailing group hastily followed his example.

The missile whined overhead.

Jack was already up and running. As he neared whoever it was, they threw the weapon at him in the hoping of slowing his advance. A blur went horizontal as the pair tumbled over in a violent struggle.

When we arrived Jack was standing, holding the would-be assassin by his lapels in one of his massive hands, the other drawing back ready to deliver a crushing blow.

"Hold it!" the Colonel shouted. "We need him conscious for questioning."

"Dick," Dominic said through gasps of breath, "go and fetch Constable Bracknell."

The policeman looked unbelieving. "Shot at you, did he? Now I wonder why he would want to do that." His radio crackled as he called for an armed response unit.

"I can't imagine," Jack retorted. "That's your job to find out, copper."

"According to his passport, he's French. Now why would a Frenchman want to shoot you? Exactly what have you been up to, Sweeny?"

"Nothing."

"People don't go around shooting at folk without a good reason."

"Just a minute," Dominic snapped. "It's Jack that's the innocent party here, you're treating him as if he's a gangster."

"It seems pretty odd to me," Bracknell retorted. "He must have done something or upset somebody. Not into drugs, are you?"

"I'll dot him one," Jack yelled. "Bloody cheeky copper. I've been nearly killed and this idiot's accusing me of drug running."

"Calm down, Jack," I said softly. "Let it slide for now. We have bigger fish to fry, remember? Don't want you in a prison cell tonight, do we?"

A squad car swung to a halt. "I'm Detective Inspector Rosefield," the man said as he got out, displaying his ID card. "We'll make a run on him at police headquarters."

Without further ado, they bundled the foreigner into the back of the car, departing rapidly.

"Well, stick oi with a prong," Dick muttered. "What a right funny old do."

The Plan

*T*he moon appeared from behind clouds to shine its eerie light across the bay, reflecting off the gently rippling waves like a multitude of dancing fireflies as we arrived at the cove.

"At least we have a little light to see by," the Colonel muttered. "Danny, take your chaps get over to the far side. Careful now, try not to give the game away."

"We'll be as quiet as mice, to be sure."

"What next, guvnor?" Jack asked.

"Drummond had better get into the cave. When I signal to the yacht, he'll do his decoy act, which should bring them ashore and occupy them long enough for you to get going, clear?"

"I'll be in the water before they land, that will allow me a bit more time. I'm away to the shoreline now."

"Affirmative," the Colonel said with a nod.

"This has split us up into dangerously small groups, Colonel," Dominic pointed out.

"Calculated risk, Chantril. Are you sure you're up to tackling these thugs?"

"Wouldn't miss it for the world, Colonel," Dominic grinned back.

"There's still three of us, this side, plus I have a revolver loaded with blanks. Won't hurt anybody, but they aren't to know that, are they?"

"Jane said they have a gun on the boat, she thinks she saw one."

The Colonel grunted. "After that last episode I wouldn't be at all surprised, Chantril. God knows what Danny's men have, I dread to think," he ended with a chuckle. "Never thought I would be running a show with gypsies, but they all seem to be first class chaps, by Jove?"

"Then what?"

"If we all make as much noise as possible, they won't know where to look first. Remember the plan." He checked his watch. "Drummond and Sweeny will be in position by now. It's time. I'll take your car, they won't be able to see it properly at the cliff top."

"Be careful, Colonel."

"Thank you, Jane. That goes for all of you."

The Colonel arrived at the top of the cliffs, slamming the car door loudly to give an impression of confidence.

At that point, it was possible we all subconsciously held our breathes as he made his way down, standing in full view on the beach to start signalling, slowly waving the torch in the direction of the yacht, as Sid had done before.

Within moments the dinghy left for the beach, a wide glittering wake curving along the water of the bay, the hum of its motor clearly audible. Its bow slid onto the sand with a grating noise.

As it did, the Colonel stepped backwards into the shade of the cliffs.

"If oi belongs to Glasgow," sang Dick, staggering from the cave drunkenly, clutching a beer bottle. "Hello there moi beauties, come in for an ale, have yous?"

"Get off this beach, you drunken slob," a gruff voice ordered, "otherwise it will be all the worse for you."

"Don't be like that, here, have a sip of this here jollop, it be good for you," Dick went on, regardless of the threats.

"The fool's raving drunk," another man said.

"I don't care, there's no time to mess about with him, give me the gun?"

Bang, Bang!

"My God, they've shot him," I gasped.

A screaming mob appeared from the far side. "Yaaa," Danny's colleagues shouted at the top of their voices at the same instant as the Major and Dominic shot from cover.

Bang, Bang.

The Colonel came into sight. More shots rang out.

Bang, Bang, Bang…

"There's a bloody party going on, quick, back to the yacht."

"STOP! Or I shoot, this is the police," the Colonel's voice came loud and clear.

I dashed out. "Where's Dick. I think he's been shot."

"No, oi b'ain't be, Miss," he called, appearing out of the night.

"That was me," Colonel Masterson explained. "Thought I'd get the party going. Once they said about shooting Drummond, felt it would give them second thoughts, they would be too busy looking after their own bodies."

Giving him a cuddle, I smiled with relief. "Thank God for that, Dick. The place would never be the same without you."

"We got the blackguards," the Colonel whooped in triumph.

"My shillelaghs got a dent in it," Danny quipped, waving the great piece of wood in the air. "Sean has a terrible bruised fist." The gypsies seemed elated.

"Let's hope Jack got on alright," I mused.

"He should be here soon, if he was successful," Dominic replied.

"We did okay," came Jack's voice, and there they were, standing together on the beach.

"Damned good show, Sweeny. You're a regular trooper, would have been glad of you in my regiment."

"Thank you, Colonel. Now, next step, what about Sandcastle?"

"We shall use one of these rogues," the Colonel snorted. "Let them do some of our work for us." He grabbed one by the scruff of his neck. "You can come with me and Danny, we're going to make a telephone call to your partner in crime. Tell him there's been a snag so he must come to the beach right away."

"There's a phone box about half a mile along the road," Dick volunteered.

"I'll not make any phone calls," the crook said. "I know what's good for me."

Danny purposefully smacked his palm with the business end of his shillelagh. "You'll be doing just what I say, or by the suffering Jesus, you'll sure find out what isn't good for you."

We watched them go.

"I hope this next part goes as well as the rest has, so far. We've been very lucky," Dominic pondered.

"Don't worry reverend," Jack broke in. "It'll go like clockwork. Sit yourself down, we'll look after this wretch," he said, clenching one of his huge fisted in a threatening manner.

A smile swept over my face. Pity the man, if he tried anything with this mad lot around. "While we're waiting, Jack, tell us what happened on the boat?" I asked.

"It was an easy swim, Jane. Just ducked under as the dinghy went close by. Once there, I found the ladder they used to get on with, then crept along a side deck. The cabins were well lit, making it simple enough finding the lad. It just took a shoulder to the door, when it gave. "It's okay, young'un, I'm a friend," I called.

"You're Mister Sweeny, aren't you, Dick's friend?" William said.

"That's right, lad. Now we leave here getting you safe. It's over the side with a swim to the shore, simple as that. You're going home, my lad."

"But I can't swim, Mister Sweeny," William came back.

That had never entered my head. Looking around desperately I found a life preserver. "Slip this on, it will keep you afloat. Just hold hard onto me, I'll tug you along."

Then the lad's eyes filled with tears. "I've been so afraid."

"Yes, young man, guess you must have been. Come here, we haven't got much time, but enough for a cuddle. No time for tears though, save those for your mother, she's worried sick about you. Now we leave this rotten old boat."

As we went over the side, the sound of gunshots came to our

ears. There wasn't much I could do about that though, the main thing was getting young William back ashore. That's how it went."

"Well done, Jack. Come here with me, young William, you need a cuddle," I said.

Time dragged.

Eventually the crunch of shoes on the sand came to us.

"Who's there?" Jack demanded.

"Masterson," replied the Colonel. "Sandcastle's on his way. We have to work out a way of forcing one of these to call him down."

"That's easy," Danny put in. "Sean can twist his arm up his back nice and hard. Then, if he doesn't do what we say, by the Virgin Mary, Sean will break it off and hit him over the head with it."

"Oh, very Christian, that is," Dominic snorted. "Break an arm off in the name of the Virgin Mary."

"Have you a better suggestion?" the Colonel demanded haughtily.

Dominic paused. "No, I haven't as it happens," he grudgingly admitted.

"Have no sympathy for this scum, vicar. They're rogues, kidnapping and have been terrifying a young child," Masterson rasped.

The group lapsed into silence again. Waiting is dreadfully boring.

"Listen, there's a car coming," Jack whispered.

"To your places everybody. It's just Danny and his helpers on the beach, the rest of us to the clifftop to grab Sandcastle."

We waited again. This Sid person was a long time coming. Straining my ears for some sound or other, but the still of the night was only broken by waves gently caressing the sand.

"He's signalling," Dominic whispered.

"Go on, do your ting," Sean said to their captive.

Nothing happened. A stifled gurgle of pain emitted from the crook.

"Say it," Sean snapped.

"Come down, the boy's sick," the crook called.

"Sick? Are you sure, he was fine when I phoned earlier?"

"He's… ha, yes, he is sick."

"What's going on, why did you yell like that?" Sandcastle queried. "Are you alright?"

A scuffle broke out on the beach.

"Run, it's a trap… ahhh, my bloody arm, you've broken it."

Sidney must have dashed for his car, because the engine roared into life, headlights came flooding on piercing the night as he swung away from the cove.

Several shapes dived for cover as the car dealer drove his vehicle at them in his attempt to escape.

"Tallyho!" roared the Colonel regaining his feet. "You follow with the Irish contingent, Brageshaw. We'll take a short cut, try to head him off, what!"

We all piled into cars, Dominic swinging ours hard around with the Colonel hanging out a window shouting instruction at the Major, following behind.

"Which way?" Dominic yelled.

"Up that track, it takes us along the edge of the fields coming out just ahead of him, if we're lucky."

The car suffered terribly, bumping and lurching all over on the uneven ground.

"Nearly there, revrund," Dick hooted, his teeth chattering together with the violence of our ride.

Suddenly the hedges ended as we drove into an open field with the whole drama laid out in a panorama before us.

"There!" Jack shouted. "Sandcastle's headlights are going along the lower lane. He's way ahead, we'll never make it in time."

"If he gets to the village first, he'll warn the others. With the horsepower he has under that bonnet, he'll get clean away," the Colonel groaned.

"Oi daresay that copper'll never believe us anyway, he's got his daggers out for Jack and oi," Dick stated. "He reckons we're interfering bugger…"

"Yes Dick, we all know what he thinks," Dominic said, cutting him off. "Most unfairly in our view. Now we have William, so he can't argue about it this time."

"Yeah, that may be, but he didn't see Sid, did he. All he'll know about is the two Danny caught," Jack ended.

"Oi've an idea," Dick piped up. "What about they big round bales? They got left right at the top of the hill up here after harvest. If we could get one rolling, it'll end up on that lane, right where Slimebucket's car's a-goin'. That should put his brakes on."

"By Jingo, you're right, Drummond," the Colonel shouted enthusiastically. "All hands to the pumps," he called.

"Don't you mean all shoulders to the wheel," Jack answered cheekily.

"Come on, no time to lose, push with all our might," Danny snapped.

Lots of grunting ensued, but nothing happened. "Perhaps it's too heavy?" I pondered.

"Maybe, Jane," the Colonel agreed, "but we must get it moving. Give it everything we've got, now!"

"It's not budging," Dominic groaned.

"You're not bloody pushing," Jack yelled in Dick's ear. "Get stuck in, it was your daft idea."

"All right, all right, no need to shout," Dick grumbled.

More grunts followed.

"It moved," I yelled, "it did, I felt it."

"SHOVE!" shouted the Colonel.

It began turning, slowly, a fraction at a time, then lurched, and very quickly picking up the pace as gravity took hold on the downhill slope allowing the weight to move it forward. Faster and faster, spinning, bouncing, flying through the air with bits of bale going in all directions, to become a terrifying spectacle of doom.

"By the suffering Jesus, look at it go," Danny screamed in jubilation. "The car and bale are heading for exactly the same place, Begorrah."

"Sid's not seen it yet. Good heavens, he'll get a shock when he does. Let's get in the cars to join them there before he tries to escape," Dominic cried.

The enormous monolith tore towards the point of intersection, crushing, ripping or simply destroying all in its path, straight through the last hedge and into the lane beyond. An oak tree opposite finally brought it to a shuddering halt, laying a half broken wreck completely blocking the road.

At the same instant, the vehicle's headlights illuminated it together with a dreadful screech of brakes drifting across the field, telling us of Sid's desperate fight to avoid the obstruction.

"Ah…" came his cry of horror as the sound of bending metal from the car hit the bale squarely.

"Up and at him," the Colonel whooped. "Charge!"

Dominic tugged open the car door, grabbing Sid by his collar to drag the wretched man out.

"Allow me, reverend," Jack said calmly, laying a hand on the vicar's arm. "I'm better qualified than you at this." He held Sid up by his coat lapels, the man's feet several inches off the ground. "You'd better own up if you know what's good for you. There's no judge or jury out here, no coppers either. I'm about fed up with kidnappers and being shot at."

"What can you do?" Sid sneered.

"I'll knock your ruddy block off, that's what."

"I'll have you arrested for assault, there are too many witnesses," Sid challenged, haughtily.

"Really" Dominic said, as we all turned our backs. "We can't see a thing, can we?"

"See what, Chantril?" the Colonel asked. "Far too dark to see things out in a lane."

"Now you're mine." Jack's enormous fist drew back. "You've asked for this. Have you ever had your face smashed in before?"

"No, don't hit me," Sid whined. "I'll do anything you say."

"Right, but don't go squirming back on your word, I'll not forget. The first thing is to have you confess to Bracknell," the Colonel ordered. "Then we have to find out who this boss person of yours is."

"No, not him, not the boss. It's more than my life's worth to squeal on him. You lot should leave well alone too, he's bloody dangerous. You simply don't know what you're getting yourselves into, trying to nail him."

"So, it is a him," I snapped. "At least we know that much."

"Who is it?" Dominic demanded. "Telling might help your sentence."

"I'm saying nothing," Sid replied, squirming. "I mean… I dunno."

"Don't know! Don't give me that rubbish, you've been dealing with him on a daily basis."

"Not me, guvnor, it was Crusher at the cottage."

"Briar Cottage?"

"Yes, guvnor." Sid squealed as Jack gave his arm a hefty wrench.

"Humph," went the Colonel. "We're getting nowhere here, Chantril," he blustered. "Best we get him back to the village into the police station. We will need to be carefully quiet in case this boss chappie is hanging about. We don't want to give the game away, putting him on his guard, do we?"

"In the car you," Jack grunted, giving the luckless crook a hefty shove in his back.

Taking Them Down

*T*he church clock chimed eleven as we stopped outside the police station. It was in darkness.

"Dammit, the man's not here, never around when he's wanted," the Colonel ranted.

"He'll be in his house just around the corner. "Jack piped up. "Dick'll fetch him."

"No oi bloomin' well won't. He'll not be a-comin' out for oi a-knockin' on his door after closin' time."

"Dick's right," Dominic muttered. "I'll have to go."

"I'll come with you, my love. He's bound to reply to both of us."

It took a while before lights came on. "Yes, who is it," Bracknell's voice came through the closed door.

"The reverends, Constable, we need your help."

A bolt slid across, then the door opened revealing the policeman standing in his pyjamas. "What is it at this hour, I was in bed?"

"Dominic explained the events.

"You shouldn't go taking the law into your own hands, reverend, as well you know. Where are these supposed crooks?"

"In the car, Jack's keeping an eye on them."

"Wait there, I'll get a uniform on."

Once at the car, Bracknell got to business. "Right, let's be having it."

"I'm saying nothing," Sandcastle muttered, "other than this

thug beat me up," he cried, pointing at Jack.

"Is this true?" Bracknell snapped. "Assault is a serious matter, Sweeney."

"The man confessed to being involved with the kidnapping of Master William," the Colonel said impatiently. "A certain amount of force had to be used to capture him. I take it you'll believe me and the reverend, as well as Jane? We are all very reliable witnesses."

"The Reverend and Jane, well, yes, I suppose so. Get him inside the station, I'll call the Inspector."

The Major drew up just then.

Master William got out, pointing at Sandcastle, "That man took me to the boat, he screwed my arm up my back until it hurt, hitting my mummy." He promptly kicked Sandcastle in the shins.

"Ow! Control that bloody kid, will you, copper?"

"You leave this child alone," I snapped. "You've done quite enough damage as it is. I hope you'll get all you deserve."

"Should you say that, Miss Jane?"

"Don't you think he deserves all he gets, Dick?"

"Yes, oi do, shall oi kick him in the shins as well?"

"Best take Master William to Lady Celia. It's late, but there's a party going on, so she'll be up," Bracknell cut in. "Before I have to arrest Drummond for assault."

"What about these other two crooks?"

"We'll bring them in, Bracknell, you'll be wanting a word with them."

"Put them in the cell," the policeman said. "I'll wait for Rosefield. You lot had better get to the Manor."

There were cars parked everywhere, too many for us to go up in ours.

"Give me a hand, William," I said. "Margaret will hold your other one, you'll be safe with us."

A smile came, his fright half-forgotten now he was with friends.

Dominic rang the doorbell. "I hope she can hear it, there's a lot of noise in there.”

As the door swung opened, Celia was ready to welcome guests. She looked very surprised. “Oh, it’s you, vicar, the Colonel, too, oh, Jane with Margaret. There’s that dreadful Drummond and Sweeney with a lot of scruffs, what on earth is going on?”

“We have someone for you,” Dominic said, as he parted, allowing the Colonel to unblock Celia’s view of Margaret and me.

“I’m sure you will want to see this young man,” I whispered.

Celia’s face went through an agony of contortions, bewilderment, surprise, happiness then finally, tears of her heartbreak. Clasping William to her, she kissed his little face, while trying to wipe her tears away at the same time. “Thank God you’re safe, my little darling,” she stammered.

“Ahem,” went the Colonel. “May we come in, please, m’dear,” he asked, finally breaking the silence.

The woman was completely choked up, so nodded.

“Somewhere quiet, perhaps,” Dominic prompted.

“Yes, certainly. Go into my study.”

“I’m alright, mummy. They never hurt me much. Please don’t cry,” William said.

“My baby, thank God you’re back and unharmed.”

“Yes, mummy, I didn’t like it on the yacht, they weren’t nice people.”

“My God, the yacht!” exclaimed the Colonel. “What fools we are.”

“I’m sorry, I don’t follow you,” Dominic queried.

“There may be some clue as to the identity of this boss person, Chantril.”

“You’re right, guvnor,” Jack put in. “I didn’t have much time when on board for William, the main thing was getting the lad off.”

“Don’t blame yourself, Sweeny, you did the right thing,” the colonel replied, appeasingly.

“Shall we all go back?” I asked. “It should be safe now.”

“As long as we don’t do anything silly. The crooks are at the police station. Celia, old girl, you must go on here as if nothing has happened. Get William out of sight, he must not be seen until the last crook is caught."

"To be sure," Danny cut in, "there's the goods in the cave, too. They don't know we've found that yet."

"Who are they," Celia asked, indicating Danny and his lads.

"Danny O'Flattery, at your service, ma'am."

"Danny's friends helped get William back, along with young Drummond and Sweeney," the Colonel quickly explained. "We probably wouldn't have managed it without their help. One more thing, Celia, Sweeny here swam to the yacht to get the lad."

"You saved my son?" Celia asked Jack.

"Yes, I'm a good swimmer, Lady Celia."

"Thank you, Mister Sweeny." She turned to the crowd. "You're the gypsy people from the far field, aren't you? If you helped, then if you ever need anywhere to stay, you'll all be more than welcome here. I've plenty of land, I'll even have the gardener lay fresh water on for you, too. Thank you, thank you all, so much."

"Look here, m'dear, we're not finished yet, not by a long shot," the Colonel explained. "This boss is still unidentified and on the loose. That's why you must keep this ball going and young William out of sight. For goodness sake, don't break it up now because the boy is back."

"Have no fear, Colonel, I'll do just that."

"Would you like Danny and his friends to stay here as a guard for you?" Dominic asked.

"Yes, I would feel a lot safer, please do stay." She tried to smile, but the stresses of her ordeal showed in her face.

"Good," the Colonel said. "We're off to the cove, see you soon, Celia."

❧

The sand crunched under our feet as we walked onto the beach.

"The dinghy's still hard ashore," Jack grinned. "The old Bill haven't arrived yet, so let's get cracking."

"I'll come with you," Dominic volunteered. "Two sets of eyes are better than one."

"Take care, Chantril, this is still a very dodgy business," the Colonel uttered.

"We'll check out that box in the cave," Dick suggested.

"What box, in what cave" Colonel Masterson demanded. "You never mentioned anything about this, Chantril?"

"Sorry, must have slipped our memories in the excitement."

I shot him a glance, he was fibbing and he knew it.

Dominic smiled guiltily back. "We'll be off then."

"Show me this cave, Drummond. We can tidy this end up while they're away."

"Have you got a torch then, Colonel?" Dick asked.

"One's never without a torch in the country, Drummond, first rule, there's no light in a lane or field."

Click. The circle of light etched out a small round in the inky blackness of the cave's interior.

"There it be," Dick said, pointing as the box jumped into sight.

"Ah ha," cried Masterson. "Illicit goods, maybe the gang's been smuggling." He picked up a stone to begin hammering the lid up. "It's loosening. Come on Drummond, give a hand. Lift!"

Clunk!

"Wine!" I exclaimed. "Just bottles of wine."

"Wait, it's too deep a box for that. Take some out."

"Rightyo, whatever you say, Colonel," Dick happily replied.

"No drinking any, either," the Colonel snapped, pre-empting Dick's obvious enthusiastic intentions.

He looked crestfallen in the torches glow.

"You're right, Colonel, there's another layer," I encouraged. "It's under this sheet of cardboard."

"This isn't wine," he said as he lifted the sheet away. "It's covering packets of white powder, and look, there's a row of smaller boxes along the side. Give me one, please, m'dear."

"Here, be careful, they look very delicate."

"Ye Gods," the military man cried loudly. "A cache of diamonds! There are boxes of them."

"So that's what the men meant when Dick overheard them talking," I pointed out. "It wasn't rugs or stones, they were talking about drugs and stones, uncut diamonds I expect. They are smugglers."

"You're right, m'dear. This is some haul, there must be a small fortune here. We had better get it all back in with the lid on before the police arrive," the Colonel muttered.

"Just a minute," I said, holding a hand up. "These wine bottles have the same label on as the ones the Count donated for the fete."

"By Jove, so they have. That's a coincidence, isn't it?"

"Too much of one, if you ask me. Ah, here come Dominic with Jack."

"Well?"

"Nothing much out there to give us any leads, Colonel," Dominic said. "Just some crates of wine. Oh, I see you have some as well, with the same label."

"Now that's definitely not a coincidence, is it, Colonel?

It most certainly isn't, m'dear."

"Listen," Jack called. "The cops are here, they're coming down the cliff path right now."

"Corks," Dominic breathed, "now we're in hot water. I'll never live this down."

Another torch beam lit us up. "What's going on here," snapped Detective Inspector Rosefield.

"We found this," Jack put in quickly, indicating the crate.

"You're the lot that rescued the boy, aren't you?"

"Yes, we are," Dominic replied. "Together with the Colonel and the gypsy folk."

"Who is the one who was shot at?"

"Me, copper," Jack said.

"The guy that fired that shot is a member of a notorious

French gang. He's their hit man so you were lucky, my lad, he is usually a crack shot. One thing's certain, you've upset somebody big. Who is it?"

"Search me, guvnor," Jack muttered. "I'm in the dark as much as you are."

"Is Missus Chantril here," Rosefield asked.

"Yes, here I am, Inspector."

"I've a message for you from pretty high up in the French Gendarmerie."

"From Phillipe?"

"That's right. It reads like this… The chateaux not known in area. Man you asked about is suspected of connections within the French underworld. Very dangerous, repeat, very dangerous. Do not get involved. Regards, Phillipe."

"Good Lord," I uttered. "It's him, he's Mister Big, the top boss."

"Mister Big?" queried Rosefield. "What do you know about this?"

I explained.

"I knew it, I knew it," Jack exploded into life. "That so-called bloody Count is behind all this. Had him marked as a bad'un from the moment I clapped my minces on him. No wonder he can deck Olga out in high fashion and jewellery," he moaned. "Just a minute, Olga! She's in that house with him."

"In that case, the young lady is in great danger," DI Rosefield went on. "Look here, take note of what I say, I don't want you to go rushing in where angels fear to tread, girlfriend or not, the consequences could be disastrous, maybe even fatal for her."

Dominic sighed. "This explains a lot of things, the wine, him not being very sure where his so-called chateaux is, or even why he moved to this village in the first place. That was to be nearer the whole operation. After Jack hit him, it was an insult, that's why there was an attempt on his life."

"We need proper backup. I'll get an armed response unit here to surround the place," Rosefield said.

"But Olga might get hurt," Jack cried out. "A load of coppers with guns dashing all over the place, people are going to get shot."

"Oi don't know why you're botherin' about her, our Jack. She was quick enough givin' you the old heave ho when his nibs came on the scene," Dick pointed out.

"I know that, but I still wouldn't like to see her hurt."

"Neither would any of us," the Colonel added. "Which is why we must let the police handle the matter."

DI Rosefield nodded. "That's right, no heroics. My men will be in place within an hour, but nothing will be done until daylight, just in case..." His words trailed off. "However, we'll arrest those two at Briar Cottage quietly during the night, I'll get on the radio to arrange that now." He took a few steps away to be out of earshot, his mouth moving as he gave the necessary commands.

Dick tapped my arm. "Maureen's prediction," he uttered.

"What do you mean?"

"She said mouths talking, see, he's doing just that."

"She also said there would be a telephone box by a junction," Dominic added. "A graveyard with riches, too. Don't read too much into fortune telling, Dick."

"It's what she said," Dick insisted. "The rest came true as well."

"The rest of what?"

"Ah, well, you wouldn't understand, revrund, but it did."

"You're talking in riddles now. Go home, get some sleep," Dominic snapped.

All that Glitters

$\mathcal{A}$ tense atmosphere hung over the village as dawn's early light steadily revealed Annabel's old house, a house that the Count was holed up in, ostensibly with a hostage.

Shooting a glance at Dominic, I asked. "Are you okay, darling?"

He nodded.

"Who would have thought Annabel's old home would become the setting for high drama. Can you see any of the police, my love?"

"No, none of them, they are all very well hidden."

A metallic click of a tannoy system sounded across the fields.

"This is the police armed response unit. You are surrounded, throw any weapons you have out of a window into the garden in clear sight. Come out slowly into the lane with your hands up, palms facing us. Leave the young lady inside the house. You have one minute to comply."

"Do you think he will, revrund?"

"I've no idea, Dick. Who can tell what goes on in the criminal mind?"

"I'll bloody-well murder him with my bare hands if he's harmed Olga," Jack muttered.

"Let the police handle this one, Jack. If they start shooting, you'll stand a good chance of being hit if you're running about," Dominic warned.

Looked at my watch I viewed. "Time's dragging. It's surprising how long a minute is when you have to sit one out."

234

The silence was shattered by a window smashing into fragments.

"He's going to make a fight of it," Jack breathed.

Bang. A shot whistled overhead.

"Get away from 'ere, or sacre blieu, the mademoiselle will be killed. Moi demandes clear passage across the field be'ind this 'ouse."

"Don't be a fool, you cannot escape, we have the building surrounded," the tannoy replied.

Bang. Another bullet whined above us.

"He means it," Dominic said. "I'll crawl to the inspector, perhaps I can mediate?"

"He'll not worry about you being a vicar, he's a desperate man now," Jack replied.

"I don't think he'll shoot me."

"Please don't take any chances," my concern coming through my words.

"Somebody has to go, he knows I'll be unarmed." He ran off half bent to keep a low profile.

"Dick, me old mate, it's high time we gave the reverend a hand."

"What can you two do?" I asked, "other than get yourselves shot."

"Improvise, Jane. You coming?"

"Me!" I exclaimed.

"It's your husband," Jack retorted.

"Okay, anything to help, I don't want him hurt, either."

We ran low along beside the church wall, crossing the road near the inn, to make our way behind it, hiding in some bushes.

"What good are we doing here?" I asked.

"Yes, oi were a-wondering that?" Dick muttered. "The inn b'ain't open yet."

"Simple. He bust the window at the front of the house and fired that way to keep everybody's heads down. He'll loose off a few more shots, then come out the back door making his way across the open fields here. If he has Olga as a hostage, they dare not fire in case they hit her. Once clear, he'll probably nick a car then head for the harbour in the hope of hopping aboard a boat, harbours lead to France, don't they?"

"Crikey!" Dick gasped. "Did you think of all that yourself? You should have been a detective, our Jack, that's amazin'."

Bang, bang, bang…

"There are the shots," Jack snapped. "Look, here comes the blighter with Olga in tow. Pullin her along by an arm. I've a debt to repay, shooting at me," Jack snarled, standing up.

"*Ah, zee brave Engleesh 'ero, Jaques, 'e comes to rescue 'is beloved maiden,*" the Count mocked. "*Keep away mon ami, I have a gun pointing at the mademoiselle's ribs. She gets eet eef you try to stop moi.*"

"You bloody coward, hiding behind a woman," Jack shouted back.

It must have struck a nerve, because the Count's arm whipped out level as a shot rang out.

Jack dived into a bush.

"Are you okay, Jack?" I asked, creeping to him.

"It just nicked my arm, nothing much, Jane."

"He's makin' off, just like you said," Dick confirmed. "What'll we do?"

"To the vicarage, get our car," I cried.

"The revrund won't like that much," Dick said.

"We ain't going to ask him," Jack retorted.

"Here are the keys, Jack," I called, holding them out.

He grinned back. "You're a real sport, Jane."

We piled in, Jack twisted the key in the ignition, firing the engine into life.

Dominic's voice came drifting to us. "Hey, where are you all going with our car?"

"Just drive, Jack. I'll explain to him later."

The vehicle shot out onto the lane, tilting dangerously as Jack swung it into a sharp turn.

"Hey, steady on," Dick yelled. "You'll crash us a-drivin' like a maniac."

"Shut up, just keep your eyes peeled for them. Can you see that bloody Count yet?"

"No, oi can't, only the doctor's car in front."

"That's it then," Jack cried in jubilation.

"That's what then?" Dick seemed confused.

"That's the one he pinched. I'll try to ram him, make him swerve into a crash as he takes the next corner."

"Ram it!" Dick yelped. "We're the ones that's going to crash. Oi can see it bein' another one of those days, oi hates transport."

"Go on, Jack, do it. It's a matter of life and death," I shouted.

"Hold on tight," Jack hollered. "I'll hit the rear corner hard."

THUD! Crunch, grind…

"He's losin' it," Dick yelled.

The vehicle wobbled crazily all over the road. The Count's head popped out as another shot whistled by us.

"Shit," Jack yelled, tugging the steering wheel violently round.

Suddenly our world was upside down as the car rolled. Hard objects hit us.

"Ouch! Me bleeding 'head…" Jack gasped. "Quick, get out."

"Not bloomin' likely, that nutter will start shootin' at us. Oi b'ain't bullet proof," Dick protested.

"That's a point, he hasn't fired a shot, yet I'm standing up. Take my hand Jane, I think we're safe, he's out of ammo."

"Thank you, Jack. I wonder where we are."

"Oh, oi ache all over, grumbled Dick, holding the small of his back."

"Never mind your medical history, where are we?"

"Um, let's get moi bearings. Oh ah, well along the lower lane, almost at the road junction with the old cemetery, that's over on our right."

"There they are!" Jack exclaimed. "By the graveyard gate."

Bang…

"I thought you said he was out of ammo, Jack. We need cover, get behind this telephone box."

Jack peered out. "Sorry Jane, he must have reloaded. I think they went in."

"Oi daresay there's plenty of ways in," Dick muttered. "Oi used to come here when oi were a-courtin' our Faga… oi mean Maggie."

He got an odd look of horror from Jack. "What, in a bleeding cemetery?"

"Oh ah, nicely quiet hereabouts," Dick replied with a grin, "Don't get disturbed. It's well overgrown now since the old chapel fell into disrepair. Follow oi."

"Never mind your love-life history," I said. "Lead on, quickly."

Dick was faultless, nipping in through a gap where the wall had fallen down some time in the distant past.

It had to be admitted, the place was a wreck, now badly in need of attention with gravestones at crazy angles.

He held an arm up to stop us near a vault. "It be handy for protection," he explained. "Bullets don't go through stone."

"*Scream… 'elp me Mister Jack, I ah…*"

"That was Olga," Jack cried. "What's the swine doing to her? We'll have to split up. You come with me, Jane. Dick, go over to the right, just watch out for flying bullets."

"Bloomin' great hayricks, what am oi supposed to do against bullets," Dick protested.

"Just keep low with your head down," Jack snapped, "be quick about it."

The bushes moved behind us.

"Oi surrender," hollered Dick. "Don't shoot."

"By the suffering Jesus, don't go busting your boiler," Danny said. "'Tis only me. I heard the shooting."

"You go with those two, Jane," Jack said. "You'll be safer with two to look after you. The Count doesn't know Danny is here."

"To be sure, he doesn't. But by the Virgin Mary, he will, soon enough."

Jack went away running low, using whatever he could as cover. We could just make out his progress.

"He should be the other side of the Count now, I tink, Dick.

What now?"

An owl hooted.

"That be odd," Dick muttered. "Owls don't hoot during the day."

"I think it might be a signal," I whispered. "From Jack."

"Right, Miss. Oi'd best return it."

"Can you do an owl hoot?" I asked, rather surprised at Dick's unending talents.

"When I brung Maggie a-courtin', it was a good way to get rid of people when they came a-nosin' around, see, it sounds eerie."

"Whooo hoooo," he went. "Over here."

There was a mad scramble where Jack had been, coupled with a kind of roaring snort, immediately followed by an, "Ooof!"

Jack and the Count stood, looking as if they had been dragged through a hedge backwards. The Count's arm raised, the gun in his fist.

"Crikey, he'll shoot our Jack real easy that close," Dick cried, picking up a cricket ball sized chunk of concrete, delivering a perfect overarm throw.

The missile went sailing away, landing just in front of the Count's left temple.

"*Aaaah. Sacre Bleiu, moi pistole,*" the man yelped, letting go of his hostage as he almost fell.

Jack became a blur, using his substantial weight to drive the Count away from Olga. He bent, lifting the Count up by his neck.

"*Oh, Meester Jack, you saved me,*" Olga cried, flinging her arms around his neck.

The Count, seeing a window of opportunity, hit Jack in the stomach, and now free of restraint, run for all his worth.

"Dick, where are you?" Jack hollered.

"Right here, mate," he replied, standing up from his hiding place.

"I'll deal with this swine," Danny screamed, giving Dick a hefty shove sideways.

Dick, having been propelled to our right, accidentally

happened to be directly in the Count's line of escape.

The collision resounded around the graveyard as Dick vanished into the old vault, its wooden door, weary of life now after a century or so of misuse, and in no fit state to resist, gave in with a sickening crash.

"Yikes…" His voice faded into the tomb.

Danny grabbed the Count, hitting him squarely on his left ear with a right hook.

The man staggered a foot or two, only to bump into Jack, who had regained his wind.

"Oh no you don't," Jack growled, pulling his right sleeve up. "We've got a score to settle."

It was a really powerful blow, we all winched as Jack delivered it. Something went crack, perhaps it was the Count's jaw?

The crook collapsed, to lay very still at Jack's feet.

Danny was grinning at him. "A more deserving blow, I have never seen delivered. Are you sure you're not Irish?" He burst out laughing.

"Nah, a Londoner, me old sunshine. Now, where's my old mate gone?"

"To be sure, he's lounging about somewhere. He went that way just now."

"He was pushed through the door of the vault," I put in. "We should see if he's alright."

"I'll stand over the Count," Danny said. "You two go find him."

"It's black in there," Jack mused as he leant a hand against the splintered timbers of the door frame.

"Dick," I called into the gloom. "Are you okay?"

He groaned. "Moi bleedin' head. It fair got bashed about."

"He's complaining, so he's alright," Jack quipped with a broad grin.

"We need a light, its pitch black in here," I said.

"I've a torch," Danny answered. "I remembered the first rule of the country. Here, take it."

Click.

There lay Dick, propped up against an ancient coffin, now split open after Dicks violent impact with it, its contents spewed out all over him.

"Oi b'ain't a-covered in bones, am oi?" he asked, hesitantly, looking around.

"No, you're not," I assured him. "Here, take hold of my hand, I'll give you a tug up."

"Why is it all sparkling?" Jack asked. "Bones don't glitter in the dark."

Bending, Dick picked up some objects. "Crikey, our Jack, it's a load of old coins, broaches, jewellery and all sorts of stuff."

"This must have been a hoard," Jack muttered. "Wonder if it belonged to old man Sharpe, he was a miser."

"Misers keep the loot with them, Jack. This stuff is much older than anything he might have had, seventeenth or eighteenth century I would think."

"Who does this place belong to?"

"Oi dunno, our Jack, oi don't care, neither. It's creepy in here and moi head hurts."

A siren wailed as the police approached along the lane.

"Let the police sort it out," Dick groaned. "As long as oi don't have to pay for the door, oi got pushed through by him," he ended, indicating the Count.

The place became flooded in blue. "We'll take care of him," DI Rosefield said. "Sergeant, get a search going for that weapon."

"*Thank you, Meester Jack,*" Olga whispered. "*You saved my lifes.*" She kissed his cheek.

He kicked the ground, embarrassed at the praise as well as the very unexpected kiss. "That's okay, my pleasure. What are you going to do now?"

"*I not knowinks. Maybe goinks back home to the old countries.*"

"You can't go anywhere yet, Miss," Rosefield snapped. "We need you for a statement and witness. So, you'll have to come with me first."

Jack watched her go, his brow creased in thought.

"Cheer up, Jack," I said. "She was quick enough to drop you when that co-called Count appeared. At least she did appreciate what you did. There are plenty more fish in the sea."

He shook his head. "No, not like her, Jane. Not like her. She's beautiful."

Lady Celia

"*H*ow pleasing it is to have village back to normal at last," Dominic mused as he leant back in his swivel chair.

"How do you mean, my love?"

"Briar Cottage and Annabel's old home empty again. Dick is back home, almost cleared of crime with Lady Celia's son back at the Manor for her to look after."

"I felt sorry for Olga, so have let her stay in my cottage until she decides what she's going to do. The police confiscated her passport, she's stuck here for now. We should go to see Celia, she's acting most oddly, not like her usual old self even though William seems none the worse for his experience."

"In what way, I never noticed anything?"

"Seriously, she's still refusing to attend the WI Meetings. The poor woman seems broken by the terrible events."

"Surely that's no loss," Dominic said with a grin.

"Don't mock. I had a chat to Susie at Leggett's store yesterday, she told me Celia has no interest in the stables or horses, no interest in anything in fact, now that is most unlike her."

"Mmm, I'll need reinforcements for a job like that. We had better call at the Colonel's on the way, let him know what's going on."

"Celia down!" he exclaimed. "That's not like her, Chantril. She's always been such a sensible person. I'll come with you, better try to get to the bottom of it."

Young William answered the door to our knock.

"Hello William, how are you," I greeted. "Is mummy in?"

"I'm well, thank you, Jane. Mummy is in the sitting room. Why is she crying all the time?"

"Oh dear," Dominic uttered.

"Take us in, young man," the Colonel said. "We'll have a chat, see what's up, by Jove!"

We found her in an armchair, a damp handkerchief in one hand, the other supporting her head at an angle. She looked totally miserable.

The Colonel humphed. He was out of his depth already.

Touching Dominic's arm as I indicated the mess the place was in. "This hasn't been touched since the night of the ball."

"Perhaps you had better talk to her alone," Dominic suggested. "More up your street at the moment. Come on Master William, take us to the kitchen to show the Colonel and me, how to put the kettle on."

"Pardon, vicar?" William gave us a confused look.

"Go on…" Dominic shooed the lad out.

A hand was laid on Celia's arm. "What's the matter?"

A pair of eyes, red from the tears that had passed through them looked up. Her head shook.

"It might help to talk to somebody, me if you like, we know each other, I'm not a stranger to you. A problem shared…"

"It's no good, you see," Celia replied softly. "I can't go on, not after what has happened."

"But William is back with you now. He's a lovely lad, incredibly brave, too. All those crooks have been arrested, so there's nothing to fear."

"I can't go on," she repeated. "They destroyed me. First my jewels, then my son. How has it affected William? Will we ever know the truth of that? He may be scarred for life for all we know from his ordeal."

"He seems alright, took it with indifference, they didn't frighten him much. He's a spirited scamp, most likely gave them as good as he got, you should be very proud of him. Children are very robust providing they have somebody who loves them, as you do, Celia. Don't let him down now, he just doesn't understand you at the moment. If you wish, I could arrange counselling?"

"Counselling?" she repeated vaguely.

"Just for a while, to help you over the crisis."

A deep sigh left her. "I suppose so, if you think it might help. It's the memories, you see."

"What memories?"

"Of how it used to be. My husband, my little treasure, William, all the happy times. Just thought I had managed to put them behind me after my husband died then we moved here to start afresh. Now they've shattered those dreams, too, gone like the wind. I can't stay here, it's depressing me."

"Where will you go?"

"I've no idea, that's depressing me even more."

"Why don't you start up the ridings school again, you like your horses, such noble creatures?"

"Susie can look after them."

"Well," I went on, clutching at straws, "what about your lovely garden and grounds? You have always adored those."

"Appleyard's off sick."

"Oh, I'm sorry to hear that. Who's looking after the lawns and flower beds?"

"Nobody."

"But they need constant attention, don't they? Look, why not allow Dick and Jack to come back, Olga even, she needs work?"

Celia stiffened.

"Only until your other gardener returns," I added quickly. "They did a great deal to help with William, Dick risked his life on the beach."

"Yes, that's true," Celia admitted grudgingly.

"There you are then, that will help, plus give you a feeling of security with someone being about the place."

"Alright, but it's against my better judgement, you know what a disaster area Drummond is at times."

Dominic appeared with the tea, the Colonel and William.

A slight nod went to Dominic. "Lady Celia would permit Jack and Dick back for a while to generally keep an eye on the place," I added, as the Colonel's head rapidly swivelled in my direction. "Perhaps Olga could come to help tidy the place for her ladyship?"

Celia nodded again.

"That's great," Dominic cried. "I'll pop along to tell them," he beamed. "There's the picture, too."

"What picture," Celia asked, a sliver of interest garnered by Dominic's statement.

"The one we found in the cave," I put in. "We must have forgotten about that, what with everything else."

"We should have told the police about the body," Dominic went on.

"A body? Whose?" Celia said. "Who found it?"

"Well, me, I mean with Dick's help, we found the picture and a skeleton deep in a cave. We think it's the missing picture of Melissa Possibly the remains of his Lordship."

The Colonel went "Humph.". "We all thought Drummond had made all that up!"

"As did everybody else at the inn that night," Dominic added. "But apparently, he didn't, did he?"

"How interesting," Celia said, brightening slightly.

"The picture belongs to the Manor, that's where it hung originally," I said, hoping to encourage Celia's interest further. "The Lord should be buried, too, he shouldn't be left there."

"Why not?" Celia muttered. "He was a pretty awful buzzard, I was told. A really bad egg."

"The painting is in good condition, it should be worth a lot of money," Dominic put in.

"Money!" Celia exclaimed uninterestedly. "What good is money, only major trouble."

"Yes, quiet," Dominic uttered, confusion on his face.

We departed the Manor, having achieved a modicum of success. Olga seemed interested on returning, at least it gave her an income until the police returned her passport. Then she was free to do whatever she wished.

"Temporarily, you say, reverend," Jack mused.

"That's right, until Appleyard's legs mended," I added, encouragingly.

"How did the silly old fool go manage that, Miss Jane?" Dick asked.

"Slipped down the ladder when he was putting the rest of the ties on the Wisteria," Dominic said. "A job you should have been finishing."

"Oi were a-given the sack, remember?" Dick snorted in disgust.

"Ah well, let bygones be bygones, Dick. There's no good of holding grudges."

"You want to tell that to Rudge, revrund," Dick returned, his teeth grinding in annoyance.

"Will you go or not?" Dominic retorted. "I have to phone the police about the things in the cave."

"Oi s'pect so, if you say it's okay," Dick muttered.

Annabel

As I had promised Annabel, we went into town for our girlie day. We chose a good one, warm with plenty of sunshine which allowed us to wander to our hearts content. She was a very pleasant young woman, sensible too, much like her sister, but hopefully without Margaret's violent temper.

Annabel loved the shops. "Oi've never been in town afore, Jane. I can call you Jane, can't oi?"

"Yes, naturally, as long as it's not Miss Jane or Missus Revrund, as Dick does."

She giggled. "He be a right one for that, Jane. Oh, look at they dresses, b'ain't they pretty. A bit short, though, aren't they?"

"They would suit you wonderfully. Shall we try some on?"

"Oh, can we, oi'd like that, Jane."

"You have a very good figure, why not flaunt it a bit?" I teased.

"Have oi? Dick says oi'm a frump, looks like an old lady's washin' basket."

"In that case, we'll have to do something about it, won't we? Maybe it's time for a makeover, Annabel? You have a lovely name, let's get the rest to match it."

She chose two, came spinning out of the booth excitedly. "Look at this, do it suit oi?"

"You look superb, just need some shoes to go with it, a set of medium heels, let's show your legs off a bit."

Annabel looked a picture; her confidence began soaring, which I knew needed a boost after Dick's ribbing. Confidence can make a woman alluring. It had to be admitted, Annabel had charm as well as good looks in bucketloads.

"Can oi have another dress, Jane? They seem to suit oi, these shoes are really comfy, too."

"Have as many as you can afford. You can afford them?" It dawned on me that instant that Annabel had never had a job, so I had no idea of her financial situation.

"Aww, you're worried about oi, b'ain't you? That's lovely, Jane, you be very sweet. But oi be fine, thank you. Oi got left money when our parents passed away but until now, oi've never spent any, not a penny. Oi could probably buy the shop, not even thinkin' about it," she whispered, smiling so delicately, I knew she would crush some man's heart as soon as they saw her.

It pleased me. She had looked after Margaret, fended for her intently, in so doing had sacrificed her own future. Now she should start living, to be able to enjoy herself, be the woman as she should be. Now she was opening out before my eyes into an absolute stunner.

"What do you think about goin' a bit shorter? Could I carry it off?

"It will be the men they'll carry off when you appear, Annabel. You are going to knock them for six."

"Do you think Jack likes oi?" She suddenly asked.

"I'm not sure, Annabel. He's had the hots for Olga ever since she arrived at the Manor."

"Oh, her," Annabel almost snorted. "She's all showy flashy, teasing, leads men on. Oi've seen how he looks at her, going around flaunting herself like she do, with that split right up the side of her dress."

To say it surprised, perhaps flabbergasted me, would have been a huge understatement. For a woman who had apparently shut herself in that house the sisters had shared, Annabel had noticed an awful lot, she was plainly more worldly wise than anybody suspected. "Olga may have just acquired a deal of serious competition," I replied with a wink.

"Do oi look that good. Oi have to admit, she is a looker, so can't blame Jack for a-going after her."

"Don't put yourself down. You are as attractive as she is, now you have the kit to go with it. Do you like Jack?"

"Yes, ever since he moved here takin' up with Dick. But with him a-sayin' oi looked like the local tip, oi never tried."

"Let me assure you, that from this day forward you can forget about tips, you will be turning heads wherever you go, no trouble at all. Jack is a good man, has principles, keeps his word, too. He's looked out for Dick. I've seen clearly at times he's surely needed looking out for on many an occasion, so he's loyal as well. I don't think you would go far wrong there. Tell you what, let's look at some makeup, would you like that?"

She giggled again. "Never had any, maybe it's about time oi did, Jane?"

"There's nothing wrong with a little warpaint, even I use it now and then."

A visit to a leather shop for a good handbag together with a little jewellery, put the lid on it. She looked like a film star.

"Right, let's go to terrify the men, shall we?"

"Oi'm ready," she cried, spinning around with excitement.

"Hello Dick," I greeted cheerfully.

"What are you a-doin' here at the Manor, Missus Revrund?"

"Annabel's with me, we're just helping Celia out for a day or two. You both know what to do?"

"Oh ah, Miss. We're to cut the lawn then prick out the winter seedlings," Dick answered with a cheeky grin.

"You're on your own, do it properly," my warning went.

"Don't worry your pretty little head about us," Jack came back. "I'll keep an eye on him."

"Oh really, who's will be keeping an eye on you?"

"Some gorgeous female," he said with a laugh. "That would do me a treat."

"You are both incorrigible. I'll bring some tea out later. Then you may even get your wish, Jack," I called mysteriously, as the French windows closed.

He stood looking after me, puzzlement all over his face.

However, with Dick in the vicinity, an odd feeling hung in my heart, causing me to pause, watching the pair.

"How do oi start this here mower?"

"Turn the petrol on then pull that cord, it's so simple, even you should be able to manage it," Jack retorted sarcastically.

Thump, thump, thump, went the machine.

"Oh ah, works a treat." Dick took hold of the handlebars as he let the clutch out, the ancient machine lurched forward.

"I'll get some seedling trays round," Jack muttered. "Can be doing that at the end of this patio."

Dick almost vanished down the garden. He leant on the handles; the mower swivelled to begin the run back up.

He seemed to be doing well. I was about to leave them to it, when Jack came back into view. He sat on the stones, beginning the boring work of pricking out.

A motion beside me drew my attention. "Hello Annabel, you look fantastic today."

"Do oi, Jane? Thought oi'd come to say hello to the lads."

Goodness knows what affect that might have, I pondered, her standing there looking like a photocopy of Marilyn Munro.

Dick had reached the edge of the patio by now, about to turn back again.

"Coee!" Annabel called, as she opened the glass door, stepping out.

"Strike a light!" Dick exclaimed, as he caught sight of the vision of loveliness that came into view. "What are you a-doin' all spruced up like that our Annie? It is Annabel, isn't it?" he asked, uncertainty lingering in his words, in case another beautiful maiden had moved into the village.

"Do you like it? Had moi hair done and bought a new dress with other things," she replied.

"Oi ain't never seen you a-lookin' like that afore, Annie, not ever," he gasped, completely forgetting the metal monster he was supposed to be in charge of, stupidly letting go of it.

"Shouldn't you be holdin' onto that?" Annabel asked, nodding at the now free contraption.

"Holdin' onto what?" Dick muttered, completely stunned.

"The mower, a-corse."

"Mower? What mower? Oh, the mower," Dick screamed.

"What the hell are you yelling about?" Jack asked, finally taking notice of the situation behind him.

"She put me right off moi stroke, she did."

"Who did?"

"She did."

Jack stood gaping for a few seconds, long enough for the mower to get within his grasp. "Oh, good morning Miss, excuse me. Now get hold of this bloody mower."

Dick made a grab, caught a foot under a step, falling flat on his face.

Jack spun the machine, heading it back down the lawn, straight through a flower bed, the begonia heads gaily flying back into the cuttings box in a bright arc.

"Ooeer," Annabel said. "Oi don't think you're supposed to mow the flower beds, our Dick."

For some weird reason that nobody even managed to work out, the contraption reversed course, heading straight for the glass windows at the top of the patio.

"Stop that mower!" Dick screamed the exclamation loudly.

Jack came out of his stupor. "Blimey, where did you come from? Wow, you look gorgeous. Are you a new maid?"

She seemed very happy at the accolade. "Shouldn't you do something?"

He took her hand, kissing it.

"Oi meant about that mower."

"Mower? Oh, right, yes, the mower." He flipped the petrol feed off, soon the machine drew to a halt.

Slipping in beside Annabel. "I told you the effect you would have. Are you happy now?"

"Oi be right happy, thank you, Jane. Jack kissed moi hand." She seemed in a dream.

"How come the bleeding mower got out of control?" Jack demanded.

"You shouldn't swear in front of a young lady."

"Oh, right, sorry Miss."

"T'were Annie, coming out lookin' like an American film star. Fair put oi off moi stroke it did. Oi still can't believe it."

"Annie? Annie who?"

"Our Annabel, you great twit, Maggie's sister. That's her a-standin' there."

"This young lady? Are you sure? Yeah, she does look very nice," Jack answered in a bemused way.

"You kissed moi hand," Annabel pointed out.

"Kissed you? Did I?"

"Yes, you did, Jack Sweeny."

"I'll happily kiss you again, you're a very beautiful young lady. Where do you live?"

Dick kicked his shin. "At moi house, you great nitwit, with Maggie and me. It's Annabel, Maggie's sister, how many times have oi got to tell you?"

"Annabel?" The fact suddenly hit him like an express train. "You're really Annabel?"

"yes, oi am."

"What happened? I mean, um… you look so different."

"Jane took oi into town, so oi bought a few things. Do you like them." She twirled around.

"Like them! You look fabulous. But you usually stayed indoors, cooking and things. You have always been so… um…"

"Dull… yes, that was oi. So, Jane took oi into Exeter to look around and change moi lifestyle. Jane said I should get out a bit more."

"You have left Jack speechless," I whispered. "Believe me, you are serious competition for Olga now, isn't that good? Talking of speechless, what's Celia going to say when she sees this mess?"

"She won't," Jack put in. "I'll swap some plants from the bottom bed. They are all due to be emptied soon anyway."

Diamonds

*F*ollowing that brief encounter, several things changed in the village. Charlie banned smoking in the inn, bringing a large sitting room into service for meals. His idea proved incredibly popular, increasing the patronage to an amazing degree. It was muttered the food was good, so that was encouraging.

However, Lady Celia remained in a morose mood. We all tried hard to cheer her up, but no matter what anybody did, it made no difference. Counselling never really worked either; she wasn't a person one could easily counsel.

"I'm pleased to see Annabel isn't tying herself to the house anymore, often accompanies Margaret to the inn on occasions. She's begun to venture into the town, too, buying more clothes, shoes or anything else she thinks might enhance her appearance, which it has to be admitted, they most certainly do."

"She's gained a local following of ardent admirers. If jack wasn't her as a girlfriend, he'd better get a move on. Perhaps we should try Charlie's cuisine?" Dominic said out of the blue. "Just once in a while, would give you a break now it's a smokeless zone, it should be pleasant enough."

"Is there some ulterior motive behind this?" I asked. "Keeping an eye on Dick, for instance."

"Just thought we might join them for a meal, that's my main reason. After all, they all behaved remarkably well under duress, so a little show of support from us would be appreciated as well as demonstrating to the villagers, that we do respect them."

"I'm all for it. Dick certainly needs a show of support. When do you fancy going, my love?"

"Why not tonight, spring it on them a bit, then Dick won't be able to wangle his way out of it."

"Let's walk along to suggest it. Have the police sorted out who owns that treasure trove Dick found in the cemetery yet? It's been a few weeks now."

"Constable Bracknell said they are having problems, need to find the records. That's a point, wonder if they were in the ones we found in the belfry? I'll call that inspector."

Dick seemed surprised at our knock, but Margaret was delighted.

"All of us, go have a meal there, oi'd like that, oi think Annabel would, too."

"What's brought this on, revrund?"

"A show of appreciation for your help, Dick. You were there when the chips were down," Dominic answered.

"Oh ah, oi'll go if we're havin' chips."

Dominic never tried to correct or dissuade him. If that error got him to the inn with a group, he was satisfied.

"Good. We'll meet you at seven this evening. See you all later."

It was almost impossible to believe the difference Charlie had made. The inn was air fresh and very civilized. Tables strategically placed with comfortable chairs, our table was formed of two, once we had called booking our party, with six of us to sit.

"Evenin' Jane," Annabel greeted with a charming smile. "It be nice gettin' out a bit."

She looked radiant, mostly by her own hand after leading her into town that day. I was impressed. "Hello Annabel. May I say how beautiful you look?"

"Thank you, Jane. Oi think oi have the hang of lookin' pretty now, but all thanks to you."

Jack stood with his mouth open when he came in. "Annie, it is Annie, isn't it?"

"If you want to call oi a name, it be Annabel, oi don't like it shortened," she said pointedly.

"Oh, right, Annabel. You're a stunner, can I sit next to you?"

"There b'ain't no law against it, Jack Sweeny."

It pleased me. Plainly he was smitten, all thoughts of the delectable Olga were lost in antiquity.

"Oi see her ladyship still b'ain't a-comin' to the meetings," Margaret put in. "Thought she would have got over that to-do by now."

"She still reckons oi stole her silly jewels," Dick muttered. "What would oi want with them? T'were most likely that old tramp. What happened to him, revrund?"

"Got a suspended sentence, Bracknell told me."

"That means he's out on the loose again," Jack noted. "Probably getting up to his old tricks."

"Let's hope not," Dominic said. "He promised the judge he would go straight."

"Yeah," Dick snapped, "straight back to his old ways."

"We shouldn't judge people," Dominic tried to quantify. "He should be given a chance."

"When oi were in town last, oi saw some lovely jewellery in the pawnbrokers window," Annabel put in. "Were tempted moiself."

My ears pricked. Why was lovely jewellery in a pawnbroker's? If it was valuable, it would be in a jeweller's shop. I determined to go look next day. Dominic didn't know it yet, but we were about to become detectives again.

The meal ended, we bade them goodnight, going home.

"Shall we go into town tomorrow, darling, will you come?"

He nodded. "I'm at a loose end, why not, have a look around."

Luckily, it was a sunny day, making the drive in easy, as well as finding a parking spot. I had elicited the name of that shop from Annabel last evening, so guided Dominic in that direction, knowing there was a religious shop nearby, so it proved a simple task.

"What are we stopping at a pawnbroker's for?" he asked, gazing up at the sign hanging outside.

"Just a whim, I fancy. Oh look, isn't that jewellery beautiful? Doesn't it remind of someone's?"

"Good heavens, that's CHS's!"

"Mmm, you could be right. Surely she's not reduced to pawning her valuables?"

"Lady Celia would never do that," he retorted. "I'm going to ask who pawned it. Come on."

Dominic put the point.

The dealer was reticent, but agreed once the police were mentioned. "A Mister Bono Isiah," he replied, looking down the list.

"Don't you mean Isiah Bono?"

"That was the name he gave, vicar."

"What did he look like?"

"A scruffy individual. Needed a good bath if you ask me."

"Didn't that make you suspicious?"

"Said he'd been forced out of his home, but had been left the goods by a wealthy aunt so decided to cash them in."

"We know that person. He's a local tramp, he's been up to no good for a while. In that case they are probably stolen goods. Please take them from display immediately. Would you go to phone Lady Celia and Bracknell, please, my love?"

There was a call box nearby, getting in touch with the Constable first, who could then inform his local station. Celia said she would come straight away to identify the goods.

"Well done," the Inspector said to us. "We rely on the public keeping a sharp eye out for stolen goods."

"It means Dick will be free of suspicion over this," Dominic replied.

"He never did it, as he continually said," I pointed out.

"Now," the Inspector said, "I need a description from you of this person, shopkeeper, then we can put out a warrant for his arrest."

Celia arrived. "Yes, Inspector, they are my missing jewels. How wonderful to see them again." She turned to us. "Thank you both for helping. I must apologise to Mister Drummond, too. The poor man has been put through hell over this."

"I'm sure he'll be delighted, Lady Celia."

She smiled. "Please, just Celia. You have been so very kind to me." She seemed to wander. "If only… oh well."

I wondered what she meant by that? If only… if only what? Was there something else? Her son was back, jewels returned with Dick exonerated. Celia should be able to get on with her life now, bring the riding school up to form again, caring for her beloved horses, grounds and home. Yet, she hesitated, seemed apart from life, at least the life that had existed prior to recent events, apparently unsure, a fact that was completely out of character. "We need to talk to Olga. Let's go now, please."

Her look of surprise at our knock, meant it needed a smile to put her at ease. "Hello Olga, lovely day."

"Yes, it beink is, very sunny, no?"

"May we have a word, please?"

"Come in, beinks, pleases." She ushered us into the sitting room. "What doink for you, can I?"

"We wondered if you would return to the Manor helping Lady Celia permanently now. She's still low of spirits, I believe you two got on well."

"That okay, I like der lady, she kind to me a lot. But me not knowink now, not all her other worry on her minds."

"What other worries?" Dominic asked.

"Oh, I not of said, lady may be cross."

"Sit down Olga, let's talk this over. We all want her to be happy again, taking part in the community here, as she used to. What worry has she? You can talk to us, we are discreet."

"Well, Jane, der ransom paid she to der crooked people. A lot of money beinks, she has so little left."

That was news to my ears. "How much was it, Olga, do you

know?”

"Million by pounds."

"Do you mean a million pounds!" Dominic exclaimed.

"Da, millions of pound. She has no money any mores."

"No wonder she's worried. That place costs a packet to upkeep, then the fees at the school for young William, staff wages, plus the animal feed. I wondered why the Volvo had vanished. Look, if you can help, you can stay here for free, at least until Celia has a chance to sort herself out."

"You are kind lady, Jane. I vill go see der Manor Lady. Police still keep my passing ports anyway."

We left for the vicarage. "What on earth is Celia going to do? Can't the police get that ransom back?" Dominic mused.

"Probably went to some Swiss account, they wouldn't be foolish enough to keep it here. The police should be asked though, they might locate it. Bracknell might be able to help."

Rolling in It

*T*he Constable shook his head. "That's a lot of cash, Jane. She must have hocked the Manor to raise that amount. No wonder she's so upset. I'll phone through to headquarters, can't do much from here about that. I got a letter from them yesterday, too, they want a word with Drummond for some reason. I hope he's not been up to no good again?"

"What do you mean, again? He hadn't done anything in the first place, it was your lot that decided he had, without the slightest foundation, either." The accusation was sharp, their attitude all through had piqued me, especially Bracknell's. "I always thought it was innocent until proven guilty, not the other way around."

"Oh, well…"

"There are no 'Oh wells'," Dominic added. "You were wrong on every count. You should give him a full apology. Especially after the bravery he showed in the kidnapping case."

"You lot should have left that to us," Bracknell retorted.

"We tried telling you if I recall correctly, you weren't interested in the least, even accused Dick of being drunk when he came to the station and ignoring young Williams plight. He could have been killed if it hadn't been for us," Dominic snorted.

"We'll have to wait to see what headquarters need to see him about. Something you aren't aware of, most likely."

"I really don't believe you," I snapped. "He's been cleared, now all you're trying to do is try to pin some other crime on him. Leave him alone, he deserves better."

We left. But my insides were seething. Why was Bracknell being so biased? Dick was not well educated, we all knew that, it was not his fault, but that didn't make him a natural criminal. If anything, he had tried hard to make a go of the marriage, even taking Annabel under his wing. It wasn't a surprise to me his heart wasn't in bettering himself if people treated him like this.

"I'll pop into the church, my love, need a little solitude," Dominic said as we got to the vicarage gate.

He was upset, too, he had a habit of praying for a situation in the hope it might help. "Alright, my love, take as long as you want."

A knock came. It was Dick and Margaret.

"Hello Dick, come in, both of you."

"Thank you kindly, Miss Jane," Dick muttered.

He was obviously in a low mood. Why was that?

"They won't leave him alone," Margaret burst out. "That rotten copper just called demanding moi Dick attend the station tomorrow. Oi asked him why, but he wouldn't tell, said it was heading quarters."

"Headquarters, Margaret, of the county police. That's pretty powerful stuff, coming right from the top. I wonder why?"

The door slammed as Dominic returned. I explained why the pair were here.

A deep sigh left him. "This is monstrous. I'll get onto my lawyer, Dick. You need proper representation in this affair. We'll come with you as well for support. Try not to worry. As I've said before, if you tell the truth you'll have nothing to fear. Now be honest with us, you haven't done anything, have you?"

"Revrund!" he exclaimed. "You knows oi always tells the truth."

"My advice is not to push that point," Dominic replied with a grin. "But as long as you've stayed within the law, you have our full backing. Isn't that so, my love?"

"Yes, absolutely. That blankety Bracknell is being far too high handed with you, Dick. It's about time he was shown the error of his ways.”

Dick cheered up noticeably. “Thank you, revrunds. Oi know oi’ve been a bit of a lay-about in the past, but it t’weren’t possible to get any work, oi did try. Then oi got painted with a black bush, see.”

“You mean tarred with a brush, Dick. It’s time that was stopped. Go home, try to rest. If you go for a drink, please don’t overdo it, you must be sober tomorrow for this meeting.”

“Very well, revrund, thank yous both.”

“Where’s Jack?”

“He’s taken Annabel out to the pictures in town, Jane,” Margaret said. “Oi think he likes her a lot now,” she finished with a giggle.

It was great news to me. At last the young woman had come out of that shell she had gone to hide in after her terrible experience at the altar. A silent prayer passed my lips.

Dominic’s lawyer arrived in good time to be briefed on the matter.

“That’s police persecution, they can’t keep picking on a person without evidence. As long as he’s free of any guilt, he has a good case. He can sue, I’ll help with that.”

Good, I thought, take them down a peg or two. Ever since coming here Constable Bracknell simply assume Dick was guilty of something time and again, it needed nipping in the bud, or in this case, a full-grown briar rose.

“Ah, Mister Drummond,” the detective in charge opened. “Who are all these other people?”

“Witnesses to clear moi name, from whatever you’re going to accuse oi of all this toime.”

“Perhaps there has been a misunderstanding, Mister Drummond. We are not accusing you of anything.”

“Why all this cloaky dagger stuff then, Bracknell demanding oi turn up here today?"

"We actually requested, I'm sorry if it came as a demand, that was never meant. Possibly put across incorrectly by the staff here." He glared at Bracknell.

"So, he's not being accused of anything?" Dominic asked.

"Who are you?"

"The vicar here, he is one of my faithful parishioners, if I may say so, an honest one."

"We're all very pleased to hear it," the detective answered.

"Then what's it about, copper?" Dick was getting edgy.

"Didn't Constable Bracknell explain?"

"Nobody's explained anything."

"He was told to, fully, rather than bring you here unprepared. Allow me to apologise, Mister Drummond. It's about the odd cache of treasure you found accidentally."

"T'weren't moi fault the door got bust, oi were pushed into it by that crooked Count," Dick retorted.

"Yes Sir, a very brave act on your part, helping to capture that man. He was extremely dangerous, well done. Now about that vault, we traced the person who was buried there. It seems he was a relative of yours, a Barnham Drummond."

"So, what am oi supposed to do about it?"

"We did try to locate people who may have owned items in there, but that was hopeless. It means you own it, Mister Drummond. It's worth a considerable amount of money."

"Is it? An hundred pounds or so?"

The detective allowed a smile to flicker across his face. "You should sit down, sir."

"Here Dick," I said pulling a chair over.

"Are you ready?"

"A-corse oi am, just get on with it. As long as Bracknell isn't going to hold oi responsible for whatever it is, like he always does."

"Mister Drummond, you are the owner of twenty million pounds worth of very valuable antiques."

A silence hung in the room.

"Did I hear correctly or had just dreamt that? "Did you say twenty million pounds?" I asked.

"Yes, that is correct. Mister Drummond is a very wealthy man. Congratulations sir," the detective said with a grin, holding a hand out. "Such items as brooches with diamonds in them are worth an absolute fortune each.

"How much is that, revrund?" Dick muttered.

Poor Dick was in shock.

"It's what the police said, twenty million. Where is it deposited?" I asked.

"We set up an account for him at this bank," the man said, handing me the sheet of paper. "It is entirely up to him how he wishes to dispose of the goods to realise that sum, but collectors will be queuing up, make no mistake. The horde could be worth much more, that is our experts estimate at base value."

"Good heavens," I uttered. "You're a very rich man, Dick. I hope people will look up to you now, as they should have all along."

After that, much hand shaking went on. As the lawyer was known to Dominic, Dick decided to have him handle any transactions, a wise move, because plainly Dick hadn't a clue about money.

Margaret was beside herself. "Wait till our Jack and Annabel hear about this, they'll be over the moon," she giggled.

"It means you are also a wealthy woman, Margaret." You're married to a multi-millionaire can't be a bad thing."

"Oh ah, Jane. Oi'd best keep an eye on his spending, then."

"He'll have a job of spending any, the interest alone will pay for expenses or else anything you all need."

"Will it? Oi hadn't thought of that. You mean, the interesting comes in faster than he can get rid of it?"

"I guess so. Isn't that wonderful for you all, no more money worries."

"But oi'd feel guilty about that, Jane. Don't seem right to oi.

After all, t'were ill gotten gains, weren't it?" Margaret replied.

"He can donate some, but only he can decide that. He needs to get over the shock first," I whispered in her ear.

"He do look a bit stunned." She burst out laughing.

Here's another matter I would like to clear up, Mister Drummond, while we're all here, if I may?"

Hello I thought. What are this lot coming out with now? Not more unfounded accusations?

"There's a casefile pending about an arson accusation."

"He was cleared of that, Mrs Brisket was found and corroborated the times. You have no right to bring that up again." Dominic cried loudly, plainly annoyed.

"It takes time for witness statements to be verified, vicar," the detective said. "But we finally got it all sorted officially."

"Well?" Dominic demanded. Hostility was growing by the moment.

"Mr Drummond is cleared of an involvement whatsoever. Another person has been arrested on that charge, vicar."

"Dick, you free of any wrongdoing at all. That's wonderful," I cried, giving him a hug.

"Well done, Dick," Dominic joined in. "It's taken long enough though. May we know who it is, seeing as how Mr Drummond has suffered so much."

"You'll all know who's been charged sooner or later. It has to be proven in court of course, but with the witness statements and self-confession, that should be an open and closed case. The man got drunk a few night's ago, getting into an argument, stating he would do the same to this person's house as he did to Mister Sharpe's. When we checked around, two more witnesses came forward confirming the facts. They had just been to frightened of having their homes burned down, to come forward."

"Who is it?" I asked.

"Mister Rudge. He's securely locked up now."

We all left the police station in a state of shock after that. Although I wasn't surprised. The man had been a loud mouthed nuisance causing lots of trouble continuously. He would get just deserts at least."

Helping Hand

*I*t took several days for the enormity of the event to sink in. Which wasn't a surprise, the amount was vast, far beyond Dick's comprehension. What surprised me more than anything, was he didn't dash to the inn to celebrate, instead stayed home quietly.

Margaret seemed more practical about it than her husband, who she told me, had taken to sitting in his armchair, simply staring ahead.

Possibly anybody would, after receiving that kind of shock, as well as being total freed from any other lingering guilt.

"The news has spread around the villages like a wildfire, even farther, judging by the number of begging letters that have begun arriving," Dominic said.

"Poor Dick is numb," I agreed. "He had no idea the complications wealth might bring, after all, he had spent most of his life living hand to mouth. Luckily the lawyer has mail redirected to his office, setting up a department to deal with it, which was a very wise move."

"One thing Dick has done, is paying for any repairs to the church that might need doing. The roof's stopped leaking very quickly once the lead was reinstalled. He's also got us a new car and another for the doctor, after the Count had crashed it."

"So, you got your Volvo after all, the car he had desired so much," it was said with a tease.

"It was very generous of him," Dominic nodded. "The next good deed was giving Jack a few million, changing his lifestyle dramatically. They'd been best mates for years, so it pleased both of us that they should remain that way, my love."

I realised that kind act gave Jack and Annabel a much brighter future, too.

Other than that, Dick was at a loss.

However, there was one person we knew needed help, so took a walk to chat to him.

He listened intently. "She chucked Jack an' oi out on our ears," he muttered.

"But she has apologised, Dick, even before she knew of your windfall, so it wasn't to get into your good books, she really meant it. Celia is an important part of the village, we miss her at committee meetings and poor Susie might lose her job, as well as all the staff at the Manor. She sold that painting to pay them for a while, but it's a big establishment to run. She was forced to pay a million ransom to those crooks, but that's never been recovered. That's where the trouble started. Please Dick, let bygones be bygones, help her out. If you won't go to see her, I will, for you."

He sighed. "I guess you're right, Missus Revrund. Oi can't see all they people chucked out of work, oi know what that's like moiself. Okay, let's take a walk. You a-comin', revrund?"

Olga opened the door. "'Ello, how you beinks?"

"Is the Lady Celia home?" Dominic enquired.

"You be vaitinks moments, pleases."

"I wonder how she'll take this?" I whispered to Dominic. "She can be very independent."

He shrugged his shoulders.

She appeared little different to our last visit when she entered the hall, downcast, lost, worry weighing heavily upon her. She tried to smile. "Good morning, can I help you?"

"Perhaps the opposite, Celia," I returned. "We have discovered why you're so worried, financial problems, it seems."

She started. "Who told you that?"

"A well-wisher. That is unimportant, what is vital, is you need help, Celia."

"Yes, I have, it's very serious." She sank onto a chair. "They ruined me, nor can the ransom be recovered. I'm at a loss what to do. Selling the Manor is about all that's left, Jane."

Stepping to her, I laid a hand over hers. "We can help, by we, I mean Mister Drummond can."

A light smile went his way. "You found your relative's treasure, I understand?"

"Oh ah, that be right, m'Lady. T'were a lot of money, oi'm told, so oi wondered if you would accept a gift. It would sort your problems out, lettin' you stay put here, as well as all your staff. Miss Jane explained about all that and a few other things. It means a lot of people rely on your employment, but you can't pay them now, can you?"

A nod came from her. "That is most kind, Mister Drummond, but to keep the Manor would cost a small fortune."

"Oi know that, the revrund's explained it. Would say, five million help?"

In all the time here, I had never seen Celia so dumbstruck or speechless. It took a while for an answer to come.

"Ber… but that's an awful lot of money. Are you sure?"

"Oi'm told oi've more dough than oi can shake a stick at, so yes. Oi know we've not always seen eye-to-eye afore, but that's in the past. Let's look to the future now, a-corse that's what Miss Jane says. Is that okay?"

"I… I don't know what to say. Thank you, um Dick, may I call you Dick?"

"It be moi name, oi'd rather that than some of the things oi've been called in the past," he said with a wide grin. "Here, oi've made a cheque out."

Something happened at that moment. Celia seemed to come alive, a healthy flush took her cheeks and standing, took Dick in a hug.

Nobody was more surprised than him, not by the expression on his face.

We left Celia to reorganize her life, a revitalized woman, just as she used to be, which was a delight to see.

"Olga will stay now, so her passport is not such an urgent matter. She likes Master William apparently, they get on well. Now the riding school will start again, so Susie keeps her job, another great piece of news. She's going to take on more staff now her finances are stable, especially in the garden. So, all's well, that ends well with that problem, my love," I said as we arrived back at the vicarage. "Perhaps life will settle now?"

We had just sat, when a knock came. "Hello Jack," Dominic greeted. "What can we do for you?"

"I want to get married," he blurted out.

"Really… I mean, that's wonderful," Dominic said. "Who to, you do need a bride, you know," he ended with a laugh.

"To oi, revrund." From beside the building stepped Annabel. "B'ain't that nice?"

From my position behind Dominic, I caught the crafty wink she gave me. "Congratulations, Annabel, and to Jack of course," although I realised that she had got her man. After all, there was nobody more deserving, either.

She curtsied. "Jack asked oi last night as we walked along the lane. T'were a lovely night with that big moon a-shinin' down on us, right romantic. Then he stopped, popping the question on one knee."

"Come in, both of you, we need to sort a date out," Dominic suggested.

It took but moments. Next month then," I muttered to Dominic after they left. "How lovely, having another wedding here, especially after all the upset the whole village has been through. Let's hope it will settle to a peaceful one again."

"Mmm," he mused. "Don't think I can ever recall it being that, not from the moment I came here. Still, it's been interesting," he finished with a wide grin. "Not many vicars can claim to have done what we have in the line of duty."

The month shot past. We were looking forward to a quiet life without any more dramas, there had been more than enough of those. I was in the church tidying up a couple of days before the wedding, when Annabel walked in. "Good morning, Annabel"

"Mornin', Jane."

She sounded very downcast, on looking I noticed a tear on her cheek. Taking a hand, led her to a pew. "Sit down, Annabel, tell me what the problem is, please."

She burst into a flood of tears.

"What on earth has happened, my dear Annabel?" I asked as sympathetically as possible, placing an arm around her shoulders in comfort.

"Yer…yer… you don't think he'll hop it at the last minute, do you?"

"I assume you mean Jack? Why should he? Believe me, he is smitten. Jack has principles, he has never let Dick down, has he? Not even under the direst circumstances, nor anybody as far as I know, he's just a very reliable, solid chap. Is this because of your previous experience?"

"Why, yes, Jane. How do you know about that, oi b'ain't never told a soul?"

There was a need to think quickly. Margaret had told us in confidence and I didn't want to destroy trust between them. "It was noted in some church records, that's all."

"Oh, oi see. Well, yes, t'were an horrible thing to happen to any girl, Jane. A-corse of it, oi never went out again, as you know. It wasn't until recently with you. Then Jack asked oi to marry him out of the blue. Oi said oi would, but now oi'm terrified it might go the same way. It would break my heart."

"I'm sure it would, I understand, Annabel. Has Jack behaved oddly?"

"No, he seems happy. But then so did that last swine, he just buggered off, leavin' oi there alone."

It was the first time I had ever heard Annabel use bad language, bringing home how hard the incident had hit her. "Would you like me to talk to Jack?"

"Oh no, that might be worse, it could frighten him away."

"Goodness, Annabel, I wouldn't ask him straight out, that would be awful. Just in little ways, to get an idea of his feelings. To see if he's thinking ahead to after the wedding."

"Oh ah, that be a good idea. Oi'm sorry a-comin' here like this, oi were just so worried, oi didn't know who else to turn to and you've been such a good friend to oi, Jane."

"It's part of a vicar's wife's job. We can't have you torn up inside, can we? You're far too precious to us all for that. Now go home and try to relax, have a nice cup of tea. I'll be in touch soon."

"Am oi precious? Oi never thought oi'd ever be that."

"Of course, you are, my dear sweet Annabel, you deserve lots of love as well as a wonderful husband."

She cheered up. "Oi'll go off home, then. Thank you, Jane. Oi'm glad you came to live here, you've been a really good friend to oi all through. She gave me a hug."

On consideration, it might be unwise to talk directly to Jack. Dick would be better, as he had known him ever since his arrival from London when they had chummed up. I went to his home.

"Hello, Miss Jane," he said, rather surprised at my knock.

"Where are the girls?"

"Out at Leggett's store Miss."

"Have you a moment or two, Dick?"

He grinned. "It's all oi seems to have nowadays, after that excitement. Be a mite too peaceful here, if you ask oi."

"God forbid we have to go through that again. How's Jack after his fight with the Count?"

"Our Jack be fine. He seems to have forgotten all about that maid at the Manor now he's been a-goin' out with Annabel. Fair struck on her, he be."

That was good news. "The wedding's only a couple of days away. No getting drunk, none of us want a repeat of your weddings."

That cheeky grin took his face. "They did get a bit excitin', Miss, didn't they? Nah, Jack'll be okay, oi'll see to that. Oi'm his best man, Charlie will do the honours givin' Annie away Tis all organized Miss, stop worryin'."

"How is Annabel?"

"Why do you ask that, Miss?"

"Just wondered." It was a guarded question in case anything had been said in the house here.

"A-corse of that other do when she got let down, you means?"

"Oh, you know about that?"

"Everybody do, Miss Jane. Is that why you came?"

Dick, as I had discovered in the past, was a cute soul who rarely, if ever, missed a trick. "In a way, I had concerns."

"Our Jack won't let Annie down. He loves her to bits, really does. Oi'm surprised, a-corse oi never knew he had it in him. He thinks the world of her and has been bustin' a boiler to get wed. You go home to stop gettin' in a tizzy."

Relief must have shown in my face.

"Maggie and oi have bought Maggie's old home and are a-movin' back there now it's been made bigger, so Jack and Annie will live here. It's all sorted. Oi've got a shop in town to do the caterin' with a few special cars for the day."

"Special cars?"

"You'll see. Annie is goin' to wear her bride's dress again, it'll be perfect."

"I sincerely hope so, Dick. Okay, I'll leave it in your capable hands." Then immediately regretted saying that, but on thinking about it, he seems to have farmed all arrangements out for others to organise. As I left, the girls left the store. A wave, sending a smile along with a nod to Annabel, hoping she would get my drift.

The day was bright, bringing memories of my own wedding last year, when Margaret joined me at the altar. A lot of water had gone under the bridge since then, but Dick and Margaret had stayed firmly together.

The door knocked. On opening it, I found Jack standing wringing his hands. "What is it, Jack?"

"Can I have a word, please?"

"Of course, come in." Taking him into the kitchen as Dominic was busy is his study.

"It's like this," he began, fiddling with the handkerchief he held his enormous hands. "I was wondering, um… if Annabel would… err, go through with it?"

"Why on earth shouldn't she?"

"Well, I'm not much of a catch, Jane. I'm sure she could do a lot better than me, she's so beautiful, kind and thoughtful, an angel in my book."

"Jack, go to get ready, oh, you are. Well, just don't be late, or that threat I made once shall be put into action, by finding the biggest and heaviest object I can lift, then hit you over the head with it. Annabel loves you, you silly thing, that's why she said yes. She wants nothing more than to stand by that altar today by your side, saying Yes again. Okay?"

"Wow, really?"

"Yes, really. You two are the giddy limit, yet for some reason, I'm very fond of you both. Don't let any of us down. Now go, do what you must."

"What was that about?" Dominic asked as the front door closed.

"The pair of them have butterflies in their tummies, that's all. Are you ready?"

"Just got to slip my vestments on."

It was amazing, the place was packed. Everyone together with their auntie were there. Dick was well known for calamitous weddings, but not Jack, unless the news of Annabel's disaster was far better known than she realised. Having peeped in to check Jack was in position, which he was, waited for Annabel's arrival, remembering mine only too well with Margaret on that other amazing day.

A line of Rolls Royce cars drove into view, decked out with

ribbons and flowers. Goodness knows where they had come from, together with bridesmaids and chauffeurs, Dick's mysterious 'special' cars no doubt. He had done them proud.

Out stepped Annabel, looking truly a picture in a dress that had probably been made for her. Oh, of course it had been, Margaret had just borrowed it for her big day.

"You look terrific. How do you feel?"

"Is he…" Her face was pained with concern.

"Stop worrying, yes, he is, you shall wed him today. Now, how about one of those wonderful Annabel smiles."

The relief was plain and true to form, she returned a dazzling smile of happiness. "Oi can't wait, Jane. Thank you for all you've done for oi."

"As long as you're happy. Not much longer. Need to go in now. See you soon." I gave her a gentle hug, being sure not to ruffle her dress.

It happened, just as Annabel wanted so dearly for all those years. Plainly they would be happy together, not only together, but with Margaret and Dick, too. They were all made for each other, to live happily ever after in peace.

Life settled into the one I had yearned for when first moving here. No more wild escapades, no more drunken or calamitous weddings, thank goodness. At least, I sincerely hope not. I strongly believed everybody had had their fill of those events.

The End

And they all lived happily ever after.
Even Dick, who at last settled down.

Other books by this author.
The Forest Mist Series.
Book One
Warrior Women

Book Two
Acts of bravery

Book Three
Back to the Future

Book Four
Destiny

Book Five
Tragedy

Book Six
Vespasian

Book Seven
Occupation

Book Eight
Swords of Legend

The Maid and Minister Series.
The Maid and Minister I. A Challenges
The Maid and Minister II. Putting Ghosts to Rest

Lost Loves Series
Book I. Elise
Book II. Trials and Tribulations

Hela, first born of Odin. A teenage prehistory warrior Series
Hela. Becoming a Warrior
Hela. The Journey

Some Cockney slang

Almond Rocks (or almonds)	Socks
Apples and Pears (or apples)	Stairs
Barnet Fair (or Barnet)	Hair
Bottle (and glass)	Arse
Chine plate (china)	Mate
Daisy Roots (Daisies)	Boots
German bands (Or Germans)	Hands
Hobson's Choice (or Hobsons)	Voice
Mince Pies (Minces)	Eyes
Plates (of meat) (or plates)	Feet
Rory O'Moore (or Rory)	Door
Round the Houses	Trousers
The Frog (and Toad)	Road
Tremble in fear (or tremble)	Ear
Uncle Ned (or Uncle)	Head

Non Rhyming

Hooter	Nose
Prawn	Fool/idiot
Off your trolley	Mad
Shooter	Gun
Six under	Buried
Shell-like	Ear
UXB	Unexploded Bomb

Seafaring

Brig	Prison
Bulkhead	Wall
Companionway	Passage
Deck	Floor
Deckhead	Ceiling
Drogue	Sea anchor
Hatch	Door
The Cat	Flogging implement
Keelhauled	Punishment

About the Author

This is a recent picture of me. I spent many years holding a naval commission and on leaving the Service, took a three year retraining course in horticulture, going on to bring several large estate gardens to excellent condition over about twenty years in Surrey and Hampshire. From those counties, I moved to west London, England and began writing, completing the series in south Wales. The journey has been an interesting, if long a one, but enjoyable, mainly from the degree of research required and intense interest generated, even maybe an overactive imagination.

Email: angela_jane_halliday@yahoo.co.uk

Angela Halliday on Facebook

Angela Halliday on Twitter